the
HEIRLOOM

PUTNAM
— EST. 1838 —

G. P. PUTNAM'S SONS
Publishers Since 1838
An imprint of Penguin Random House LLC
penguinrandomhouse.com

Library of Congress Cataloging-in-Publication Data

Names: Rosen, Jessie, author.
Title: The heirloom : a novel / Jessie Rosen.
Description: New York : G. P. Putnam's Sons, 2024.
Identifiers: LCCN 2023056474 (print) | LCCN 2023056475 (ebook) |
    ISBN 9780593716052 (trade paperback) | ISBN 9780593716069 (ebook)
Subjects: LCGFT: Novels.
Classification: LCC PS3618.O831455 H45 2024 (print) |
    LCC PS3618.O831455 (ebook) | DDC 813/.6—dc23/eng/20231208
LC record available at https://lccn.loc.gov/2023056474
LC ebook record available at https://lccn.loc.gov/2023056475
p.   cm.

Printed in the United States of America
1st Printing

Book design by Ashley Tucker

the
HEIRLOOM

a novel

JESSIE ROSEN

G. P. PUTNAM'S SONS
NEW YORK

For all the original owners of all my precious heirlooms.
And for Geanna, for helping me write this one.

the
HEIRLOOM

ONE

U P UNTIL THE MOMENT JOHN PROPOSED, I DIDN'T know the human body was capable of feeling two opposite emotions in the exact same second. The tips of my fingers tingled with elation, and yet my legs felt like newly hardened cement. I was squarely inside pure joy and somehow watching it all unfold from above, so tense I felt dizzy. On one knee before me was the man I loved, asking a question I'd hoped was coming for months. He'd picked the perfect spot—the quietest corner of the High Line, my favorite five square feet in all of Manhattan. He'd somehow found a way to get us here from Los Angeles without me suspecting a thing. And the universe delivered him a pink-skied July where the city air was still somehow crisp. But more than all that, John was choosing me as the one person in the world he wanted to commit to for the rest of our lives. Tears clouded my eyes. *Yes* was what I should have been screaming as I leapt into his arms. But instead I was staring at the only bad part of the surprise, the one in his hands.

"Shea . . . you haven't answered me," John said, words absolutely no man wants to say after *Will you marry me?* He held the ring box up to my still-frozen face. Inside its silk-lined top were the three words that had triggered my panic: *Hudson Vintage Collectors*. They sat above what should have been the more important item inside: a gleaming emerald-cut engagement ring. But it was not shiny with brand-newness, according to the *vintage* in the jewelry store's name. It was an heirloom passed down from another woman—from another marriage. A stranger's marriage, because I knew there wasn't any jewelry being passed down from John's family. That made this a deeply meaningful piece of jewelry with a completely unknown origin. An object filled with a lifetime of karma that I was now expected to wear into my own hopefully happily-ever-after. And most important, my personal proposal nightmare.

TWO

T HIS WAS NOT SUPPOSED TO BE HAPPENING THIS WAY. In fact, I'd done my part to prevent it since the day John and I met.

"There are four, and only four, truly nonnegotiable things about me," I'd said on our first date. "Do you, John 'Middle Name' Jacobs, want to know them?"

We hadn't gotten to middle names by that point. We were three hours into what would be a twelve-hour date that started because my mouth was, per usual, working faster than my brain. I saw a man reading *No Country for Old Men* several stools down the coffee bar from me and couldn't resist telling him I thought the movie was better. It turned out the book's reader was the most attractive man in the room, if not all rooms. Meanwhile I was a sweaty post-workout mess. That was rare; I always gym-showered post-workout. And my coffee bar sit-down was rare; I'm a preorder-on-the-app type. But oddest of all was John "Middle Name" Jacobs's reaction to my unsolicited comment: he picked up his coffee and said, "Prove it."

I did, or at least I proved *something*, enough for John to suggest we keep the conversation going with a stroll to a second spot: a bookstore with a wine bar, the right kind of cheeky. It was one of the many gold flags I'd clocked, golds being the opposite of reds. There was the magnified blue of his eyes. The fact that he had some-but-thank-God-not-too-much product in his wavy hair. The way he tucked his corporate-ish shirt into his tight-ish jeans but knew adding a belt would have been one step too far, especially for a Saturday. And actual important stuff too, like how polite he was to the server who came by our table a bit too often and his responses to questions he asked me about my life while still sharing just enough about his own. That's why I decided it was time for me to share the four life-defining things—or the conversational thread I'd been using as first-date detective work for a decade.

"Fine," John said. "But if one of the four is that you're *cats*, not *dogs*, I'm out."

It was the kind of response I was always finger-crossing to hear: cute, but not in a condescending way—a Harrison Ford–character response.

"I'm dogs," I said. "And thing number one is that I will live in Italy someday."

John's eyebrows did a little rise-and-fall. It made me want to kiss him immediately. "Why's that?" he asked.

"First, I'm one hundred percent Italian on my mom's side. Second, if I could live inside a movie it would be *Roman Holiday*. But mostly because my nonna and pop once took my sister, Annie, and me there for an entire month. We stayed on

Nonna's family farm outside Salerno, picked wine grapes every day, and made pasta every night, and I swore on the plane ride home that I'd live there someday."

"Noted. And approved," said John, then quickly, "Not that you need my approval." *This guy is good.*

"Moving on to number two," I said, sliding ever-so-slightly closer to John in the circular booth we were sharing. "If I had any real singing ability—and I do not—I would be a singer. Like drop-out-of-college-to-tour-shitty-bars-across-the-country style."

"But you said you work at a film festival. Why not in music?" John asked, demonstrating excellent listening skills.

"Too painful," I joked.

"Gotcha. So this second one is more a warning if you someday wake up from a coma with the voice of . . . ?"

"Kelly Clarkson," I said.

"Kelly Clarkson," John repeated, eyes honest-to-God twinkling. "All right, so far, I'm not running away. Gimme number three."

This was where the rubber usually met the man never calling me again.

"Three: I think extreme wealth is immoral. Or is it *a-moral*? I never remember."

"I think it's *i-*, not *a-*, and how rich are we talking?"

"Bezos, Musk, and Zucks, obviously. This hedge-fundy cousin Stew on my dad's side. Essentially people who've amassed more than they'll ever need and hoard it. That's one reason I love my job: we take money from big brands and use it to help small filmmakers."

"Interesting," John said. My mind rushed back to the details he'd shared so far: *middle school math teacher* hadn't screamed *trust fund*. Then a second stat flashed: *hometown, Costa Mesa, California*. Orange County. His parents probably owned a chain of luxury car dealerships and sat on the board of "the club." In that case, this was potentially the last moment John "Middle Name" Jacobs and I would share together. I considered smooching him before it was too late.

"Well, I spent seven years working for a hedge fund run by a guy like this cousin of yours before the market crashed," he started. "Probably seven years too long by your standards, but the whole thing was so gross that I went back to school to become a teacher."

"Oh good. Very good!" I said.

"Are these things of yours some kind of test?" John asked, wisely.

"Yes," I said, because I was too buzzed off sauvignon blanc and this man's pitch-perfect answers to lie. "Now, I want to issue a disclaimer for the fourth and final thing: it's about marriage, but don't read into it."

John leaned his very solid body in, squinted his baby blues, and said, "Try me." My heart actually fluttered in my chest. I'd always thought that was just an expression.

"Number four: I am superstitious about many things, but most important among them is heirloom jewelry. I don't like it. I don't trust it. So if someone was to propose to me with an heirloom engagement ring, I would say no."

"What's an heirloom engagement ring?" John asked.

"An antique ring you buy at a vintage jewelry store that

was previously worn by an unknown woman in an unknown marriage."

"And what is there to be superstitious about?"

"Bad karma. I believe the ring carries the energy of the previous wearers' marriages."

"And then what? Gives it to you?"

"*Exactly!*" His quick grasp of the concept was reassuring.

"Okay, but *why*?" John asked.

"I'm not one hundred percent sure. In my mind the energy needs to move and so it sort of jumps—"

John laughed. "No, I mean, why do you believe this?"

"Oh. Because of my nonna. She was the queen of superstitions. No shoes on the table, no owls in the house, if you gift someone a knife you have to also gift a penny. But her rules around marriage were legendary."

"More legendary than the penny/knife thing?" I had never seen a man's brow furrow quite so adorably.

"Oh, every Italian knows that one. But Nonna owned a bridal shop, Bella Vita, and the rumor in town was that if a bride followed all her rules, she'd end up happily married. Never wear a gown without a veil, never wear pearls with your gown unless they're your mother's, never say your new name before *I do*, and never accept an heirloom engagement ring."

"And you believe in all these?" John asked. His tone suggested curiosity, not judgment, but either would have been fair. I'd had plenty of people question my "belief system" over the years, including my mother, who had believed Nonna's rules were optional, and my sister, who became fully anti-superstition after a degree in psychology.

"Well, veils are pretty, I already hate pearls, and I don't want to change my last name, so we're just left with the heirloom thing, which actually makes the most sense to me." It had always been as simple as that to me—a fact as true as the sky being blue. John nodded, taking it all in. Then he said the six words that sealed our fate: "I guess that does make sense."

I tipped across the booth and kissed him just long enough to know that the longer version would be very, very good. We parted and smiled teenage smiles, then I looked deeply into John's eyes. He had amassed so many gold flags by this point that I'd lost count. But this was my favorite, the sense that I could see all the depth, warmth, and pure goodness at his core. *This is the feeling I've been waiting for*, I realized in that moment. *This is the kind of man who could be my person.*

THREE

"SHEA? YOU'RE FREAKING ME OUT...," SAID JOHN.

The willows in the planter box beside me were poking against my arm, nudging me. And out of my left eye I saw a few tourists gawking. Even they looked nervous.

I could see straight through John's anxious eyes down to his cliff-teetering heart: he was dying inside and doing so while holding a piece of jewelry that would make any girl swoon. *He must have been saving money for months*, I thought. *Maybe that's why he took the job coaching his school's Science Olympiad team?* I focused back on John's sweet, hopeful face. His purchase was suspect, but my silence was rude.

"My answer is yes. I want to marry you," I said. "It's just..." I couldn't exactly say what I was thinking: *Why did you pick this ring? Were you just not listening when I said no heirlooms no less than five times over the course of our relationship!?!?*

John somehow stood up and scooped me into his arms in one motion. "Okay! Yes! But *shit* was that scary! Okay, I'm good. We're good." Then he stopped, looked directly at the ring, and closed the lid on the box. "Right. I should have said this first: I know the ring is vintage."

"An *heirloom* . . . ," I said, still reeling.

"Right, and I know what you've said about them." *So he heard but ignored me?* "But I searched for months, and I'm telling you, Shea, this is it. I saw dozens of rings. I even bought another one and returned it because it didn't feel right. I was looking for one connected to a sign because I know that's how you would have made this decision. That's why it had to be this exact ring, because—wait for it—I found it at the shop where you first said 'I love you.' Remember? That jewelry store in Hudson?" Now that *Hudson Vintage Collectors* inside the box made sense.

"That *does* seem like a sign," I offered slowly.

"No, wait, it gets better," said John, on a roll now. "I wasn't even supposed to be in Hudson, but my tire blew out on the drive from Saratoga to Manhattan, remember? I stopped for lunch at Baba Louie's while it got fixed. And earlier that day— *I swear to God, Shea*—I had booked our flights here, to New York, because I knew I was going to propose, but I still didn't have the ring! I walked up and down Warren Street, waiting for the car, until I just randomly stopped in front of the *I love you* spot. Just like you did that day. Remember? I had been talking about some field trip I was taking my students on? You grabbed my arm to stop me and said, 'I love you,' then we looked to our left, saw a window full of engagement rings, and died laughing." Of course I remembered. "Well, it was *that window* where an old man put this exact ring onto a stand the exact minute I walked by! And it was this rectangle cut like you told me you like! I mean, come on!" he finished. One of John's finest qualities was his inability to lie, or even exaggerate. These events had happened, all of them, and I could not deny that it was the kind of impossible coincidence that I'd follow almost anywhere. *Almost.*

"Emerald cut," I said. "And I will never forget telling you I loved you for the first time."

I took the black velvet box from John's still-trembling hands and opened it again. Perched inside was a positively gorgeous diamond surrounded by tiny baguette stones radiating outward, like a very organized starburst. I hadn't been sure exactly what kind of ring I wanted to wear when it was my turn, even after a decade of examples via every friend's bling-shot moment. For a few years, I even wondered if I could ask my future fiancé to propose with a watch like my best friend Rebecca had with her wife, Teres. But now that I saw this one, I understood the appeal.

"I knew you'd love it," John said confidently, if not 100 percent correctly.

He took the ring from its box, preparing to slip it on my left finger. I heard one of the tourists say, "*Awww,*" and wondered if someone, or everyone, was taking a picture. But my brain flipped to panic as the gold band touched my skin: *No, don't, it's not safe.* Was Nonna's ghost screaming at me? But then—

"Hmm, it's a little loose," John said. He was right. I could feel the band starting to slip off my finger. And with that sensation, a solution appeared.

"I don't want it to fall off," I said. "What if I wear it on my necklace chain to be safe, for tonight?"

THE NEXT THING I knew we were floating out of a cab for dinner at Cafe Lalo, the cozy dessert bar where Tom Hanks first sparks with Meg Ryan in *You've Got Mail* (gold *fiancé* flag!). Two seconds after that, I was bawling in the arms of my sister, Annie, who'd flown all the way from Los Angeles to be with us. In the room behind her were Rebecca and Teres, down from Boston; even more of our college best friends; and my New York City crew. I both could not believe how far John had gone to make this so special and wasn't surprised in the slightest.

"Thank you, thank you, thank you, and how in the *world* did you pull all this off?!" I sobbed.

"Welcome to the club, kids," Annie's husband, Mark, said as he handed John a beer.

Then my big sister grabbed me by the shoulders, kissed me on the forehead just like our mom would have, and immediately clocked the engagement ring *not* on my finger.

"Bathroom?" she asked.

"Bathroom," I said.

FOUR

T'S *BEAUTIFUL*," ANNIE SAID AS SHE HELD MY NECKLACED ring.

"I know, but . . . ," I started.

"Stop. You love him. *I* love him. Because John Jacobs is undeniably worth loving and marrying. Let the superstition go, Shea."

We were squeezed inside a single bathroom stall. She was seated on the closed toilet; I was pacing around in the square foot of remaining space, just like always.

Annie and I had been hiding in bathrooms ever since she was tall enough to reach the locks on their doors: ages six and two, respectively. Mom thought we went there to play, which doesn't seem very hygienic in hindsight, but we were typically dealing with one of my numerous neuroses. Once, my favorite doll had been left at home and I was worried about who would take care of her while we were at the Olive Garden. Another time, I spotted my school crush sitting in a nearby pizza parlor booth and decided that I couldn't *possibly* eat while in his presence. And when Mom and Dad fought—over the cost of the dinner bill or the rude way he'd talked to the hostess or the way he'd claimed she flirted with the waiter—Annie whisked us both away. Annie always joked that she became a school counselor because she already had decades of training with me. This was not the first time the topic of heirlooms had come up in one of our "sessions."

"But, Annie, you know what Nonna always said," I argued. "And you—*and* John—know that *no heirlooms* is one of my four things. *In life*," I said.

"Your life is bigger than four things, Shea," Annie tried.

"Dozens of people know this about me! They're *all* going to react. They're going to ask me about it. I've literally convinced other women to be anti-heirloom because of my own superstitions!"

"Which are *Nonna's* superstitions," Annie said. "The same woman that had our grandfather *BB-gun an owl* in the backyard because she thought it was bad luck." Annie tucked her pin-straight hair behind her ear like she always did when she knew she'd made an excellent point.

"I know, but the heirloom thing was always the one that made sense to me. The karma. The spirits. Annie, another woman wore this ring every single day of her marriage. *What happened in that marriage?!*"

"Breathe, Shea."

There were times when my sister's calm, wise nature was just the balm I needed. Right now it was like claw nails on a chalkboard. I half breathed to appease her. "Be honest. How bad would it be to just ask for a different ring . . . ?" I fluffed my opposite-of-straight hair, like I did when I already knew the answer to my question.

"Today?! First, I'm going to need you to be a little more grateful for the lengths this man went to!"

She was right. But the stubborn little sister in me still wanted to make her case. "Fine," I said. "But I don't love the imbalance of power here. The man just gets to dictate what the woman wears for the rest of her life, without feedback? Where's the feminism in proposals?"

Annie stood up from the toilet, nearing the end of her rope. "Marriage is a give-and-take, a lifelong series of compromises. You said yourself that John put a ton of care into this choice. It's a symbol for him, too. And not of some random spirits that are going to seep through your skin. You said he bought it where you first said *I love you*. Jesus, Shea! Either I'm walking you down the aisle to marry this man, or I'll divorce Mark and we can switch spots!"

She hair-tucked hard after that one. But she also triggered a thought. A single tear streamed down my face as I realized that I'd been too thrown by the excitement to remember the gaping holes in this life-changing moment.

"How did you do this all without Nonna and Mom?" I asked.

"I had you," Annie said, pools in her eyes, too. "And now you have me."

We lost our nonna—the feistiest five feet in all of LA's South Bay—to a bad heart when I was sixteen and Annie was twenty. We lost Mom—Nonna's sweet and sensitive only daughter—to cancer four years later. Pop the stoic—maybe because he could never get a word in—held on for a few more, but Annie was without all of them when she married Mark. They'd known each other since high school, but I think she waited until they were thirty because it was too hard to imagine her wedding day without our people. I'd walked her down the aisle.

Suddenly the memory of that moment made my teeth clench.

"Oh God, Dad," I said.

"It's fine. John asked if we should include him tonight, but I knew you'd say no."

As far as I was concerned, our father was just one more person in our life who was gone.

I squeezed Annie tight, bumping us both up against the stall door.

"Thank you," I said. "For coming here. For talking me off this ledge. For everything."

"You can thank me by having the time of your life," said Annie. "And for the rest of the night, if anyone asks, *Is that an heirloom?* you're going to say, *Technically, but now it's only mine*."

I laughed, a very good feeling. "How long you been working on that one?"

"Since the minute you walked in the door," she said. "Now go try it out on Rebecca and Teres, who drove down from Boston at six a.m. for this."

.   .   .

THE LINE WORKED. As did Annie's bigger piece of advice: I put
my superstitious thoughts in a drawer inside my brain. I felt
grateful and relaxed and truly, truly loved by everyone in my
life, and I found a way to keep that exact feeling going all the
way back home to Los Angeles.

And then, I had the dream.

FIVE

THE FIRST THING I NOTICED IN THE DREAM WORLD was the floral pattern on my dress. It was the same one I'd been wearing on the day John proposed. But I wasn't on the High Line, or even in New York. I was alone in a sea of gold-carpeted floor that smelled like old Clinique perfume: Bella Vita Bridal.

Suddenly the room shifted shape, or was I transported somewhere else? There was a mirror now, with three panels. *Yes.* This was where Nonna brought each bride to see each gown. I'd spent hours after school looking at it from a different angle, typically tucked away under the crinoline of a giant gown. Now I was on the platform. Now I was the bride.

"Here we go! All classic ball gowns first," I heard a voice say. I spun around to find Nonna in her uniform of pink slacks and a crisp white button-down, but this wasn't the version of her I'd known at the end of her life. This woman's olive-toned skin was smooth and her hair still jet-black. I opened my mouth to speak to her, but no words came out.

"I know you're not a ball gown girl, but every bride should see herself as the queen of the day."

I looked in one of the trifold mirrors, trying to see if I was the younger version of myself, too. Instead I found Annie sitting in one of the wingback chairs positioned just off to the side. The chairs for the spectators. She was younger, maybe twenty? But I didn't linger on her face because in the next seat was our mother, alive and glowing with mother-of-the-bride pride.

"Just try them, Shea," Mom said with a knowing wink. "Make your nonna happy."

I looked to find a row of dresses hung up to the right of the mirrors.

"Go ahead," Nonna said. "Take any one you want."

But my dream self was still silent. Or maybe she couldn't speak?

"Let's go, Shea . . . ," I heard Annie say. "There are literally three dozen to go . . ."

Nonna came close to me. The rest of the room dissolved into a blur.

"You just do what I always taught you, and the choice will be clear," she said.

"*Ascolta il tuo cuore*," I heard myself whisper.

"Exactly. Close your eyes and *listen to your heart*."

I did as she said, as she'd *been* saying since Annie and I were very little girls. *Ascolta il tuo cuore* applied to things as little as deciding on our annual Halloween costumes and as big as figuring out how to apologize after I'd blown up at Mom or Dad. And when it came time for my first crushes and dates and heartbreaks, it was *ascolta* still. Nonna was like my very own Jiminy Cricket.

I turned my attention from her expectant face to the long row of dresses: a wide, three-tiered taffeta skirt with an elegant ballerina-style top; a fully beaded corset and A-line bottom that looked fit for a European ball; a simple off-white boatneck silhouette in ecru raw silk that felt like it couldn't be worn without a crown. Not one tugged at my heart.

"Just start from the left," Mom said, pointing to the *Swan Lake* style. I felt myself zombie-walk toward the rack. Was I watching this happen or was I in this room? I slipped the lace straps of the gown off the hanger's arms and lifted it toward me, going through the motions. *Poof.* It vanished. I turned back to the rack—maybe I hadn't actually grabbed it? But the dress was gone. Nonna shrieked. Mom clutched her hand to her chest. Even Annie looked freaked. *Wha*— I felt myself try to say, but the words stayed trapped behind my lips. Panic flooded me.

"Okay. It's fine. We're fine. Just try another," Mom said soothingly.

I grabbed the next option in line, holding its tulle skirt more tightly as I took it from the hanger. It evaporated even faster, gone like movie magic.

"What is this? What's happening?" Nonna looked up for some kind of answer from the heavens, like she did if a light mysteriously went out. Then she turned toward me, face panicked. "Shea? What have you done?"

I did not know, and worse, I couldn't tell her. It was like my lips had been sewn shut. I flipped back to the mirror, but my face was fine. I opened and closed my mouth. Meanwhile Nonna, Mom, and Annie were searching the row of dresses, exchanging anxious whispers. Unnerved because of me. It made me panic even more. *Why can't I speak?* I stared into the mirror, begging for some kind of breakthrough. Then I took in a huge breath, tightened my center, opened my mouth, and tried over and over and over again to scream.

Suddenly I was awake and shaking. John was beside me in the bed, sound asleep. I was safe. Heart pounding, I opened my mouth and easily whispered *hello.* I touched my fingers together, remembering the feel of the dresses that had disappeared between them. Then I turned to my nightstand to check the time. Instead I saw a sparkle lit by the half-moon shining through our bedroom window: the ring. A vision of Nonna's face from the dream shot across me like a gust of wind. I'd had nothing but happy dreams about my grandmother since the day she died. But then, I'd never done something she'd so certainly disapprove of . . .

We draw the line at ghosts directing our dreams, I told myself as I grabbed my phone from the nightstand. On the screen were five new email banners: two from work and three from WeddingWire.com—because obviously the Internet started eavesdropping the second I got engaged. *The dream was just wedding overwhelm,* I thought as I crept out of bed, careful not to wake John. It was five a.m., late enough to excuse getting up. I'd distract myself with a giant cup of coffee and some final prep work for our ten a.m. pitch to woo a big new client for the festival. Another perfectly reasonable explanation for a stress dream.

I grabbed my laptop from the tote bag in the corner of the room and my robe off the hook behind the closet door. I left the ring on my nightstand.

SIX

D ID YOU SEE THEIR FACES WHEN YOU WALKED through the partnership with the Academy Museum?" My boss beamed like he'd just coached me to a spot in the Olympics. "You closed the deal right then. We'll hear from them with a yes in an hour, Anderson, tops."

"You think?" I asked, grateful now for my predawn prep sesh, despite how much coffee it had required.

"I know," he said.

Jack Sachs was a New Yorker turned Angeleno, and he still wore the suits to prove it daily. We'd worked together at the New York Film Festival, my first real job out of college, and I was part of the team that wooed him to join us in LA at what was once the fledgling LA Cinema Fest. Jack Sachs—a classic two-names-always guy—was a marketing genius. He'd taught me everything I knew about turning corporate money into an indie experience, playing our version of Robin Hood to fledgling filmmakers in the process. One time I had a few too many open-bar beverages and told him I wished he'd been my dad. Jack Sachs was a good enough guy to never bring it up.

"Shea Anderson just hooked a very big fish," he announced to the bullpen full of cubicles as we left the conference room. "Our first-ever streaming platform sponsor. And she convinced them to invest their dollars in a brand-new activation specifically highlighting Asian and Pacific Island filmmakers, previously our most underserved artists." My co-workers cheered, even moody Julie, who'd wanted in on the pitch for this deal. I struggled not to look down, uncomfortable with the attention. I had always been type A on the outside but very worried about what people thought of that. But I sipped in a quick breath to remind my body we were grown up.

"Thank you," I said. "I'm excited to get to work on this one." I had done what Jack Sachs said, and I was incredibly proud.

"HAVE A MINUTE, Anderson?" Jack asked in a suspiciously low tone as we continued down the hall.

"Sure," I said, matching his volume.

"Looks like Christy is moving on from director of brand integration."

"Really . . . Going to a competitor?"

"Don't know yet, but I want to see if I can push you to fill her shoes." I stopped walking, shocked. Jack moved me along with a look.

"Sorry, but director? She has years more experience than I do."

"You can do the job, and you deserve to try," he said, hur-

rying us into an empty cubicle at the sight of potential eaves-
droppers. "But I'm going to need to pitch this up the chain, so
can I send you to New York for some competitive research on
our old stomping grounds during their festival? I want to be
able to point to all the knowledge you have across the space."

"Absolutely," I said. "That's in two weeks, right?"

"Yep. And good. If my master plan works out, in ten years
I'll be retired and you'll be me."

Jack Sachs left me with his signature somehow-not-creepy
wink. He'd given me good news. Potentially *great* news. I
should have been bounding over to my desk trying to hide my
total glee. Instead I stood, arms crossed tight across my chest,
staring at Jack as he disappeared down the hallway.

ANNIE AND I had a standing monthly lunch date. I'd been
anxiously awaiting today's spot since we started: Koreatown's
Prince pub, recognizable from the classic seventies film *Chi-
natown*. The location was a convenient ten minutes from Annie's school and fifteen from my office. But staring into space
had made me fifteen minutes late.

"Sorry, sorry, sorry," I said, rushing to meet Annie at the
table. "Traffic."

"I'm familiar," Annie said. "I also live in this city." She
quick-crossed her arms, annoyed.

I let Annie kick things off with a major vent about the in-
sanity of the Los Angeles housing market. She and Mark had
been trying to buy something with any proximity to any beach

for almost a full year. It was maybe hurting more than helping that Mark was a Realtor. His pride had taken a beating.

"You're saving at least twenty percent of your paycheck,
right?" she asked me.

"Yes," I said.

"Good. We should have been doing that the minute we
started working, but the closest thing Mark and I had to a
wise financial mentor was the cartoon owl on our mobile
bank app. All right. You're up. Tell me something uplifting."

I figured it was wise to start with the potential job promotion instead of the weird dress nightmare. Annie's reaction
proved me right.

"Wow, Shea! That's incredible!" Annie said, lit up with
motherly pride. "You're on a serious roll."

"Thanks. It is great. I just had a weird moment after he
told me, but now I think that's because I'm still thrown from
my insane dream about Nonna's bridal shop."

"Oh no," Annie said with a face that suggested she already
knew where this was going. Her look did not shift as I re-
capped.

"I knew it!" I said, story complete. "This is my subconscious fears about the heirloom talking! I shouldn't let it go!"

Annie took one last bite of salad, then sat back in her
chair. "You know I hate playing therapist to you, but since you
refuse to hire your own, let's do this: Shea, do you honestly
think that the potential bad karma *maybe* held in your engagement ring is stronger than your actual relationship with
John?" My sister was good, which is why I didn't need my own
therapist.

"I'm sorry, but *maybe* . . . ," I said. "All I'm saying is, would you buy a secondhand couch if you found out someone had died on it?"

"Fine, but what if no one ever died on the couch?" Annie asked.

"What do you mean?"

"You're assuming someone died. That the karma is bad. What if it's not? What if it's actually good?"

That question made a synapse fire somewhere deep inside my head. I'd assumed the worst, but a happy history was a possibility and my best-case scenario. *What if I could find out whether the karma is good, not bad?*

"I'll just find out who owned the ring," I suddenly said. I felt a spark running through me now, like I'd just been plugged in.

"Wait. What?" Annie asked.

"That's it! That's what will solve this. I'll find who owned my ring before me, so I can find out if the story of their marriage was good or bad! There's got to be a way, right?"

"Oh my God, *no* . . . ," said Annie. She dropped her head between her hands then shook it back and forth.

"You don't think I can find out?" I asked.

"The no was for me," she said, refusing to meet my very eager eyes. "I just accidentally walked you to the entrance of the rabbit hole."

"Maybe," I said, stealing a fry from her pile. "But we both know me; I would have found my own way there eventually."

Annie responded by pushing her entire plate of fries over to my side of the table, admitting defeat.

SEVEN

THAT AFTERNOON I LEFT THE LONGEST, RAMBLIEST message on what was hopefully Hudson Vintage Collectors' answering machine.

Hello, I'm Shea. My boyfriend—sorry—fiancé! Sorry. That doesn't matter. Anyway! A man named John Jacobs recently bought a ring from your shop. Emerald-cut diamond, baguettes on the side, gold band. I'm wondering if you can give me any information on the person who sold the ring to your shop. Because . . . well . . . it's a long story! I'd just love to chat about the ring. Whether or not you have info. Okay. Call me back. Please. Oh, and I'm Shea.

I forgot to leave my phone number. I literally had to call back and say it on a second message. A good night's sleep was becoming a medical necessity for me.

I intended to tell John all about my new plan over dinner. Annie hadn't been the most excited audience, but I envisioned him being supportive. He'd once followed me all the way down the rabbit hole of figuring out who once lived in my apartment through their old junk mail. The answer was a local dentist with a thriving practice whom we now saw for cleanings! *This could be like that!* I reasoned to myself on the drive home. But John blew into Dr. Rachel Fine's former apartment that evening with a plan of his own.

"We don't have anything tonight, right?" he asked, hitting me with a quick kiss before running into the bedroom.

"No. I was thinking we could order in ramen and chat about some things," I said.

"Hmm, I was thinking we could go see a wedding venue," I heard from the other room.

"I'm sorry, what?"

John popped his head back into the hallway, a proud smile plastered on his face. Meanwhile my lips were a line.

"Trust me," he said. "You'll love that it's a surprise."

"We got engaged like a minute ago. Shouldn't we chat about what *we* want before scheduling venue tours?"

"It'll be quick," John said. "And fun, no matter what." His eyes were always his tell—and right now they were wide with excitement. Whatever he had planned had turned him into a kid on Christmas morning. Or maybe more like a parent with the ace-in-the-hole gift under the tree.

"Okay," I said, letting go of the rest of the arguments I'd been lining up in my head.

OF COURSE THERE was plenty of time on our drive to this mystery location to come clean about the jewelry store voicemail, but the mood—or maybe just *my* mood—didn't feel right. Instead I told John about my potential promotion.

"It's huge, Shea," he said. "You should be really proud. And we should be condo shopping . . ." He trailed off at the end, knowing it was a touchy subject. *Maybe that's why Jack's news about the job hit me weirdly,* I thought, *because I knew John would jump to this?* John was not someone who got anxious about money. He'd grown up comfortable enough and his parents never talked about their finances. Meanwhile my dad counted out Mom's weekly allowance at the breakfast table, then checked in on how she'd spent it over dinner. It had taken me forever to even tell John what my salary was. And I'd told him I thought all married people should keep separate checking accounts. Maybe I was just anxious about the reality of combining our lives in that way?

"I just don't want to be stressed about money since we'll be saving for a wedding," I said.

John nodded; there was something he was not saying. I threw him a look that let him know I knew.

"I think my parents want to pay for the wedding," he confessed. "The whole wedding."

Kay and Bob Jacobs were incredibly generous people, but I could imagine their conversation with John went something like, *We'd like to pay for your wedding; now please plan it, stat.* They'd been pressing him to get engaged for at least a year. Kay kept "casually" dropping the fact that she and Bob were engaged after nine months and still very happily married. But this was good news. A huge gift and a help to our future. *Then why is my mouth oddly dry?*

"What exactly did your parents say?" I asked, but that was just as John pulled into the parking lot of what was either the actual wedding-spot option or a very mean decoy. "We're here? Your surprise spot is the Hollywood Bowl!?" I squealed.

"Yes," John said as we parked right next to its famous twelve-foot marquee. "The world-famous Hollywood Bowl, home to decades of LA music history and a bit of our own."

"You can get married here?" I was still in disbelief.

"You can if you teach with the wife of the congressman who covers this district. But ceremony only, and not on the night of a scheduled show." I reached across the car and squeezed John's hand so hard I left a mark.

He'd taken me to the Bowl for our third date, a warm August night with just enough breeze to give my new bangs a sexy bounce. We'd shared our mutual love for the famed amphitheater on our first date, both agreeing that it was one of the only tourist spots in the city that actually belonged to us locals. The show that night was Tom Petty and the Heartbreakers, another mutual favorite. The smell of meat-and-cheese picnic spreads wafted through the seats, and the famous half-moon stage was lit up in an electric blue that vibrated against the clay canyon background. That night the Bowl became one of our special places. And like all its biggest fans, we both knew it was technically an LA County park, meaning the entire venue was open to afternoon picnics, the thriftiest date spot with a world-class view.

"Did you ever imagine something like this when you thought about our wedding day?" John asked, the breeze just warm now, three years later.

"I honestly didn't," I said, walking up the hill toward the entrance.

"Well, what were you thinking?"

I felt my legs stop moving, then a troubling thought dropped in: I'd never actually pictured the site of our wedding, or of any wedding. I'd dreamed up our honeymoon many times—two weeks traversing Italy from the heel to top laces. I had also envisioned the house we'd buy once we could finally afford a down payment—a classic Craftsman with a big front porch and an old wood door I'd paint yellow. But I had not imagined how, where, or with whom our wedding day would unfold. *Ever?* I racked my brain for some childhood vision, but there were only movie images and other friends' weddings. *My grandmother owned a bridal shop! How have I not given any thought to being a bride?*

"I think this would be really special," I finally said, which was true but didn't exactly answer the question.

John and I did pick up ramen on the way home that night, but I never brought up my new ring search plan. More wedding talk felt like too much for the night. Part of me even wondered if it would be better to never hear back from Hudson Vintage Collectors at all.

The next day I left my phone charging at my office desk as I ran from meeting to meeting. *Better to not be distracted by it*, I thought. When I came back at the end of the day, I saw three texts from John and one missed call from a number in upstate New York.

EIGHT

CCORDING TO SIMONE, THE EXTREMELY GEN Z granddaughter of the man who sold the heirloom to John, there wasn't just information on my ring, there was a handwritten note. She had to start the call with a pointed rant about her plan to propose to her future partner with first-class tickets to Paris. But the TED Talk was worth it for the intel she'd collected: My heirloom was sold to the shop by a woman named Carmela Costanza, who had left a message *in Italian*. John already thought his purchase was fated; this would seal the deal.

"It's short," said Simone. "Just one line: *Per la prossima donna fortunata*. I did a quick Google Translate and it means 'For the next lucky woman.'"

I shot up from my desk chair and threw my pen in the air. "Lucky woman! Yes! Luck is good! And this makes *me* that next lucky woman, which is *very* good! This is exactly what I needed to hear! I was just looking for some kind of sign that the ring contained good-not-bad vibes so I could wear it in peace. And this is it." I felt my body start to unwind for the first time in two weeks.

"Yeah?" Simone said.

"Yes! Of course! She's saying this ring brought good fortune! She's leaving it for the next lucky woman! Me! Which means she can't be some miserable divorced lady whose epically sad love story filled my ring with all sorts of bad marriage karma. The energy *must* be good. Simone, this is lifesaving information! God, I just wish I could thank this woman!" *I could thank this woman*, my brain repeated. Then my body plopped me back down on my chair as if to say, *You're going to want to be sitting for this*. I'd accidentally triggered a thought I could not unthink.

"I could try to find Carmela . . . ," I heard myself say.

"*Ooohh*," said Simone. "Fun!"

"No . . . Wait. I don't need to do that," I backpedaled. "That is opening a whole can of worms."

"Mmmm. You mean a Pandora's box . . ."

"Yes, exactly. Better to keep it closed."

"You think that because you don't understand Pandora's box," Simone said in her signature know-it-all tone. "It's fine, ninety-nine point nine percent of the world doesn't. Fortunately, I'm the point-one percent. I'm studying *the classics*."

"Fine," I said. "Enlighten me."

"Long story, but what you need to know is that Prometheus—the guy who ultimately creates man from clay— pissed off Zeus, king of the gods and heaven. They talked it out, then Zeus gave Prometheus's family this woman, Pandora. He said it was a peace offering, but turns out Pandora arrives, opens this jar she always keeps with her, and just leaves it on the ground. Yes, *jar*, not box. Twist! Anyway, from the jar comes sickness and death and tons of other unspecified evils. Which is a pretty baller move on Pandora's part when we consider that she was probably pissed about being a pawn in some male god's bullshit. But still, Zeus flips out, flies in, and orders Pandora to close her jar, *ASAP!* And she's like, *That's a bad idea because there's one more thing inside, and it's pretty important.* And he's like, *Bullshit! Everything has been horrible so far, and I don't trust women.* Long story short, Zeus wins, the jar gets closed, and one final thing remains inside. And guess what that final thing is?"

"Oh, um, I don't know. Famine?" I tried. I'd honestly lost the string somewhere around Pandora's arrival.

"Wrong. It was a something that *the classics* scholars now believe to be called *hope. Hope!* Incredible, right?!"

I went with my honest answer: "I don't think I get it." I could hear her slump down in disgust.

"The point is that anyone who fears they're opening the box-slash-jar is actually doing a brave thing, if they can stand to leave it open long enough."

I WALKED ONE full loop around my office block before making the decision to start searching for Carmela. I even employed Annie's recommended box-breathing tactic for reducing anxiety. None of it worked because I wasn't nervous, I was excited. *Thrilled* even. I felt like some portal had been opened by Carmela's letter. Choosing not to walk through would feel like denying destiny.

I started with a simple Google search: Carmela Costanza + Hudson, New York, assuming she lived in or directly around the town where the jewelry store was located. A Costanza Floral Boutique in Red Hook, New York, popped up. It was the exact last name, and I mapped Red Hook at just a few miles from Hudson. I clicked over to their website to find it was run by a woman named Helga, who looked as far from Italian as it gets.

Next stop: social media. I reasoned that Carmela-aged people had accounts, even if they weren't active. A quick check of *Carmela Costanza* in all of New York State netted eighty-nine results, so I knew the name wasn't rare. But none were remotely close to Hudson. Either she didn't live there anymore, she wasn't online, or—I suddenly realized—she was dead.

I typed Carmela Costanza + Obituary + Hudson, New York next. Did you mean Carmela Costanza Preston + Obituary + Hudson, New York? the nav bar taunted me. I clicked through to very bad news. Not only was Carmela Costanza dead, but her obituary included a mysterious additional last name: Preston. *Then why did she write "Costanza" on her ring note?* I clicked through to read the full obituary. Instead the link took me to a grainy photo of a serious woman with dark curls wearing a grandma-floral dress. She could have been any one of my relatives. Below the image was one very confusing line of text: *Carmela Costanza Preston is survived by her loving daughter and husband.* She'd passed just four months prior, leaving me no way to ask her why in the world she'd sold her ring and omitted her married name.

I leaned back in my desk chair, taking in everything I'd just learned. Logic told me that you don't leave off the last name of a beloved husband when dropping off his engagement ring. *Maybe Carmela never legally changed her name?* That would be odd for someone of her generation, but not impossible. Luckily years of stalking potential online dates had prepped me for this moment. I could find a second source of Carmela intel.

One hour, three pages of notes, and an unknown number of browser tabs later, I had a new name to help me put the pieces of this stranger's life together: *Gianna Preston Miller*, the "loving daughter" from Carmela's obituary.

Better yet, Gianna appeared to have uploaded old family photos onto the Hudson Garibaldi Society's very dated website.

My hope was to find a photo of Carmela and her Mr. Preston together to give some visual sense of whether or not they were happily married, or married at all. Three clicks in, I found something even more confounding. Pictured was a very happy Carmela cutting an anniversary cake beside an older, square-jawed man. On her finger was a diamond ring that looked absolutely *nothing* like the one currently secured around my neck. *If that ring was her engagement ring, then what is my ring?*

I clicked around all the sites I'd found with Gianna's info until I finally found one that included her email. *Carmela left me a note*, I reasoned. *Maybe she always hoped I'd reply?*

Hello, Gianna, I typed. I've recently learned that my fiancé

proposed to me with your mother's former ring. Forgive the in-
trusion, but I would really love to know a bit about her. I'll confess that I have a superstition about heirlooms from my own
Italian grandmother. Maybe you can relate? Thank you in advance for anything you're willing to share. All the best, Shea
Anderson

After ten drafts, I pressed SEND, then closed my laptop
and took the first deep breath I had in hours, if not days. That
was seconds before I remembered I was going to New York in
a week. I'd be just two hours south of where Carmela had died
and Gianna still lived. The chance of it all gave me chills. *Who
in their right mind could deny this coincidence?* I thought as I left
my desk for another crucial walk around the block.

NINE

M Y NEW YORK TRIP KICKED OFF WITH SEVENTY-TWO
hours of intense film festival recon. The event had
totally exploded in size since my time there, five years
ago now, and something felt lost along the way. I noticed more
large-scale activations—a new street fair featuring local businesses and a warehouse converted into one of those social
media–focused art exhibits, this one dedicated to famous
movie moments. But there were fewer and fewer chances to
interact with actual filmmakers and way fewer small films in
the lineup. In fact, one whole category of micro-budget movies had been replaced by upcoming streaming TV shows. I
noted it all in my *Harriet the Spy*–style notebook, excited to
share findings back in LA.

By Saturday afternoon I was officially off the clock. I'd
wanted to pop by the High Line for a stroll by our proposal
spot, to relive the moment without the stress of how I felt that
day, but the window of the trip was too tight. I barely even had
time to connect with John until I got on the train north.

"It's all going to be fine," he said without my prompting. John could tell my level of anxiety by the way I said hello. A lack of worry about anything surrounding the ring had been his attitude since I'd finally come clean about Carmela right before booking this very train last week.

"You didn't need to sit on the whole plan," John had said. "I would have been for it then, and I'm not worried now."

"Even about the last-name stuff?" I asked, a twinge annoyed by his laissez-faire–ness, or maybe jealous.

"Plenty of teachers at my school go by their maiden names," he'd said.

I didn't have the heart to tell him that those teachers were not from the same generation as the previous owner of my ring, or that as of that morning, I still hadn't heard back from Gianna. That was now the very last thing I wanted to think about, two hours south of trying to find her.

"Okay, distract me with some middle school drama," I said to John as apartment buildings turned to town houses outside my train car window.

"Easy," he said. "I just received an email with the subject line *Crop Tops: A School-Wide Concern.*"

———————

THE AMTRAK TO Hudson was like a theme park ride through a landscape painting of 1920s New York: misty, rolling hills met the Hudson River; stately mansions sat along the tracks; painted-on towns with lantern-lined streets were just beyond each station. No matter how much I fought the feeling, it reminded me of Dad.

I spent the first fifteen years of my life begging him to take me on the California version of this route. He commuted on the Coast Starlight from our home in Santa Barbara down to Los Angeles from Monday through Thursday most weeks. It turned Mom into a single parent for 75 percent of the time but afforded us a lifestyle far beyond what she'd grown up with under Nonna and Pop's roof in El Segundo. Annie and I went to private school in Montecito right down the street from Oprah's compound. I knew we were wealthy. I knew that was because Dad worked for the biggest importers of Japanese whiskey in the US. But I had no idea that he was on thin ice for most of his career, that Mom somehow got his work done when he was too drunk to do it himself, and that most of our "money" was thanks to credit cards. But at some point, I was old enough to realize my dad couldn't be passed out on the couch three days a week and also at his big, important job in LA those same days. Ironically, that's when things between Mom and me got ugly. I took all my rage at him out on her. She didn't deserve it.

The sound of the train horn dragged me back to the present. I focused in on the widening Hudson River gleaming outside my window. It was dotted with boats filled with people taking advantage of the lingering summer. This was not the Coast Starlight. Neither Dad nor Mom was here. *And it would not help to bring their past into my future,* I thought as I got up to shake things off in the café car.

TEN

IT WAS ONE OF THOSE STICKY LATE-SUMMER AFTER-noons in "the country" when I arrived—the kind that added a half-inch frizz halo around my hair and made my skin feel like I was five minutes post-shower. Still, walking felt right. I wanted to put myself in Carmela's shoes, strolling these streets. Had she come here for dinner with her husband? Or ventured here solo for a little antiquing and a quiet lunch? Was she a former city mouse? Or had Mr. Preston's family been local and encouraged them to live nearby?

My whole body was glistening by the time I reached the lion-flanked doors of Warren House, which would have made an excellent set for a remake of *Clue*. I used the serpent-shaped knocker to announce my arrival, then heard a scream straight out of an actual murder: "Wen-*deeeeellll*!" The double doors flew open. Inside was a teeny-tiny purple-haired woman in a purple velvet jacket, holding a dog with a purple plaid bow tie.

"You're Shea!" she screamed. "I'm Winnie! This is Wally! Wendell is *somewhere* . . . Let me show you to your room, and then we'll have coffee and talk about this whole *ring* situation. Simone's got the whole town talking! Lots of ideas! Lots of suspicions! Actually, Wally, show Shea to her room! Go, go, quick, quick! I'll make the coffee."

And with *all* that, an eight-pound dog led me up an overwhelmingly grand, purple-carpet-covered staircase to my purple-walled room.

"SO HOW LONG have you two lived here?" I asked as Winnie poured what appeared to be liquefied black tar into my violet-covered teacup. Wendell had finally joined us—a rumpled yin to his wife's elegant yang. We were several minutes into our gathering, and I still wasn't sure if he spoke.

"Five years the first time, and now twenty-five the second," Winnie answered for them both.

"Where were you for those years in the middle?" I asked.

"Well Wendell went to New Mexico to work on God knows what; it's still classified. And I went to Acadia, Maine, to open a B&B with my sister."

"Oh. You were in separate places?"

"Yes. Divorced. And both *re*married." Wendell had yet to react to any of this information. He may have been asleep.

"And so now you two are . . . ?"

"Married again! To each other. To be clear."

"*Wow*," I said. "Also, if you don't mind my asking, *how* and *why*?" Winnie added a tablespoon of sugar to her coffee, then mine. This explained her energy.

"Well the first time was right at first, then not. I think we were too young. But there were no hard feelings. We kept in touch, and we ended up missing each other. And by the second time, we were who we should have been to make it work the first time, so it stuck. So far! Right, Wen?" Wendell shrugged one shoulder.

"That's . . . wow," I said. *How would I think of a ring's karma if it held Wendell and Winnie's story?*

"But here's the thing for *your* thing," Winnie said, plowing ahead. "I insisted on a new ring for the second go-round. New proposal. New marriage. New ring!" She pointed to a wide gold band on her left ring finger with a row of inlaid amethysts, of course, then she looked down at the diamond around my neck. "Smart to keep it there until you crack it wide open. The story, not the diamond! Diamonds are very strong. Though, that's more Wendell's territory than mine. Anyway. We support you no matter what! Don't we, Wen?"

Then, *finally*, Wendell opened his mouth to grace us all with three words that made up for all his silence. "Metal conducts energy," he croaked.

"Exactly!" Winnie said. "You know, one time I was wearing a—"

"Wait. What did you say?" I asked, turning to Wendell.

"Metal conducts energy," he repeated. "And your ring is metal."

"Would you mind giving me a little more of a lesson on that?" I asked.

Apparently, *lesson* was the magic word. Wendell proceeded to speak like a Wikipedia page come to life—light on the *life* part.

"Under an electric field, free electrons move through the metal like billiard balls knocking against each other. They pass an electric charge as they move. The transfer of energy is strongest when there is little resistance. The most effective conductors of electricity are metals that have a single valence electron that is free to move. This is the case in the most conductive metals, such as silver, copper, and gold, like your ring."

"And what exactly is being conducted?" I asked, hoping I'd followed.

"Energy, dear," Winnie said. I got the sense she was worried her husband would power down, what with all this conversing.

"Right, but what exactly is *energy*?" I directed my query to Wendell. It was worth it to me if my questions tired him out so much he slept for an entire week after this.

"Energy?" he repeated, animated for the first time since we'd sat down. "It's what's we're made of—who we are. It's everything. And metal holds it, until it passes it along."

Wendell's slumped posture and straight lips said, *It's all very simple*. But to me this was an earth-shattering confirmation of what I'd believed forever. The first piece of truly affirming information I'd heard in decades of carrying around Nonna's warning. And it was science! Facts! My favorites.

"Thank you both so much," I said before Winnie poured yet another cup of tar. "But I have to go meet Simone."

"Right! Two o'clock at Hudson Roastery!" The town gossip truly did know all. "There's a bike on the rack out front for you to use. The purple one!"

I felt airy all over thanks to Wendell's encouraging tutorial. So much so that I decided to check my phone one more time for a reply from Gianna. My pulse quickened as I opened the email app: at the very top was the icon for one new message. Next to it was Gianna's name.

Hi, Shea. Congratulations on your engagement. Unfortunately, I'm not in a place to help you. That's not the ring that my father gave my mother. In fact, my mom would never tell me who gave her that ring. It was a secret she chose to keep forever. Hard as it's been for me to live without knowing, I believe I should honor her wishes now that she's gone. My apologies, but good luck.
—Gianna Preston Miller

ELEVEN

I SHOULD HAVE DITCHED THE "BIKE" FROM WENDELL AND Winnie's the moment I found it leaning up against a rusted piece of fence. I was already feeling defeated after reading Gianna's note. Riding a purple hunk of metal up a mile of cracked sidewalks was not the answer. Within five minutes, a grinding clank was coming from the wheels, and a frustrated moan from my body.

"Something's wrong with your bike," I heard a voice behind me say.

"Ya think?" I answered. I would have looked back to roll my eyes, but I was too afraid I'd fall on my face.

"It's the chain." The bike-splainer's voice was male and deep in an Adam Driver way. Normally I would have found that attractive. Right now I wanted to throw something in its direction.

"Anything I can do about that without falling off this heap?" I called out.

"No," was his one-word reply. With that I turned around to snap back and—*obviously*—fell off the bike.

"Oh man . . . saw that coming. You okay?" not–Adam Driver asked as he glided my way. He was my age-ish and rumpled-ish, but still handsome without qualification—the kind of guy I would have shot a look at across a bar in my dating days. I felt myself stop my eyes from doing their old thing right now by default.

"I'm fine," I said as I picked myself up. He made a delayed effort to help, awkwardly grabbing my arm to hoist me off the sidewalk. My body fluttered at his warm touch, another old reflex.

"Why are you even riding this?" the stranger asked.

"They gave it to me at the inn up the street," I said. If he wasn't going to introduce himself, then neither was I.

"I thought that was you from the train station earlier," he said with a coy smile. "If I'd known you were headed to Grey Gardens, I would have warned you about the bike . . . and Winnie's coffee." So he was a local-ish?

"Mmm, you think Winnie is Big Edie and Wendell is Little?" I immediately regretted encouraging him, but that *Grey Gardens* reference was just so perfect.

"No, it's obviously Winnie as Big and the dog as Little," he said. I laughed out loud, then instantly regretted that, too. This man looked like the type that made sport of getting women to laugh.

"So, could you maybe help me fix this bike chain issue?" I asked.

"Nah. Sorry. That thing's way beyond repair," he said.

Then he hopped back on his own bike and started to pedal away. It made my ears hot, but I stopped myself from reacting, figuring it was exactly what he craved.

"Cool! Guess I'm walking," I said.

"Enjoy!" he called back from yards away. "It's a nice day!" Then he tipped his nonexistent hat in the most annoying manner and sped off. *Humming.*

I spent the next twenty minutes dragging myself to the coffee shop, trying to imagine how Nora Ephron would have rescripted that scene to give me the last, perfect word.

TWELVE

SIMONE WAS EXACTLY WHAT I'D PICTURED THROUGH the phone, the central casting version of upstate artsy: short, chic black hair; dewy skin without a lick of makeup; wearing a linen jumpsuit in—*obviously*—black. I was so intimidated by her that I withheld the disappointing Gianna info.

"So . . . remember I mentioned my cousin Graham? The one helping me get Grandad's files organized at the jewelry store?"

"No," I said.

"Hmm, well. I have this cousin Graham, he's a feature writer. Been published all over, including the *New Yorker*," she said with obvious affect. "He comes up here from Brooklyn on the weekends, and he was really into your story when I told him about it, so he did a few things to help you out." Simone's tone had shifted from too-cool to guilty kid sister. I knew it well.

"What kind of things?" I asked.

"Um. He can explain . . . because he's coming to meet us. Warning: he's kind of . . . intense."

"Wait. Simone. Before he gets here, there's something I really need to tell you about Gianna—" I started, but then a very familiar character glided up to our table.

"You?" I asked, suddenly tense.

"You," he said, as if he'd known all along.

"What is happening?" Simone asked.

"We already met. Sort of. Your cousin stopped to inform me that my broken bike was broken, then disappeared."

"Was I supposed to carry it and you on my own two wheels?" The question was rhetorical, and he delivered it while pulling a third chair over to our two-chair table, grabbing a piece of Simone's croissant, and dropping a bomb: "Anyway, I found Gianna Preston."

"Told you he was good," Simone tried.

Graham pulled out a tattered notepad covered in hieroglyphic handwriting while I tried to decide if I was livid or thrilled.

"Address is 51 Outlook Lane, Red Hook, New York. She's an Italian teacher at the high school there. She has a tutoring session with a kid after last bell today but should be home after four o'clock, so we'll go then."

"Whoa. *Hold on. We* are not going anywhere," I said. "At least not until I know how you got this done."

Graham finished Simone's croissant, then replied, "I've got a guy at the hall of records. And a guy at the school board. And a teacher at the school. Can't share any source names, obviously." I would have hated this man if I weren't pretty damn impressed.

"This is huge!" Simone said. "You two can go talk to Gianna about the ring. I'd offer to join, but people tell me I'm polarizing."

The timing of my reveal that I'd already "talked" to Gianna was now further from ideal.

"I heard from her this morning," I said. "She doesn't want to discuss the ring, so this whole thing is over."

Simone's face fell. Graham's ears perked up.

"Read me the message," he said.

"I just told you what it said," I barked back.

"No, you told me what *you* said it said. I want to read what *she* said."

Graham didn't seem like the relenting type. I pulled up the message and handed over my cell phone.

"Doesn't say *stay away*. Doesn't say *I'll never talk about this*. You still have every right to doorstep her. Any good journalist would," he said. "Sorry, *doorstepping* means—"

"I know what it means," I said. "I've seen *Spotlight*. But I don't want to invade her privacy. It's rude."

"Look," he continued, "do what you want, but I'm sure we can crack this woman."

"What's in this for you?" I finally thought to ask.

Graham didn't skip a beat. "A big article, I'm hoping."

"I told you not to tell her about that . . . ," Simone whispered. I went to shoot her a big-sister death stare but got caught watching Graham add more hieroglyphics to his little notepad. *Is he writing something about me?*

"Look," Graham said. "I just finished a travel piece for the *Atlantic*." His emphasis made my skin crawl. "But I want to get back into personal features, and I think you have a good one."

"So you're using me and my story," I said.

"While you use me and my ten-plus years of journalism experience," he replied.

I sipped my coffee, stalling. Then I looked at Graham, trying to get a sense of whether he was going to help or hurt. In his eyes, I saw an excitement that I immediately recognized: *mine*. In fact, Graham was the first person who seemed as intent on solving this mystery as I was. And I wasn't in a position to be turning down help.

———

I WATCHED, HEART racing, from the front seat of the beat-up Volvo we'd borrowed from Simone as Graham made good on his promise. His plan had been to throw himself under the bus with Gianna. Apologize for putting me in this awkward situation, then beg for her mercy and understanding. I could literally feel the charisma dripping off his body from twenty feet away. But he appeared to be up against a tough opponent. Gianna was tall, obviously thanks to the Preston side of her heritage. I remembered a picture of Carmela's husband towering over her petite frame in one of the photos I'd found online. But she had her mother's exact coloring—the jet-black hair that caught every ray of light and deep olive skin. And Carmela's piercing eyes. Right now they were still staring daggers at Graham, but I watched as they slowly softened while he made his case on her doorstep. Five minutes later he was running back to the car.

"You're good to go," he said, slipping into the driver's seat. "You'll get more out of her solo—plus I've got to run. Call Winnie for a pickup when you're done, and email to let me know how it goes." Then he produced a slip of paper torn from the front pocket of his shirt. It was all like some kind of weird magic act.

"Whoa. Okay. How did you—" I started, but Graham's smug face answered the question and made me question if I should, in fact, email him.

Five minutes after that, I was sitting at a kitchen table with Gianna, or Gia, as she'd told me to call her—hopefully a good sign? The old, cozy farmhouse was filled with framed photos of Tuscan landscapes and that famous lemon-printed pottery from Amalfi. I knew both because the home of every cousin on my mom's side looked the same. It relaxed me, which helped because Gia's expressionless face did not.

"Where in Italy is your family from?" she asked as she poured us espresso from an old Bialetti. It was my fourth cup of the day, but oddly the caffeine was taking the edge off my anxiety.

"Campania," I said. "Salerno specifically. Yours?"

"Just north of Florence. Have you been?"

"Years ago. You?"

"We go every year, but not to the town where my mother

was from." *That's ominous,* I thought, suddenly wishing Graham were here to take notes. "I'm sorry I was short in my message," Gia said, settling into the kitchen chair beside me. "Especially because I understand what you're doing. We Italians can let our superstitions rule us. My mother insisted I pass on a gorgeous house my husband and I found because the Realtor opened an umbrella in it during our tour."

"Which is exactly why you brought her with you to see it, right?" I asked.

"Of course," Gia said with the first real smile I'd seen yet.

"Do you think that's why your mom left the note with her ring in the first place?"

"I do," she said. "And I think she'd love that an equally superstitious woman got it." I felt myself smile, then my whole body unwound. *Maybe I was meant to be here?*

Gia spent the next few minutes telling me more about Carmela Costanza Preston. She'd had a green thumb and a hot temper, especially when it came to defending her one, beloved daughter. She cooked three hot meals for the family every single day but never, ever used a recipe. And as far as Gia knew, she was happily married to one man until the day she died. Naturally he died of a broken heart two months later. Carmela sounded like someone I would have loved. But all this also made me feel deeply connected to Gia.

"You know, I lost my mother too," I confessed. "And she took some mysteries with her." The eerie connection sent a ping to my heart. Gia nodded, then her eyes went to the ring hanging on my necklace. *Her mother's ring.* After that they met mine and she nodded again, seemingly ready.

"I found it in a box way in the back of Mom's top dresser drawer. I was probably ten. Too young to know that you don't ask your mom about the gorgeous engagement ring she's hiding, but old enough to know she's lying when she says it belongs to some old *zia* back in Italy. On my wedding day, I finally got out of her what little info I have. I think Mom was feeling sentimental about her past. There was a man before my dad. They'd met when she was very young, still in Italy. He either proposed with that ring or just gave it to her; I'm not sure. All she said was that he was her first love and the reason she left home."

"But not the man she married . . . ," I said, now perched on the very edge of my chair.

Gia was leaning far back in her own chair, as if keeping herself just a little distant from it all. "I know. It's this giant question mark on the person I thought I knew best in the world. And I think it has something to do with why she became estranged from her family."

"Do you think your mom would have wanted you to have a relationship with them? Especially now that she's gone?" I asked.

"I don't know, but I'd love one. She had one sister, my *zia* Maria. I've been thinking about her so much since Mom died. I feel like she should know, if she's still alive."

"I'm sure we could find out," I heard myself say. I'd never been known to leap before I looked, but a plan was forming in my mind faster than I could question its sanity. "What if I reach out to your aunt, like I reached out to you? I'd be a curious, newly engaged woman who did some research. We wouldn't even have to tell her that you and I met, if you think it would put her off."

"You did get me to talk somehow . . . ," Gia said, wheels clearly spinning.

"Then maybe she'd be willing to, especially in honor of a sacred Italian superstition," I offered.

Gia gazed across the kitchen to the living room, where I saw a painting of what could have been the rolling hills of the very town where her mother was raised hanging above the red brick fireplace. "What's the chance of all this . . . ," she said to herself, a look of absolute wonder enveloping her face.

THIRTEEN

I T'S THAT REAL FOR YOU?" JOHN ASKED. "YOU'D FLY clear around the world to go maybe meet a complete stranger because of this superstition?" His questions made his own position on the matter abundantly clear. So did his tone.

We were making our way up the trail at Ernest E. Debs Park on the Monday morning after my return. The hike was our Sunday a.m. ritual—our "church"—but we'd woken up early to fit it in before the workday. The perfect chance to talk about all I'd learned, I'd thought. Turns out big conversations are best had on flat surfaces.

One of the first ways I knew how much I loved John was the fact that I couldn't imagine keeping things from him. Everything from *I ate all the rest of the lasagna!* to *I hate how your friend Jim talks to you* came out without my worrying about the impact. That honesty, which I'd relied on so heavily, had been off-kilter since we got engaged. I hadn't been clear with John about my apprehensions around his parents' having too much wedding leverage if they paid for the whole event. And I still hadn't shared any of the details of my bridal shop nightmare. Answering the question on the table with complete candor felt like a test, for myself.

"Yes," I said. "My superstition is that real. It always has been. It's a huge part of this whole next step we're taking together, John, and I really hope you can understand that."

John slowed to press up a steep section of the trail. I watched as his lips twitched like they always did when he landed on a tougher thought. *What is he thinking?*

We rounded the bend before the big downtown LA overlook with nothing but the sound of labored breathing between us. John was the first to plop onto the wood bench at the cliff's edge—the one with all the couples' names carved in it, including ours.

"I haven't brought this up because I don't want to go there," he started. "But you needing all this proof that the ring is safe to think we're safe . . . I've kind of been here before . . . you know."

I did know, and the fact that I hadn't connected the dots until now dropped a weight of guilt through me.

"Carrie," I said.

"Yeah," said John. "I know it's not the same, but . . ." His silence told me that in many ways, it was.

John and his ex-girlfriend Carrie had dated for almost four years. They broke up because she felt like they were growing apart. She wanted to try living abroad; he wanted to get tenure in his existing school district. John told me that the worst part of that breakup was feeling so stupid for not seeing the signs until it was too late. But from what I'd heard over the years, Carrie was hiding the signs. That was the exact history I was trying not to repeat.

"I'm sorry," I said. *I understand*, is what almost came out first, but that wasn't true. John was the first real relationship of my life. I'd had two high school boyfriends, both conveniently around prom time, and one of those classic unrequited college loves. But my early twenties were filled with three-date wonders and fun flings. I did not know what it was to have your heart broken in that way.

I reached across the bench to lace my fingers through John's, then I scooted closer toward him. I was obsessed with metaphoric markers—birds flying over big moments or symbolic songs playing on the radio. John needed actual evidence, signs he could build into a clear-cut case.

"I want to be with you, John," I said. "But I feel like I can't start thinking about a wedding until I've gotten all my fears about this ring out of the way. That's all this is: me resolving my superstition, so we can move on."

"Okay," he said. "I needed to hear that. And look, I don't want to be pushing us faster than you want to go, but aren't you just ready to cross *getting married* off the list so we can start the next phase of our lives?"

Something about John's way of seeing it bumped me. I let my fingers loosen from his.

"Do you think it's going to be that different than this phase of our lives?" I asked.

"I don't know. Maybe? We'll be married. We'll buy a house. We'll start to really organize things for our future, right?"

"Right," I said, but that was a reflex. I'd never really considered how becoming husband and wife would make us any different than we were today—how that step makes anyone different. Had anything changed about Annie and Mark, or Rebecca and Teres? What would any of those three women say if I asked them what it felt like to be a *wife* versus a *girlfriend*? How had I never asked that question?

"I didn't mean to get us off track," John said, squeezing my hand. "Back to Italy. Go if you need to. But you said the note from Carmela was positive. She said you were lucky. Isn't that all you were trying to find out?"

The correct answer was yes, but that's not what came out of my mouth as I looked into John's expectant eyes.

"I feel like I need to know more," I said. "And I'm asking you to trust me."

FOURTEEN

I VAGUELY REMEMBER DRIFTING OFF TO SLEEP AFTER A massive cup of chamomile tea that night. But then I was back inside a bathroom stall, maybe the very one from our engagement party in New York. Suddenly the door swung open.

"Annie?" I asked, squinting to make out the blurry figure of a woman.

"No, Shea," the shape replied. Mom. Or at least her voice. I still couldn't make out more than the outlines of the body two feet from my face. It was as if I was looking through a window caked with dirt.

"Mom, hi! Why can't I see you?!" I reached out to try to touch her skin, but the space between us suddenly widened, as if to say, *Don't you dare.*

"Take this, Shea. Now!" Mom said as she thrust her hand toward me, then uncurled her fingers. I somehow focused in, only to see that there was nothing inside her hand.

"Take what?" I asked. "There's nothing there."

"Shea, stop! Now!" Mom said. "Just take it and go! *PLEASE!*"

One of the most impressive things about our mother is that she never, ever yelled, even when Dad was yelling in her face. Even when he tried to do the same to Annie or me. She'd make her voice as calm and quiet as possible to fight back, which turned out to be deadlier than any outburst. Something was wrong here. I moved toward her again. Her cloudy shape slipped out of the stall, like smoke through a chimney. I pushed through the door to follow. Now we were on the Debs trail bench, but Mom was even wispier. A ghost.

"I don't want to push you faster than you want to go, but don't you want to fix this?" she asked. *What is she talking about? And didn't John just say that?* Mom opened her hand again, but there was still nothing but the deep purple veins of her palm. "Take the ring," she said. I flew back from her, suddenly understanding exactly what she was trying to do.

"*NO,*" I yelled. My long, deep cry lingered in the foggy air between us, and it made my mother vanish.

I WOKE UP cold this time. John had all the covers. I sat upright, breathing slowly to calm my racing heart. I didn't need to check my surroundings to be sure what I'd just seen wasn't real. Maybe because this nightmare was so connected to something that had actually happened.

I grabbed my robe, then left the bedroom. I didn't want John to wake up and ask me what was going on. I didn't even know if I was ready to try to answer that question for myself.

I splashed warm water from the kitchen sink onto my

chilled face, then took myself to the couch. My legs criss-crossed down onto the center cushion, then my eyes started to close, as if by instinct. I felt myself almost wanting to trans-port back to that dream—like my brain was finally encourag-ing me to move toward a long-buried memory, rather than protecting me from it. Maybe it had constructed that whole dream as a first nudge.

I drifted back to the very moment I'd spent years avoiding: Mom and I in the shabby Redondo Beach apartment where she lived until the very end. I was visiting after work for one of my weekday dinner-and-bedtime shifts. I'd found Mom in her bedroom, coiled over the top of her old rattan dresser. She'd set up a dozen or so pieces of jewelry, like an indoor yard sale. She was slow and quiet by then. The cancer had taken over about 80 percent of her blood vessels, making every tiny task a Herculean effort. She leaned against the gray metal walker that she needed to shuffle around the house. The rainbow tie-dyed sweat suit I'd bought her the week prior swallowed her vanishing frame.

"I know this is a little strange, but I wanted to make it special," she said as she walked me over to see what was ar-ranged on the dresser. "And you, Annie, and I don't keep se-crets from each other, but this is a *just us* thing, okay? I'll give Annie her own set of special pieces, with all their own stories."

Mom loved ceremony—marking important moments with a little grandeur so they'd be even more memorable. She'd in-sisted on splurging for high tea at the Casa del Mar on the day I got my first period. When Annie moved in with Mark she surprise-filled their whole new living room with balloons.

And one year she even learned Nonna and Pop's wedding song on the piano—"As Time Goes By"—then made Annie and I sing it as she played for their anniversary.

"I want you to know the stories of these things," she said. "And I want you to wear them on as many adventures as you can. You've got your whole life ahead of you, Shea. And you'll make all the right choices because you're braver than me."

The speech was stilted. Mom was searching for her words, trying to make them make sense in her foggy mind. But I knew what she was trying to say. And deep down I appreciated the moment she was trying to create for us. I just couldn't bear it. It meant Mom knew her time was running out, and I refused to accept that was true.

"Mom, no. Not now. We should be outside! At the beach! Or—*oooh*—we could go to Huckleberry for the Green Eggs and Ham. Your favorite!"

"Oh, pretty irresistible . . . ," Mom said. "Let me just share a few things with you about some of these pieces, so that after I'm—"

"Later, Mom! I promise! It's just the nicest part of the day, and Dr. Charles said vitamin D is really good for you right now. Let's pop out and we'll talk about your jewelry after."

I won. We went to Huckleberry. We ordered the Green Eggs and Ham. Mom ate three bites, then was too tired to even hold her fork. Within minutes of us getting home, she was asleep on the hospital bed in the living room. That's when I finally returned to the dresser to examine the items she'd laid out, too curious to actually ignore what she'd wanted to present. My eyes landed on a single glisten in the center of the display, and my body immediately went hot. Nestled in a white, square box was the last thing I wanted to see, let alone inherit: the thin gold band and square diamond setting I'd come to loathe over the years—Mom's engagement ring from Dad.

We'd had many arguments about her insistence on wearing it after she finally left Dad. I couldn't make sense of her holding on to their relationship after it was finally over. My teenage move had been to pretend the ring didn't exist. I avoided looking at it completely. And Mom knew it. *Why in the world did she think I would want it in my life?* I thought that day.

My eyes opened as I realized I was having the same exact thought right now, over a decade later. If anything, it was stronger now that I was starting to envision my own future marriage. *I would never. How could she?* I felt my throat tighten as the rest of the details of that day came flooding back before I could stop them.

I'd planned to ask Mom what she was thinking the moment she woke up—to say a firm *no thank you*, then remind her that she shouldn't waste a second of her sweet time left thinking about that man. But I couldn't bring myself to do it when she woke, weak and groggy. Two weeks later Mom was gone. The ring was buried with her, as was any way of knowing how she'd answer the *why* that I was never brave enough to ask.

Hot tears streamed down my face. This was the first time I'd let myself feel the searing regret of my mistake since the day of Mom's funeral. I squeezed the pillow into my chest, trying to wring out all the feelings still wound inside me. Under all the pain was a thought: I couldn't turn back time to that afternoon in her apartment. But maybe the heirloom from John was a way to correct a cosmic imbalance?

FIFTEEN

"MISS, IS THERE SOMETHING I CAN GET YOU? MAYBE a hot tea?" the flight attendant asked, leaning over me with clasped hands like the kindest of kindergarten teachers.

"Oh, I'm sorry. Did I accidentally call you?" I quickly scanned the buttons on my armrest.

"No, you just looked . . . well . . . I just wanted to check in. It can be hard to sleep, but sometimes a hot herbal tea helps."

I looked around to find that I was the only wide-eyed passenger on the middle-of-the-night flight, then caught a glimpse of my twitching foot sticking out into the aisle.

"Yes," I said, "tea would be great, thank you."

I was Italy-bound once again, "thanks to the heirloom," John had pointed out as he drove me to LAX. "That's got to go in its plus column."

His kindness was killing me, because I was going without him. We'd debated waiting for John's next school break but both agreed a two-plus-month delay would let my anxiety run away with me. My compromise was to use my rainy-day account, not our shared big-trip savings, and to only be gone for a week. Things were slow enough at work that I could pop away on short notice, and Jack Sachs even gave my mission his fatherly blessing. Though that may have been because I referred to it as "an important family matter."

"We can still go back there for our honeymoon, right?" John asked as we crawled toward the international terminal. "I was hoping for a repeat of our first trip minus you planning every single detail."

"Hey! That's what you get for hijacking my vacation," I said.

"Funny. I remember it as you drunk-inviting me to go away with you after three weeks of dating," he replied for the win.

I smiled at the memory and the truth of how it actually unfolded. "Now might be a good time to confess that I wasn't drunk at all. I just didn't want you to think I was the insane girl inviting you across the world after four dates." I didn't say *as a test*.

Pop used to say that if you could spend two weeks in a foreign country without a major fight, you could go the long haul. I saw that in action when Nonna had her wallet stolen on day one of our trip to the motherland. In it was $300 of her traveler's checks, which Pop had tried to insist she wear in a hide-a-bag tucked inside her sweater. She was mortified, but he didn't once say *Told you so*. In fact, he waited until she was napping that afternoon to go replace the funds, then tried to convince her he'd "found" the money on a park bench.

"Is it weird that our seventy-year-old grandfather is my ideal man?" I remember asking Annie that day.

"No, it's a relief because he's mine too," she'd said.

I was terrified to test Pop's theory out on my new relationship with John, and things started off rocky when I discovered that his Italian accent was just as loud as it was *horrific*, but he was nothing but kind when he used it *everywhere*. John also brought along travel skills in categories where I was sorely lacking, i.e., metro system maps and exchange-rate math. Together we made it to every single stop on my very detailed itinerary.

But it was the things I'd never thought to plan that made that time together so special. John found a walking-tour app that took us to all the places famous Americans had once lived in Rome. When I said I was obsessed with the hotel soap, he tracked it down in a Florentine department store. And he upped my restaurant game with his food obsession; John asked if the chef would be willing to share their recipe every time we fell in love with a specific dish. By the time we flew the thirteen hours and ten minutes back to LA, I was pretty convinced he was *my one*. *Italy is not going to be the same without him*, I thought as I let the salve of hot tea run through my still-jittery body.

"Bump into my armrest again, and I'll kill you," the voice next to me barked. And with that I realized—once again—that the trip definitely would not be the same *with* Annie.

SIXTEEN

I 'D EXPECTED A LONG LECTURE FROM MY SISTER TRYING to convince me not to go on this trip, which is why I crafted a very specific, Annie-oriented argument before sharing the news at our bonus workday lunch. It included words like *compelled* and *fated*; key points of persuasion like *once-in-a-lifetime journey* and *Nonna would insist*; answers to the questions I knew she'd ask, like *plenty of saved up vacation days* and *budget-friendly hotels*. The only thing I held back was the details of my most recent dream, and more important, the memories it inspired. I'd kept my promise to Mom and never told Annie about the time she tried to give me her engagement ring. As far as I was concerned, there was no point bringing it up now. Especially now.

Annie had listened to the entire Italy-trip rationale, then responded as if I'd just told her I needed to go to the mall.

"Fine, but I'm coming." Her argument: "You've been making a lot of impulsive choices over the past few weeks. You need a chaperone." My eyes insta-rolled at the preach in her voice. But being in Italy together as teens had been pure magic, and I couldn't argue with the idea of having a little help on hand.

Luckily we had something of a head start. "Big-shot" journalist Graham had set us up with a friend who worked for the Rome bureau of the *New York Times*. She was already at work trying to identify individuals with the last name Costanza living in the town where Gia believed her mother had grown up, little Borgo San Lorenzo, just fourteen miles north of Florence. Still, things were bound to get tricky in a language that neither of us spoke. I'd also have to contend with the issue of Travel Annie, her Mr. Hyde self.

My sister was much more homebody than world traveler. Her calm, rational nature evaporated the minute she stepped foot in an airport. Also, she got *extremely* motion sick. But Annie's mood since leaving LAX had been even more unpleasant than usual.

"If I don't eat something the minute we get into the city, I'm going to pass out," she said after we cleared customs.

"They served us like six meals on the plane. Why didn't you eat any of that? We need to get to the train station so we can book tickets to Borgo," I said.

"Then you go. I'll find a café, and we'll meet at the hotel."

I bought us time with the world's most delicious airport pizza—the first *only in Italy* moment of the trip. Then we cabbed over to quaint little Piazza Santo Spirito for a full meal. I'd done my research and booked us a hotel off the tourist-beaten path.

Despite the long flight, moody sister, and very strange circumstances of this journey, I was back in my happy place. My feet glided across the treacherous cobblestones of the ancient streets as if they had been raised here. The aroma of sharp coffee and soft cheese crept into my nose, making my mouth water. The bouncy melody of Italian echoed everywhere I turned. I loved Italy most because it reminded me humans have five distinct senses, and they can all be lit up at the same time.

"Order me something," Annie barked after we were shown to a plaza-facing café table. "Mark's called me a thousand times, and I need to call him back."

Apparently, there was trouble on the home front, so much that Annie kept getting up and down to call Mark. Once during our antipasti course—*prosciutto di Parma* and *calamari alla griglia*, of course. Once during the *primi*; I insisted on *tortellini en brodo*, the hardest thing to find in the States. And *twice* when we were supposed to be eating *bistecca alla Fiorentina*, a crime considering it arrives to the table at a pitch-perfect temp and costs an arm and a leg.

"All right. Enough," I finally said. "What is going on with you two? Is this about the house hunt? Or is something else wrong?"

Annie's already giant eyes widened. She looked . . . caught?

"No. It's not the house thing, and there's nothing wrong with Mark and me. It's just—" Her face went sheet white, then green-gray, then she stood up from the table, *again*. "Hold on. I need to—" I jumped up from my seat to loop my arm around her teetering body.

"You need to sit down before you pass out! Are you sick?"

But Annie did not have the chance to answer before she threw up all over the ancient cobblestone piazza.

"I'm not sick," she finally said, more mortified than ill by this point. "I'm *pregnant*."

"OKAY, HOW LONG have you known? And when are you due? And is it a boy or a girl? And do you want a boy or a girl? And—wait—why the hell are you in *Italy* with me right now?! This is the land of wine and soft cheese and strong coffee! This is the worst babymoon . . . and your husband isn't even here."

We'd rushed to check into our room for quicker bathroom access. Annie was now fully horizontal, with a hot towel on her head. I was lying next to her, propped up on my elbow like the most eager girl at the sleepover.

"You know Mark's more the Corona-on-a-beach guy," she said. "And I know we can technically travel together when I have kids, or *a kid* given how this pregnancy is going. But it won't be the same. I'll be worried about them the whole time, calling Mark back home every hour to make sure he's keeping them alive. I wanted to gallivant around Italy with you wearing fabulous scarves like we did when we played *Only You* on our first trip."

"*Awwww*," I said. "Now we have to watch it while we're here!"

The criminally underrated Marisa Tomei and Robert Downey Jr. rom-com was beloved by us as the Marisa Tomei and Bonnie Hunt sister comedy.

"Oh man, remember how mad that old cousin of Nonna's was when she found out we'd borrowed all her scarves for our side trip to Sicily?" Marisa and Bonnie had a scarf for every scene, so we had to make do.

"I do," Annie said, "but I can't laugh about it right now or I'll puke."

It was only eleven a.m. in Florence, given the red-eye from LA. We were supposed to be using this time to recover for the mission ahead, but now I had a second, more urgent task to pull off: a perfect Florentine sistermoon.

Annie and I "ran" around the city for the next three hours. We hit the Uffizi and did a five-minute spin around the *David*. We saw Il Duomo and Il Ponte Vecchio. We made it to two *chef's kiss* gelato spots. And then we went straight to the source—Prada Firenze—where I bought scarves for us both, despite Annie's (weak) protests. Some moments were worth the splurge, I told her, then warned her I'd raise her child to believe the same. By four p.m., I'd fully triumphed by getting us all the way up to Piazzale Michelangelo to see the monks of San Miniato al Monte do their evening chant.

"I get why living here someday is one of your four things," Annie said as we strolled back down the hill toward our hotel. "Please come back to the States often to visit your niece or nephew."

"Oh, I don't know if I could live here for long once there's a mini you running around LA," I said.

Annie saw the sign first. Literally and metaphorically.

"No way!" she said, then she spun me around until I was facing it too: *Bella Vita Bridal*. My heart caught in my chest.

"What's the chance?" Annie asked. "We have to go in! You have to try some dresses on!"

"Yeah . . . I'm not sure that's such a good idea given that nightmare I mentioned to you . . . Remember?"

"Of course I remember. That's exactly why we need to do this. The real experience will erase the nightmare." Annie sealed the assertion with her classic hair tuck.

"Based on your psychology degree or your sisterly hopes?" I asked, but I was already being pushed through the lace-curtained door.

This Bella Vita specialized in Venetian lace, making each gown look like it had been spun out of snowflakes. I held a few in my hands, savoring the weight of their layers, but really testing whether or not they would vanish. Annie and I used to step into the wedding dresses in Nonna's shop, holding them onto our little-girl bodies, but I realized now that I'd never actually stood in front of a mirror and seen myself as an adult bride. Outside of that dream.

"How are you doing?" Annie asked. "Any favorites?"

No was the honest answer. I liked some, but more as examples of something a bride should or would wear than dresses I could actually envision donning on the day. I turned to one of the classic trifold mirrors and gave myself a focused up-and-down. What kind of bride was I? A classic Kimberly Williams from *Father of the Bride*? Regency-age Gwyneth à la *Emma*? One of the five options Julia served in *Runaway Bride*? Or one of the eleven Jennifer Lopez gave us on-screen and in real life? My face stared at me in reply, blank.

"I'm not sure anything in here really feels like me," I called out to Annie, hoping that would end this shopping experiment. Then I turned to myself in the mirror, perplexed. *Why do I need an actress to help me see myself?*

Annie and I strolled back to the hotel arm in arm, like all the pairs of Italian grandmas doing the same.

"I can't believe Mom never got here," Annie said. Nonna and Pop had taken us solo so Mom could focus on her last semester of nursing school. She'd gone back to college sometime around my tenth birthday, when Dad's drinking cost him yet another job.

"I know," I agreed. "She would have driven us crazy taking pictures and done that thing she always did when her meal was yummy."

Annie broke into the impression: *"Incredible! My God! So good! Can you believe how good, girls? This is . . ."* We said the last part together. *". . . the best bite of my life!!"*

"How many best bites of her life do you think Mom had?" I asked through a laugh.

"Not enough," my sister said, then she grabbed my hand so we could bear yet another tiny heartbreak together. "Shea, I know we've had different opinions about your ring so far, but in case it's been on your mind, I think Mom would love that you're doing this," Annie said.

"Really? What makes you say that?" I asked.

"Mom loved that you always went for it, whatever you wanted. I've never seen her brag about something more than you moving to New York. She'd just tell people, unprompted, 'You know, my Shea is living in New York.'"

I laughed again, picturing that very thing happening at

the dry cleaner or the grocery store. "Thanks for saying that," I said. "I was always afraid she thought I was running away from her. I could be . . . feisty when it came to her."

"Oh, I know," Annie said. "But I think she respected that about you, too."

Her words brought all the details of my most recent dream to the very tip of my tongue. I almost told her about it. Instead I veered us toward a gelato shop on the corner, one last stop. Better to save us both from the angst that would come from reliving the past, I decided.

SEVENTEEN

I WOKE UP THE NEXT MORNING TO TWO MESSAGES FROM John: a photo of the first official lemon on my beloved patio lemon tree and the words *Buon ciao!*

"I think that means 'good hello,'" I said once the video on our phones connected.

"Uh-huh. Just as I intended," said John. "Where's the mom-to-be?"

"Deep-breathing her nausea away in the shower," I said.

I'd texted him the news seconds after Annie's reveal. He'd raced over to Annie and Mark's with a bottle of bourbon to celebrate. *Gold future-uncle flag.*

John once told me that the worst part about being an only child was the fact that he'd never get to be an uncle on his side. He considered it the best family position available, which may or may not have been because John Candy's *Uncle Buck* was his favorite "film"—something I'd let go when we first started dating. Part of the reason John taught middle school is because that's when he believed kids stopped thinking it was cool to be kids; it was the fun uncle's job to convince them that was wrong.

"How's the trip going otherwise?" he asked.

"It hasn't really kicked off yet. I was planning to do a little digging around yesterday, but Annie and I went on a big Florence tour instead."

"Well, I miss you. But I did sleep diagonal across the bed last night," John said.

"I respect that. And I miss you, too."

"Good luck today. How do you say that in Italian?"

"I'm not sure. My grandparents always used this weird expression *in bocca al lupo*, which literally means 'into the mouth of the wolf.'"

"Weird. Why?"

"It's like our version of *break a leg.* Humans going into the mouth of a beast, a challenge ahead. And the bad thing—whatever you're up against—is supposed to get swallowed, while the good thing, which I guess is you, survives."

"That makes no sense," John said.

"Yeah, it's odd," I said. But the truth was that I thought I finally understood it.

I hung up with John, then took my turn to enjoy the giant Carrara-marble hotel shower before our train out to Borgo. If there was one thing I'd learned from my years of precision trip-planning, it was to never skimp your way into a tiny hotel bathroom.

"Hey!" I heard Annie call once I stepped from the hot-water bliss. "You've gotten like a dozen calls from this same

New York number in the past five minutes. Is something wrong?"

It was eighteen calls, to be precise, all from Graham. And something was very wrong.

"I'm downstairs," he said once my call went through, as simply as if it were *hello*.

"I'm sorry, you're where?" I asked.

"Downstairs. At your hotel. Come meet me, and I'll explain."

Ten minutes later, he was still trying and failing.

"*Again*, you can't just follow me halfway around the world without asking!" I said.

"*Again*, a good flight popped up, and if I'd called you would have said no, but now that I'm here you'll be grateful I came," he said. Graham had a certain slick confidence that I'm sure played very well in journalism circles. I knew the type from my New York days: overly at ease, with a loose interpretation of the truth. The guy who says he *just threw some button-downs in a duffel bag*, but they were a hundred bucks each and he sends them out for laundering. And even after a transatlantic flight, Graham was pulling off unkempt nineties J.Crew model.

"When exactly will that gratitude set in? Because so far, *I* bought *you* a cappuccino and you're about to make me late for a train."

"You need me. You just haven't seen it in action yet," Graham said as he waved down the barista for a second coffee.

"I'm here with my sister. And this is a very personal journey. What if I just don't want you tagging along?"

"Look, respectfully, you have no idea what you're doing, and you gave yourself way too little time to do it. Five more days is impossible without a professional."

"You know my itinerary? Who are you?"

"A very good journalist." My expression flipped from annoyed to fully creeped out. "Relax. I ran into Gia in Hudson. *She* approached *me* to see if *we*—her words—had found the name of the restaurant her mother's family owned yet. So then I did. Caffè Degli Artisti."

That stopped me. "All right, Klute—" I started.

"Klute was a detective, not a journalist," Graham interrupted.

"I know that!" I said, skipping over the impressive fact that he did, too. "I want to know why the hell you care so much about this. Because it is not cheap to book a last-minute flight to Italy, and I know you said you used miles, but that means you used them on this."

"I told you in Hudson. I think we've got something here that will make a really interesting article. I need that. You need me. It's business, not personal."

"Don't *Godfather* me in Italy," I said. Graham smiled in a way that said he liked this tête-à-tête a little too much. "All right. I want a guarantee that you're not going to write something about me without my permission."

"Fine. Hand me an NDA, and I'll sign it." He was bluffing, but I had backup.

"Will do," I heard Annie say. I spun around to see her standing behind us, midtext. "I texted Rebecca for you. Her paralegal will have one over in ten."

"You must be the sister," Graham said.

"Yep," said Annie, now one foot from his face. "The big sister. If you're good, you stay. If you're a dick, you go."

Graham responded by raising one eyebrow—*of course*—then jotting in a notepad he'd pulled from his back pocket.

EIGHTEEN

I T WASN'T GREAT TO LEAVE ONE'S BRAND-NEW FIANCÉ for a trip to Italy intended to determine whether the ring he gave you will or will not ruin your marriage. But it seemed worse to have a strange man suddenly join the party. I called John from the café car the minute we boarded the train. Unfortunately, it went straight to voicemail.

"Hey, it's me. Um, all good here. Not calling from an Italian prison! Just call back when you can?" was my choice of message.

"How was that?" I asked Annie.

"Not super reassuring," she said, head buried in her own phone. I'd asked her to speed-read some of Graham's writing while he was in the café car, for verification's sake.

"The guy's a good writer. He did this beautiful piece about a woman who vanished from her entire family days after she inherited a mysterious house in British Columbia. And another about a man who kept trying to steal an old watch from the governor of New York back in the twenties. I guess his beat is family mysteries involving very old things?"

"That's weird," I said. "But maybe good?"

"Don't worry. I've got my eye on him," Annie said, just like she was visiting me at college to play wingman again.

THE TOWN OF Borgo San Lorenzo sat just fourteen miles northeast of Florence. It was only thirty minutes by train but, as Gia had explained, the people who live there consider it a thousand miles away. That's because the town is nestled inside a region settled by artists who fought for its independence and their own.

"Like Greenwich Village?" I'd asked her back in Hudson.

"In spirit," she said. "But my mom always said it looked like Napa Valley."

I understood the moment our train slowed, approaching the terra-cotta-colored station. In every direction, I saw rolling green hills dotted with sharp Italian cypress trees, dozens of pale pink stucco villas, and postcard-worthy church steeples.

"I can't believe Carmela ever left this place," I said as we stepped off the train.

"She must have had a good reason," was Graham's response, then he jotted something down yet again.

I'd already run Annie and Graham through everything Gia had told me in our pre-trip phone call. Her aunt, Maria Costanza, was the younger sister of Carmela Costanza Preston. She was born and raised in this town, just like her parents and parents' parents and every generation they could trace. The Costanzas had, and hopefully still, owned Caffè Degli Artisti—a traditional Italian coffee shop that we only knew about thanks to Graham's pre-trip research. Gia couldn't remember the name but knew that Carmela and her sister, Maria, worked there together from the time they were very young. But something happened either among the family or between the sisters before Carmela moved to the States, and they barely spoke for the next sixty-plus years. The last time the two had been together was for their mother's funeral in 1983.

"Italians love drama," Annie said as we walked toward the town. "I remember that from Nonna and her sister, Aunt Lucy. They were always fighting."

"But loyal, too," I said. "Remember Nonna took Lucy in at the end instead of moving her into a nursing home?"

"Yeah, well, apparently Maria reached her breaking point," said Graham. There was an edge to his tone, like the comment came from somewhere specific, but I didn't have the brain space—or expertise—to play journalist to the journalist.

WE THOUGHT THE first part of our mission would be simple: find the café. How many Caffè Degli Artistis could there possibly be in what amounted to three square miles? The answer was zero. We asked at a small hotel beside the train station. We inquired with a man behind the counter of an Italian bodega. We walked into a chic new café thinking they must have known all the competition in town. Finally, I just started asking random people on the street.

"*Scusami*, where is *il* Caffè Degli Artisti?" I called out to anyone who made direct eye contact, and even a few who avoided it.

"*Non esiste*," one Nonna-type finally yelled back.

"If *esiste* means 'exist,' then we're screwed," Annie said. Graham huffed at us both, then slipped himself into super-charm mode as he approached the woman.

"*Ciao.* When did this café—" And then he made the hand signal for *no more.*

"Oh, *non*—" She made that same signal back. "*Nome cambiato.*"

Graham turned to me, "Okay, open your—"

But I was one Google ahead. "*Cambiato!* The name changed!" I said.

"Where now?" Graham asked our newly minted tour guide, looking around for dramatic effect.

"Caffè Maria!" she said with a smile. "*Andiamo!*" Which apparently meant *I will take you there, but only because one of you is cute.* Minutes later we were on the outskirts of town at a coffee shop the size of a Beverly Hills closet. It was a brand of cozy more associated with kitsch than comfort.

"Why does a restaurant *inside* Italy need so many souvenirs *of* Italy?" Annie asked.

There were plastic Tower of Pisa salt and pepper shakers; Italian-flag place mats, napkins, and curtains; grated cheese held in gondola-shaped bowls; and an entire map of the Tuscan region painted on each table. Though that all paled in comparison to the living décor—a four-foot-something woman covered head-to-toe in red, white, and green. A living, breathing Italian flag.

"*Gio! Mamma mia! Porta la pasta a tavolo tre! Fretta, fretta, fretta!*" she screamed.

"What's going on?" Annie asked.

"I think maybe Gio is in trouble," I said.

A skinny, slick-haired boy screeched up to a table holding a bowl full of pasta.

"I have a feeling the woman doing the yelling is your Maria," Graham said.

He was correct, we learned after the woman spotted him snapping pictures of her with his cell phone, grabbed it from his hand, and tossed it into a flowerpot. *My* Maria indeed.

NINETEEN

THIRTY MINUTES AND ONE BROKEN-ENGLISH CHAT with Gio later, Annie and I—and only Annie and I—were permitted to talk to Maria.

"I'll take the notes," Annie whispered. "Yes, because I'm terrified to talk."

The scowl on Maria's face justified Annie's anxiety and made my plan for explaining who in the world we were and why in the world we were here even trickier. The plan idea had come from Gia; I'd tell Maria that she was a good friend who had insisted I visit the magical town of her ancestors. She'd told us to find the family café. We were just here to say hello for a quick chat . . . that I would somehow transition into a conversation about their decades-long family drama. Making matters more difficult, Maria did not have a strong command of English-language flattery, so Gio "agreed" to serve as our translator.

"We're here because we're good friends of your niece, Gianna," I said slowly. "We met through a connection I can explain later." Annie shot me a look that I ignored; there had to be an order to this, and I'd decided revealing Carmela's ring was not first.

"I barely know my niece," Maria said through Gio.

"I'm so sorry for that," I said. "But she thinks of you often. And my sister and I wanted to visit Italy because—" I was prepared to throw down the pregnancy card—a Nonna ace in the hole—but Maria cut me off.

"Sisters?" Maria asked, pointing between Annie and me.

"*Sì*," I said. Maria responded with a question that Gio quickly translated.

"She wants to know where you and your sister live."

"Oh, we both live in Los Angeles. But our grandparents are from Campania. I know that's not near here but—"

Before I could finish, Maria was kissing both Annie and me on the hands, aggressively. And then suddenly speaking *plenty* of English . . . she, too, had an order to things.

"See, you are smart. Loving. You do what God wants sisters to do!" Maria said. "I had a sister—Carmela. Maybe you know? She was Gianna's mother." A look of wistful longing landed on Maria's face, but she snatched it right back. "She was not loving. She was selfish. Or she became selfish . . ."

Annie squeezed my hand under the Italian-map-painted table. This was my moment.

"Yes . . . Gia mentioned that," I said. "We're so sorry to hear. How—if you don't mind my asking—did she become selfish?"

"Because of a man, of course," Maria barked. Annie squeezed my hand *much* harder. Yes, it was possible this was

the man who had given Carmela the mystery ring—my ring—
but I was going to have to do a lot more eggshell walking to
confirm.

"Was this man Carmela's boyfriend?" I started.

"Worse," Maria said. "They were going to be married. But
then—well—it is a long story . . ." *Bingo. A fiancé.* This time I
squeezed Annie, so hard she jumped.

"We have plenty of time," Annie said, too loud.

"And we'd love to hear it," I added, looping my hand
through my sister's to emphasize our closeness.

Maria smiled at that move, then waved Gio over for another round of espresso. We were in.

The man at the center of this—we'd been warned—long
story was a painter who had come to tiny Borgo San Lorenzo
to work on his art, "like all of them," Maria said with a scowl.
Of course, she never saw his paintings. Maria doubted that he
was even an artist at all because the only thing he seemed to
do over his six months in town was woo her precious sister.

"I called him *il ladro*!" she said. "The thief! Because he
steals the heart of Carmela."

"She didn't love him?" I asked.

"Who knows! It happens so quickly!"

"Do you remember his real name?" asked Annie, keeping
us focused.

"*Of course!* He was called Gianluca Marzullo."

We officially had a name, which Annie scribbled down immediately. *If only Graham could see me now*, I thought. But
something told me that he probably could. I turned around to

find him watching from a nearby bench. The man was committed.

Meanwhile Maria downed a *doppio espresso*, then continued.

Carmela was in love from the moment *il ladro* sat down at the table under the olive tree, she told us, the one positioned just high enough on the slope of the hill to give him a view of the town below.

"It used to be our best spot but after they left, *maledetto*! Cursed!" she cried.

This was not a word I wanted to hear, but once again, Annie was attuned to the more critical detail.

"*They* left?" she asked.

"*Sì, il ladro* took my sister back to Roma, and that is the beginning of the end."

It was a simple enough story to an American ear. Girl meets boy. Girl falls in love with boy. Girl leaves tiny town for big city with boy: the plot of too many movies to start running down the list. To the Costanza family, it was sacrilege, so much so that they all refused to get to know this man, little sister Maria especially. She did not speak of him when Carmela called home. She did not ask about the status of their relationship when they visited Borgo San Lorenzo for Christmas. She did not want to know Gianluca in any way, which was very inconvenient for my specific goals. I needed intel, which meant a fast-forward to the real heart of the matter.

"But Carmela died married to a Charles Preston," I said. "When did she divorce Gianluca?"

"No divorce," said Maria. "They never married. Two years of engagement, then it's over. Because I was right. *Cursed!*"

"But you're sure they were officially engaged?" I asked, not loving her continued use of the word *cursed*.

"Of course," Maria said. "Carmela ran around this town showing that diamond ring off to everyone and their dogs!"

I clutched my hand to my neckline. The ring was safely tucked under my sweater, and I now thought it should stay there until we were far away from Maria.

"But what happened?" I asked, getting back to the mystery. "Why didn't they marry?"

"I didn't know, and I didn't ask. I thought, better not to speak his name in case the fates could hear! But it was too late. He'd ruined her."

A year later, Carmela announced she was moving to America. She had everything set up in the States to try to open a spot just like Caffè Degli Artisti. She said she wanted to bring their food abroad, to have a great adventure beyond their tiny world. And she made the mistake of explaining that it had all come into focus when Gianluca first took her to visit New York.

"*Oof*," my own sister and I said at the exact same time. Annie hadn't loved when I left California for college in Manhattan, then ended up staying for almost a decade. But that hadn't been an ocean, culture, and language away—or, more important, pre-FaceTime.

"Do you remember when this all happened?" I asked. "Maybe how old Carmela was when Gianluca arrived? It would be helpful for us to figure out what year this happened because—"

"He comes here in *marzo* 1968. He takes her to Roma in *maggio* that same year. They are engaged in 1969 and done in 1971."

Apparently the experience had left quite the mark on Maria's memory.

"This was very helpful," I said. "*Grazie* for taking all this time to talk with us."

The sun was setting behind the café, leaving our table almost completely in the cypress-tree shadows. Maria had answered so many questions, but as I let my hand brush across the top of my sweater to touch the ring below, I realized there were still two very big ones unanswered. The first was whether this ring was actually from Gianluca. The story was likely connected to what Gia had shared, but I had to be certain, and only Maria would know. The second question I would only consider if the answer to the first was yes.

"Now you'll tell Gianna to come see her old *zia*?" Maria asked.

"We will," I promised with a smile, proud to be a small part of this family's reunion. "But there is one more thing before we go."

I looked to Annie for support, hoping she'd have already read my ring-focused mind. Her eyes said, *Yes, do it* and also, *I'm terrified*.

"I'm sorry that I haven't told you this yet, Signora Costanza," I started. "But I have what I think is Carmela's ring from Gianluca right here."

Have felt like the safest word given the circumstances.

Maria's face turned dark as I held the diamond up for her to view.

"There it is," she said. "*Mamma mia . . .*"

With that piece confirmed, I went the final step further.

"I have to ask: Do you think this ring is *maledetto*, too?"

Maria looked at me with eyes so serious I almost broke out in chills, then she delivered a line that finished the job: "It's a little late for that question, no?"

TWENTY

I TOOK THE BLAME FOR EVERYTHING THAT HAPPENED between meeting back up with Graham and finding our "hotel." Trip planning was one of my specialties, but I tended toward the rare when it came to accommodations. And who wouldn't want to experience a "picturesque former monastery overlooking the rolling hills of Tuscany"? The answer was Annie and Graham.

"'Knock on the gorgeous carved wood doors upon arrival!'" I read off the website. This was after we trekked up and down said rolling hills to find the unmarked building, in the dark. We knocked. And knocked. And then knocked louder. And then Graham started slamming his entire body into the admittedly gorgeous carved wood doors while Annie slumped down to sob in the grass. I actually considered running back into town to beg Maria for help but then, finally, a very tall, thin man in a seafoam-green robe opened the door—a bathrobe, not a priest robe.

"*Benvenuti a Convento dei Cappuccini di San Carlo*," he said. "Do you want rooms or confessions?"

"*Both*," said Annie as she shoved past me through the door. "I recently wished death upon my sister."

We settled into our rooms, which were about the size of confession boxes anyway. They featured wooden beds, foam "mattresses," and life-sized crucifixes. Perhaps this was what the website meant by "the feel of monastery life."

Annie was sound asleep within minutes. I sat up, sleepless again and kicking myself for saying *sì* to Maria's insistence on a third espresso; I could literally feel my heart beating in my thumbs. The idea of roaming around a pitch-dark Italian maze wasn't thrilling, but still better than sitting in bed while my mind raced with a thousand thoughts of Carmela's failed love story. Plus, I still hadn't connected with John.

It took me forever to find a spot that gave me two shaky bars of service, and even then, it was in a hallway where a dozen priests' portraits loomed over me with judgment.

"Hey! There you are! How is it? How are you?" John asked.

"It's . . . a lot, but I'm good," I said. "Just taking in some art." I tilted the phone toward a man with one of those hair crowns around a giant bald spot.

"Tough look," said John. "So, did you meet the aunt?"

"Yes, we did, but I need to tell you something first," I said, ripping off the Band-Aid. "That cousin of Simone's is with us now. The journalist who helped me out in Hudson?" I wondered if John would even remember my mentioning him.

"Graham? He's just also in Italy right now?" Apparently

men do not forget the names of the men suddenly helping their fiancées.

"No," I said, pacing my two feet of cell service space. "He came to help us. Apparently, he's one of these obsessive story chasers. He thinks there's a big article in this whole thing, so he wants to help. He has a lot of experience, and—" I cut myself off before the rambling really started.

"Right," John said, then he looked away to think. "Do you want him there?" he finally asked.

"As a person, not really," I said. "He's a lot blunt for my taste. And I've already got Annie here for that. But he's already been really helpful on the research front. I don't think we'd be getting as much done as fast without him."

"Well, I like that part," said John. "But—sorry—it's a little weird for me. This guy doesn't know you. Why is he inserting himself into your life? Our life, technically."

"I know. But he signed this doc Rebecca drew up promising not to publish anything without our consent, so I feel like he'll have to be honest."

John was silent again. I could see the lines of his scrunched forehead even through the bad connection.

"It should be you here, not him," I offered.

"Yeah. I'm pretty jealous," he finally said. "But I guess if this guy can get you home faster and with good answers, then all good."

"Yes," I said, relieved and grateful not to be with a territorial type. "That is his plan."

"Thanks. Hey, I'm sorry but I have to run. Big basketball

game against North tonight." John sometimes filled in as assistant basketball coach, the chance to relive his own glory days. *Or is it just like the Science Olympiad team and his Wednesday-night tutoring shift? Another extracurricular he took on to earn some extra cash, maybe for the beautiful ring I'm running around the world to prove worthy before I wear it properly?* The thought made me want to slink down the nearest stone wall.

"All right, I miss you, and I love you," I said.

"Love you, too," said John. "And I'm glad it's going well. Hopefully you'll be home with the answers you need soon."

I hung up, moved to the nearest wall, and let my body slide down until I was sitting in a tiny ball on the cold stone floor. Then I squeezed my eyes shut to try to stop John's last line from running on a loop in my head. *What answers do I really need?*

———————

I WANDERED AROUND by the light of my phone until I found the monastery's unsurprisingly quaint sanctuary. It was small, about the size of a hospital chapel room, and held the chill of the early fall air. The four walls were the typical deep-gray stone of Italy's oldest churches, but the top third of them was covered in truly breathtaking frescoes, each of the surrounding Tuscan countryside.

"Think Gianluca painted any of this?" a voice said.

I screamed so loud there's no way I didn't wake our robe-wearing host.

"JESUS, GRAHAM! You cannot sneak up on a woman anywhere, let alone in an ancient church in the middle of the night!" I scream-whispered.

"I was here first, so you technically snuck up on me," he said. "But this works out because I wanted to get some tape on you anyway."

"'Get some tape on'?"

"Interview you."

"For the article you're only *maybe* permitted to write about me." Graham offered a resigned nod. "*Fine.* Maybe your weird brand of extreme directness will actually help me figure some things out," I said.

"Thank you," he said as he positioned his phone to record. "Now, tell me about your thoughts after talking with Maria."

"Um . . . I guess I feel reservedly optimistic?" I said.

"Oh man," said Graham. "You're one of those people who always say *yes and no* instead of just answering the question, aren't you?"

"Hey! Be nicer or I'm not going to say anything. *Yes and no* applies here. Yes, I'm worried that the ring is essentially why she disowned her sister, but I'm trying to stay hopeful because it's looking like the ring was only on Carmela's finger for a brief engagement anyway, not an unhappy marriage. We might be in the clear, especially because Maria doesn't necessarily know the full story."

"Say more about the Maria-not-knowing part." This time there was no tiny notepad in the mix. Graham was looking straight at me. His face had softened, the way it had when he'd approached Gianna. He was turning the charm on me now, albeit for selfish reasons.

"Maria thinks Gianluca was a bad guy and very bad for Carmela, but that's her opinion. I don't *really* know why Carmela left Italy. I don't have any idea why Carmela and Gianluca broke off their engagement. I'm also wondering if the ring even holds their love considering it was never made official with a marriage. But either way, I'm trying to stay optimistic about the real story and hopeful that Gianluca is alive . . . and that we can find him . . . in Italy . . . this week." Graham stared at me for a second or two. "What?" I asked, suddenly feeling very exposed.

"Nothing," he finally said. "Just trying to get a full read on you, but it's . . . tricky."

"Ouch?" I said. "I'm exhausted and a little stressed. Also, I just had to explain to my fiancé why you're my new third wheel. So, last question for the night."

"What did he say?" Graham asked, brows raised.

"He's a good guy. He said all the right things." I was not about to give this still-questionable guy the wrong kind of intel for whatever story he was cooking up.

"Fine. Last question," he said. "I want to know if you're this superstitious about anything other than heirloom engagement rings."

"Sure. It's bad luck to get married on the date or at the place of a couple that's now divorced. Obviously never wear the hand-me-down wedding dress of an unhappy wife. My nonna always said some other little stuff about a veil and pearls. Oh, and there are rules about rain on the wedding day, but I actually think that's good luck, not bad. Something about money."

"So all marriage-related things?"

"Oh. No. I'm superstitious about tons of other stuff, too."

"Then why didn't you include any of them?"

I considered his question for a moment, then answered with a shrug. *Is this some sort of trap?*

"Okay, final, *final* question: is there a single other superstition you'd fly seven thousand miles for?"

"No," I said, surprised to be so quickly certain. "Now did I just get *trickier*?"

"Yes and no," said Graham with a smirk that made my blood boil.

TWENTY-ONE

THE QUESTION OF HOW TO FIND A FOREIGN PERSON in a foreign country with a foreign language is not something I imagined encountering outside a Sofia Coppola film. I watched as Graham turned his laptop into a command station during the train ride from Borgo San Lorenzo back through Florence, then on to Rome. He was somehow having a phone call, Google chat, and email exchange all at the same time. Annie was doing her part, studying street maps so we'd be quick once we touched down. And I'd fully cleared my work inbox so I could focus on the task of double-checking all our hotel accommodations to stave off another "quaint" stay. In forty-eight hours, we'd become an efficient trio, but that was already a third of the total time we had to find one man in a city of 2.8 million, assuming Gianluca still lived in Rome. Assuming he still lived at all.

We made it to the Eternal City and our hotel without

issue. I redeemed myself with the opulent Hotel Scalinata di Spagna—the Hotel of the Spanish Steps. It had an actual lobby, rooms with beds *plus* chairs, and five-bar cell reception. But most important, it had a view of the Italian capital's iconic landmark, and on a day so postcard perfect that even the locals were taking photos. I made sure to have Graham take one of Annie and me in our Prada scarves. We hadn't made it to Rome on our trip with Nonna and Pop, and it featured prominently in our *Only You* fantasy.

"This is a really nice shot," I said as he handed my phone back. "Thank you." Then I reached my arm out to sneak a selfie of him and me. Graham groaned.

"Come on!" I said. "I may not one hundred percent trust you yet, but we should have a photo in case I do." Graham responded by grabbing the phone back and retaking the shot with his much more selfie-friendly arm.

We all finally sat down in the lobby for a planning session complete with much-needed espresso and *panini di buffalo mozzarella* for Annie—the one food that was curing her all-day morning sickness.

"This child picked the most expensive sandwich in all of Italy," she said, mouth half-full.

"Good," I said, sneaking a tiny piece of cheese. "That means I can skip food when it comes time to impart my wisdom on quality over quantity. The wisdom is *both*."

"Lunch on me today," Graham said, joining the conversation. "I just finally heard from my guy's guy at Interpol, so I'm in a good mood. Turns out there are fifteen Gianluca Marzullos currently living in the city of Rome."

"Can I order two sandwiches so I have one for a midnight snack?" Annie asked.

"Get three," Graham said. "Maybe the gods of finding Italian men will shine down on me for my generosity."

"It would be Saint Anthony, the patron saint of lost things," I said. "But I'm not sure he locates people. Our grandmother typically used him for finding keys and wallets."

"Remind me to thank my parents for being atheists," was Graham's reply.

We spent the next twenty minutes trying to sort through the list of Gianlucas, with age as the unanimously approved starting point. In the end, only four men were between sixty and one hundred. Where to go from there was a coin toss; all we'd been provided was their home addresses.

"I vote we knock on doors from youngest to oldest so we stand the best chance of them being alive," I said.

"I think we should split up and knock out three in one shot," Annie said.

"And I think our guy is this guy who lives near RUFA, the Rome University of Fine Arts," Graham said. "So we can all just go together."

We were both too exhausted to question his certainty, and by that point we had no reason. He'd done more in twenty-four hours than we could have pulled off in a month. Annie shoved the rest of her *panini* in her *bocca* and we called a car, destination: Prati, Rome.

"The rest of Rome is an urban planner's nightmare—no order, no structure, no way to find yourself after *una bottiglia di vino rosso*," tour-guide Annie read from a website as we drove, being careful not to get carsick. "But Prati was built at the end of the nineteenth century. Now it can boast being one of the city's wealthiest hubs, with the most structured layouts and most famous places to eat. With the gorgeous St. Peter's Basilica looming over, this neighborhood includes the can't-miss Pizzarium Bonci, home to Rome's current most famous slice of pizza."

It all added up. Gianluca was now a wealthy painter settled in Prati. He'd left Carmela because he knew he could not fully love her *and* maintain his life as an artist. So he essentially loved Carmela *too* much to go through with the marriage. Ring: safe.

"That or he left Carmela for a rich daughter of Prati so her parents could fund his art career," Graham said, and with that I vowed to stop sharing my theories aloud.

Whether or not it was the result of some wealthy, non-Carmela marriage, this Gianluca was definitely rich. His building looked like a wing of Buckingham Palace, redecorated by Rome. The atrium featured a topiary-stacked park. Every single screw or nail or knob in sight was gold. The resident names—including one Gianluca Marzullo—were carved into a marble slab! Of course, none of this delight made up for the fact that Graham's Gianluca pick was not home.

"I predicted this too," he reminded us. "We'll mill around for a bit in case we run into a neighbor to question, then leave a note and head out."

Thirty minutes later we were still arguing over what to include in said note. Graham was pushing for no mention of the ring at all. Annie thought I should include Carmela's name to jog his memory. And I was advocating for a full-page story, minimum. In the end, the letter-writing delay led to a very important development: a neighbor walked through the building's garden.

"*Salve, come posso aiutarla?*" an older man said upon finding us suspiciously huddled in front of the wall of gold mailboxes. This neighbor was still devastatingly handsome—an aged Italian Pierce Brosnan.

"*Ciao. Stiamo guardando Gianluca Marzullo,*" I said, hoping I'd correctly remembered the one phrase we thought we should prep just in case: *We're looking for Gianluca Marzullo.*

The man waited a moment, likely translating my incorrect Italian, then smiled. "Ah," he said. "I see. Well, he's a hard man to pin down."

That perked Graham up. "You know him, then?" he asked.

The man nodded, which perked me up even more. "That's incredible! Would you give him this note!?" I went to snatch it out of Annie's hand.

"Actually," Graham interrupted, grabbing it instead, "we should leave the note taped to his mailbox, like we always do. That's where he'll look for it."

"Oh, you know him, too?" the neighbor asked.

"We do," Graham said. "Thank you for your help. And have a nice rest of your day." Then he stuck the note back on the mailbox and started to walk away.

"Wait. Maybe this kind gentleman has more to say about our . . . friend," I started.

"We're late, Shea!" Graham called back.

"It seems like he knows what he's doing," Annie whispered, then started to follow Graham out of the atrium.

"I'm sorry. And *ciao* . . . ," I said to the neighbor, but he was already inside the elevator.

"What the hell was that about?!" I yelled the moment we were out of earshot.

"Rule number one of journalism: trust no one," Graham barked back. "You don't know that guy. You have no idea if he'll ever get the note to Gianluca. He could put it down on the counter and forget it 'til next week."

"But he knew our guy! One Kevin Bacon away!" I said. "And also, this means Gianluca's still alive!"

"He knew a guy who's one of four guys who still might not be our guy," Graham said, correcting me.

"Watch the tone . . . ," said Annie.

"Sorry. I'm just keeping things realistic," said Graham. "It's the only way to keep pushing." Then he walked ahead to figure out where we could grab the metro. Annie gave my arm a squeeze of support.

"It's fine," I said. "I'm staying optimistic."

"Good. But, Shea, you know there's a chance we won't find this man on this trip, right?" she said. She was being kind, but it landed with the kind of crushing disappointment that always made me feel like a little girl again.

"Yeah, I know," I said, half lying.

"So maybe it would help to start thinking about what you'll do if we don't. Just so you're not caught off guard."

"Yeah," I said. Then I let myself acknowledge what she was more likely trying to say. "I guess there's also a chance I won't find him at all, huh?"

Annie was too good a psychologist and sister to answer that question.

TWENTY-TWO

OUR LUCA LUCK DID NOT IMPROVE FOR THE REST of the afternoon. The three remaining options on the list were: 1) Gianluca Marzullo of Monti, Rome, age sixty-five, which would have been young for Carmela but was not impossible given that Maria said he'd traveled to Borgo as a young artist. But Graham had done some extra digging that revealed this Gianluca was a retired men's tailor, so the connection felt wrong. 2) Gianluca Marzullo of Centocelle, Rome—a neighborhood much farther outside the city's hub but known for its multicultural restaurant scene. This Gianluca was eighty-five, so likely too old, but living in a neighborhood rich in culture like a former artist might. And finally 3) Gianluca Marzullo of Pigneto, Rome—his age was yet undetermined but his address appeared to be a church, so either he'd left Carmela for the priesthood or he was some kind of secular chapel employee. He was oddly our best bet.

We decided to press on with a door-knock at the Monti Marzullo's apartment first, after we spent an extra forty-five minutes trying to find the exact building. Map girl's nausea was affecting her navigating skills. It was all a waste of time in the end. Gianluca number two was not home either, but a woman answered the door on our very first knock. This was thrilling, until she revealed herself as his *moglie*—wife—of forty years. Mrs. Ana Marzullo did not know a Carmela, and *her* Gianluca had never even been to Florence, let alone Borgo San Lorenzo.

"It's still progress, even if we're crossing people off the list," Graham insisted.

"Since when are you the Pollyanna of the party?" I asked.

"You're right. It's not natural, and I hate it, so could you go back to being the cheerleader?"

"You know, Shea was a real cheerleader," slipped Annie. "High school captain, in fact."

"I did know," said Graham, "first because I did a full background check on her, but second, because I've met her."

"You stalked me?" I asked, incredulous but also sort of honored.

"Of course," Graham said. "Who goes to a foreign country with a perfect stranger?"

That made Annie laugh so hard she almost puked, again.

"*Hysterical,*" I said. "And I defend my cheerleading! There is nobility in the work of energizing a crowd. Though you probably never went to a single high school football game because you were too busy . . . hmm . . . I'm thinking speech and debate team or cross-country?"

Graham stopped short, impressed, and maybe honored. "Both," he said. "Nice work."

. . .

IT WAS ALMOST ten p.m. by the time we made it back to our
hotel, where there was, of course, no return note from
Gianluca Number One. Annie was exhausted and Graham
had other work to do, so I went down to the patio bar for a
solo nightcap, a Negroni—the cocktail I'd first discovered on
my trip with John.

School would have just let out in LA, so I tried his cell,
hoping he'd pop up on my screen from his classroom desk,
reviewing the next day's lesson plans with his definitely-plaid
shirt finally untucked and both boat shoes kicked off. I got my
exact wish.

"Boy, do I wish you were here right now," I said.

"Tough day?" asked John. I could practically see him lifting his socked feet onto the desk on the opposite side of the
screen.

"Yeah. We have a list of names that could be Carmela's
guy, but the most progress we've made is a note taped in the
lobby of one guy's apartment."

"What does that note say?"

"Practically nothing! Graham thought we should keep it
short, so we didn't scare him off."

"Funny . . . I seem to remember you having success with a
very long, *very* dramatic note that should have probably scared
a man off . . ."

I smiled at the reference, a much-needed mood lift. "It
could be too tricky to tape eight pages of folded paper to a
mailbox," I said. "Plus, I think the tear stains on the page were
really what sold you, no?"

"Shea, it's been years. Time to finally admit those were ice cream stains," said John.

He was referring to the letter I wrote him after our first real fight. We'd been at the Tar Pit—the third location from our impromptu first-date tour—celebrating our one-year anniversary. John had made a sweet ordeal of making sure we sat in the exact same booth at the front window. I remember feeling truly, deeply grateful going into that night, like everything in my life was finally in its right place. Apparently John did not feel the same contentment.

"I was thinking . . . ," he said. "Maybe it's time to get a place together? Save money on rent and start fresh with something ours?" My face reacted before my brain could stop it. "Wow. So that's a *hard* no . . . "

"Sorry. No. Not a hard no. It's just . . ." I could not believe the words coming out of my mouth but I could not stop the full-blast faucet of honesty. "I *just* got my apartment exactly the way I want it. With that wallpaper from the restaurant in WeHo that I'd been searching for all year. It's so perfect now. And it's the first place I've ever lived alone."

"So you're saying you don't want to move in together because of one wall of wallpaper?"

"Well it's two walls, technically, and—"

"*Ouch*, Shea. But I guess good to know. I'll go ahead and renew my lease." John didn't bruise easily, but when he did it came out sharp and sarcastic, my least favorite tones.

"Hey. You sprung this on me!" I said.

"Sprung this?! Shea, we've been dating a year. I was kinda wondering why you hadn't brought up moving in already."

"Why, because I'm the woman? Sorry I'm not the type crying into my Instagram because all my friends are getting married and having babies!"

I was losing it, and I knew it. This conversation had triggered something deep.

"You know what? Let's skip dessert. I'm not hungry anymore," I said. I meant to save us from digging any deeper into this hole, but it did not land that way with John.

"Unbelievable." We drove back to my apartment in painful silence. Five minutes later, I fled to Annie's. One hour and one whole box of tissues after that, she suggested I write John a letter to get my real thoughts down.

"It's not a letter you'll give to him," she said, "but it sounds like you don't really know what you're feeling. Writing it down might help."

"Are you secretly giving me the advice you give your kids at school?" I asked.

"My certification technically extends to middle schoolers, which is what you acted like during your dinner with John, so yes."

"Fine," I said with a pout. "But I'm going to need a pen, paper, and several hours of alone time. And more vanilla ice cream."

I sat with pen and paper, quieted my racing mind, and listened to my heart. Eventually I found my way to the feelings underneath my big reaction. I wrote that my apartment represented this huge moment of independence for me. I confessed that I'd struggled with the decision to even move back to LA, so holding on to my own, new space in a place with so many childhood memories was a feat. I even told John that in my parents' dynamic, Dad made all the house decisions because he, originally, made all the money. Keeping my space meant keeping my control. I sealed up the envelope. Then I decided that was all too important to keep to myself.

I drove over to John's apartment and slipped it under his door. He texted the next morning to ask if we could go for a walk. We met at the Hollywood Bowl and strolled the rows until we'd both gotten everything off our chests. John's bottom-line confession was that my independence sometimes made him feel insecure. Mine was that I'd grown up seeing the opposite of independence in my mom, so I sometimes held on to my own too tightly. Three months later he moved into my apartment, our cozy compromise.

"Tell this Gianluca guy the truth," I heard John say through the phone, pulling me back from my memory. "It's romantic. And any man who picked that perfect, can't-imagine-a-single-better-ring-in-the-entire-world ring is a romantic."

I spent the next hour crafting a note to convince a complete stranger to share the deepest secrets of his long-ago love life. Then I paid the concierge to translate it into Italian and call me a cab to drop it at Gianluca Number One's apartment.

TWENTY-THREE

THE FOLLOWING MORNING, ANNIE AND I MET GRAHAM in the lobby for a long trek out to the Centocelle neighborhood: Gianluca Number Three's stomping grounds. I didn't tell either of them about my second-note decision. I liked that it was John's and my little secret.

"I feel good about this one," Annie said as we approached the address Graham had been given—a pink stucco apartment building with fuchsia bougainvillea growing along and up the front. Rome meets Los Angeles. *Maybe a sign?*

"Me too," said Graham.

"Really? Why?" I asked.

He waited a beat too long to answer. "Fine, I don't. I was just trying to be nice."

"Thanks," I said, "but I actually prefer you honest."

"Then, thank *you*. You're the first. Woman at least," said Graham. He shifted away before I had to chance to try to read what that meant in his face, but my curiosity was piqued.

The Number Three search kicked off with a nosy neighbor who had a strange obsession with this Gianluca's entire life story. Marta was an Italian Gladys Kravitz. She spent her days milling about the neighborhood, sweeping the street as a spying technique, which was certainly a plus for us. According to Marta, Gianluca was kind and polite, but a real man of mystery. He came and went at odd hours ("He leaves sometimes fully dressed in the middle of the night!"). He only ever talked about travel ("Who leaves Italy so much!?"). And he'd never been seen with a woman ("It makes no sense! He is handsome and tall. Maybe too tall?"). This felt very promising given what we knew about Gianluca inspiring Carmela's wanderlust, which only made the lede Marta had buried that much more devastating: Gianluca had recently moved to a new apartment, closer to the city ("I have the address, because I'm not done with this strange man!").

Location number two featured a grumbly but helpful building super, Lorenzo. While adjusting his ancient tool belt like a fanny pack, Lorenzo reported that Gianluca was a nice man but "very worthless," a phrase I confirmed in my newly downloaded translator app.

"What man makes it through life without being able to screw in a light bulb?" Lorenzo asked. "And this man was supposed to be some kind of sculptor? Ridiculous!"

All three of us lit up: Gianluca Three was an artist.

"Are you thinking what I'm thinking?" Annie whispered.

"Yes, but you told me not to think too much about anything, in case what we're both thinking is wrong," I said.

It turned out that this Gianluca would not be found at this second location either—he'd recently moved *again*. I found this suspicious. My teammates found it annoying. Lorenzo-the-super sadly did not have the address but was willing to let us knock on the door of every neighbor in the building to see if someone did, *after* I told him he looked like Al Pacino.

Forty-five minutes and two emergency bathroom runs for Annie later, we had our answer: this Gianluca now lived in a neighborhood thirty minutes farther away, according to a very elder female neighbor who had previously watched his cats.

"So he's a cats guy . . ." I said as we reversed down the building's tower of stairs. "Don't love that sign . . ."

Annie held her hand out to Graham. "Five euro," she said. "Or pay me in a *panino*."

"Impressive," said Graham.

On the one hand, it was nice that my trip companions were getting along. On the other, we were two-to-one in the *signs* department. I made a mental note to text this dog deal to John later. He'd agree with me, or at least pretend.

"Alright, we've hit a divide-and-conquer moment," Graham said once we were finally street level. "We've got to see Three through, but there's still Number Four to hit. Annie, can you peel off to go check him out?"

"Me? Why me?" she asked.

"Because I need to be with Shea to take notes, in case we find anything."

"I can take notes. I already took notes." Pregnant Annie was even fiercer than nonpregnant Annie.

"Do I stand a chance here?" Graham asked, turning to me.

"No," I said, "but I'll miss the way you 'speak' Italian exclusively through hand signals."

He bowed a thank-you as we flagged down two separate cabs.

My spirits were high, despite the goose chase. No one had mentioned a wife connected to this Gianluca, and he was definitely an artist, even if a sculptor, not a painter. According to the barista at the café next to his building, Gianluca was currently at Galleria Borghese, a famous art gallery where he worked as a docent—a.k.a. the perfect occupation for an aging artist!

We hailed yet *another* cab to the gallery—back *toward* the city—where a very confused receptionist let me get through my entire explanation of our trip before delivering the crushing blow: Gianluca the sculptor was currently in a rehabilitation facility, recovering from major heart surgery.

"It is taking everything in me not to throw a temper tantrum in the middle of this silent room of sculptures," Annie said through shallow breaths. "What do we do now?"

"We text Graham," I said.

He replied immediately, helping us both off the ledge. This is good, he wrote. Now we know where he is. And that he can't leave that building. Graham had already slipped a note under Gianluca Number Four's door—because he obviously *also* wasn't home—so he hopped in a cab to meet us.

By the time Graham arrived, Annie was teetering with exhaustion and my head was pounding so hard I could feel it in my toes. But we were close—this could be our man. Every sign pointed to *yes*.

"Do you have your questions ready?" Graham asked as we made our way to the rehab facility's reception desk.

"Of course not," I said. "I've been too busy trying to find this ghost."

He proceeded to hand me three cocktail napkins covered in chicken scratch. "I've got you," he said.

I was so taken by the help that I didn't realize I'd jinxed the whole mission with a single offhanded word: *ghost*.

"Sorry," a very kind woman at the front desk said when I inquired about our "dear friend" Gianluca Marzullo. "*Signore Marzullo e . . . morto*."

"What did she say?" Annie asked, but the very sad look on the woman's face translated well enough for Graham and me. Gianluca Number Three, the most likely match, was dead. And tomorrow was our last day.

TWENTY-FOUR

ANNIE WAS SO TIRED THAT SHE FELL ASLEEP IN her clothes on the hotel chaise. I tried John to recount the day's failures but ended up having to leave another ramble of a voicemail instead. I decided a quick Negroni, then a hot shower was the best salve for the day. Apparently so did Graham, Negroni included.

"I'll have what he's having," I said to the bartender, too tired to even attempt it in Italian.

"Nora Ephron," Graham said.

"Fun fact, it was Rob Reiner's mother's line," I said. "But I'll let it slide given your impressive movie knowledge."

"My grandpa. Well, the old stuff was him, but it got me hooked. I would wake up an hour and a half before school every day so I could watch a movie. I kept a log in what should have been my math notebook."

"Doesn't count unless you transferred it into Excel once you got to college," I said. That reveal earned me the rarest belly laugh.

"To a fellow nerd," Graham said as my cocktail arrived, raising his. "And to us cracking this case. Don't stress too much about today. I've already been in touch with Elena about more info on Gianluca Number Four. We'll get it done tomorrow."

"Thank you, but if I hear that name one more time, I'm going to jump in a piazza fountain."

"Fair enough," said Graham. "I'm happy to ask you more questions from my ever-growing list."

"I think I deserve a turn," I said, then I took another sip of the electric orange magic in my glass. "I want to know how you got started writing. What was the first assignment that really got you hooked?"

Graham considered me for a moment, as if he was just now deciding that we were friends.

"It started with my parents' shitty marriage," he confessed. "I thought I could fix it if I figured out what was going on between them. Took me a full year, but in fairness this was pre-Internet. I was literally following them around on a Huffy bike." I suddenly had a picture of an earnest little Graham holding an even littler, just-as-crumpled notepad as he snuck around town on the saddest of all missions. It made me want to hug adult him and say, *I get it*.

"It was all pretty exciting," he went on. "Until I found out Mom had been cheating for years."

"Asshole," I said, then quickly, "Omigod, *sorry*. I didn't mean to call your mom an asshole!"

"Yes, you did," said Graham as he took a slow sip from his

own glass. "And thanks. It's the most honest response I've ever gotten to that statement."

"Well, I've been there. *Several* affairs on Dad's part in my case, plus a ton of drinking and even some bankruptcy for fun. There were *many, many* years of ignoring it on my mom's part, and a whole lot of hiding under the bed with my Teddy Ruxpin for me."

"Hulk Hogan pillow, same spot."

"Why did we hide under the bed?" I asked, lit up by the connection. "You could hear everything, and it was dirty as hell! The closet would have been way smarter."

"No way," he answered quickly. "It was scary in there. Even with the ceiling stars."

"I had those SAME STARS!" I yelled.

"Yeah, so did every kid in the nineties," said an American guy three stools down.

Graham and I spent the next Negroni round more quietly dishing on childhood noise-canceling strategies, pitting our fighting parents against each other for gifts, and even what it was like to hate the divorce we'd both dreamed of for years. We unearthed some feelings I'd long forgotten. I was struck by how easy they were to name now. My past usually brought a shame that kept me quiet on the topic. Right now I was experiencing . . . relief? Or maybe connection.

"Are John's parents together?" Graham asked. We'd taken our talk to the streets surrounding the hotel.

"Way to sneak back to your list of questions for me," I said. "And yes. They are. *So* happily. They still hold hands when they walk down the street. It's nice." Graham raised an eyebrow. "What's that for? It *is* nice."

"I could never make it work with someone who has happily married parents," he said.

"That's a pretty huge category of people."

"Almost fifty percent. But trust me, I've tried. It's like we never spoke the same language."

"Yeah, that's the point," I said. "You could learn a *way* better language." Graham raised his eyebrow again; he didn't buy my line. *What does he really know about me or John?* Then I noticed an older and a younger couple walking toward us, all four people with gelatos in hand. My mind flipped to my very first dinner with the Jacobses. It was a lovely meal at a Long Beach seafood restaurant, but I remember feeling all these weird pangs of discomfort when Kay and Bob asked me questions about my own parents. Like they were testing me. It'd prompted a little argument with John on the car ride home that night.

"They were just being curious," he'd said. "They don't care that your parents are divorced, Shea. And even if they do, I don't."

I couldn't shake the feeling. I'd called Annie after I got home that night to ask her professional opinion on whether or not kids of divorce brought more baggage into a relationship than people whose parents stayed together. She told me what I'm sure was the truth: all people have baggage. Then she reminded me that we'd spent as much time around happily married Nonna and Pop as we did around Mom and Dad. Maybe that made me bilingual?

Graham and I grabbed gelatos—*cioccolato* for him, *vaniglia* for me—then found a bench facing the Trevi Fountain. The pool below the massive stone Tritons was lit up from within, making it glow a bright sky blue against the inky night. The world upside down.

"So, I'm confused about something given everything we've talked about," Graham said.

"Wow. I've stumped the great sleuth," I said with a smirk he ignored.

"After everything with your parents' divorce, what made you so obsessed with marriage?"

"Excuse me, I am not *obsessed* with marriage," I fired back.

"Then what's this whole ring thing about?"

"Making sure it's safe to get married with *this* ring."

"So that you can have a perfect marriage."

"Not *perfect*, just not one that *ends*. I'm sure you can respect that."

"No. Sorry. I don't respect marriage at all."

"You don't *respect* marriage?" I asked. A passing man turned around at my apparent volume increase. "Like, the entire institution?"

"Correct," he said. "Don't believe in it. Don't want it."

"Wait, is *that* what this article you're jockeying to write is actually going to be about?" I asked.

"That depends on you, not me," Graham said. My ears were instantly hot, a very rare tell. *Am I being played?* I sucked in a breath, ready to storm back to the hotel, solo.

"I think we're done for tonight—" I started, but Graham reached his hand out to stop me.

"Wait," he said. "I'm sorry. I'm being a dick. I just get this way about all this because . . . I don't know."

His tone flipped me back, then I looked into his eyes to see sincerity there. I took a breath. With it I realized that we weren't just two adults in the middle of a frustrating mission; we were the remnants of two hurt teenagers with some of the exact same wounds.

"Truce?" Graham asked.

"Truce," I said. "But you're treating to the pennies we're about to throw in that fountain."

I WAS YAWNING so hard I could barely see straight as we walked through the main lobby.

"Oh, I wanted to see if they have postcard stamps at reception," I said to Graham. "Also, remind me to buy postcards tomorrow, before it's too late."

"Let's meet at seven a.m., not eight, then," he said as he walked toward the elevators. "I have a feeling you shop like you talk."

"And proud of it!" I called out as he disappeared down the hall, then I made my way to the front desk. When I got there, it turned out they'd been waiting for me.

"You're Signora Anderson, yes?" the concierge said. "I have a note here for you. From a Mr. Gianluca Marzullo."

TWENTY-FIVE

I T HAD BEEN GIANLUCA NUMBER ONE ALL ALONG.

"How do you say *told ya so* in Italian?" Graham asked.
I'd woken Annie up out of a dead sleep and grabbed him to make a game plan. His victory lap seemed like the perfect time to tell them it was my secret second letter that solved the case.

"So you're saying you took a cab alone in Italy at one a.m.?" Annie asked, now fully awake.

But Graham had a different reaction, one I hadn't seen yet: he was impressed.

FIRST THING THE next morning, we hopped in a cab to the address Gianluca had left in the note. Oddly it was not the palatial apartment complex we'd visited a day prior, or anywhere near. The car was weaving through a tiny section of the city right outside the Vatican—a place that seemed even more lost in time than the rest of Rome.

"I don't feel safe with you going in there alone, Shea," Annie said as we approached the building.

"I love you," I said, "but you and your morning sickness are not my first pick for backup right now."

"You've got to go in alone," said Graham. "That's what he's expecting. But if you weren't in such a rush, I could find a wire so we can listen."

I reminded Annie that I was a kickboxing pro and Graham that we had a train back to Florence in four hours.

THEY LEFT ME inside the portico of the oldest building we'd seen yet: a gray stone manor with crumbling wood shutters. I held my ring in my hands, closed my eyes, and said a silent prayer before pressing the buzzer: *Please, gods of romance and love and heirloom engagement rings, let this story have a happy ending.*

Moments later, I was greeted by a very familiar face.

"You're . . . the neighbor," I said, confused and suddenly concerned.

"No," the man we'd spoken with outside Gianluca's apartment said. "I was the man you were looking for. I just wasn't sure I should trust three eager American strangers, especially one with a notepad in his back pocket."

I liked him immediately.

Gianluca pointed me through a narrow hallway. It was like stepping through the tiny door into Willy Wonka's factory. But instead of the space opening up to a candy paradise, the hallway revealed what looked like an entire art museum.

Hundreds upon hundreds of paintings hung on every inch of the cream stucco walls and were stacked on top of each other to make little coffee and end tables in all the spots where furniture should go. And every other inch of the dark wood flooring was covered in easels, each holding a portrait: old, regal men; women holding babies; families posed for Christmas; and one that may have been a queen. They were classic and precise in so many ways, but with thick brushstrokes, strong features, and bright backgrounds that felt like nothing I had ever seen before—da Vinci meets van Gogh.

"*Mamma mia . . .* ," I said.

Gianluca smiled his thanks. The light from the floor-to-ceiling windows caught the still-sharp edges of his strong jaw and high cheekbones. He had that thick shock of salt-and-pepper hair I remembered from the apartment building lobby. And he was handsome; I could only imagine what he looked like back when Carmela first encountered him at her tiny café.

"Come see where it all started," he said as he led me to a smaller painting resting on what looked to be the oldest easel of the lot.

"Carmela," I whispered.

"Yes. The very first portrait that I ever painted. I was a pompous university student trying my best at pop art so I could turn myself into Italy's Andy Warhol. But I'd just been reprimanded for the hundredth time for lacking an original voice in my work. That's why I ran off to Borgo San Lorenzo."

"And met Carmela," I finished.

He nodded. "On my first morning in town. I sat down and

sketched every single thing I saw for five hours while I drank espresso and smoked the cigarettes we were all foolishly puffing on back then. And I did the same every day for the next two weeks."

"No wonder Maria didn't like you," I said.

"Ha! That and the fact that I distracted her only waitress all day long. At the end of every day, I would present my stack of works to this raven-haired country girl with the most intense green eyes. And every time she would throw out the landscapes and still lifes, and hand me back a pile of the people."

"She saw you," I said softly. "I've never even met Carmela, but I know this painting is exactly right. You saw her, too."

Gianluca regarded the canvas adoringly, lovingly. *What could have happened?*

"I don't . . . know where to begin," Gianluca said. He searched the room, seeming to wonder where we should sit to talk, or maybe *if* we should sit to talk. "Maybe with the ring?" he decided. "May I see it?"

"Of course," I said, untucking it from my blouse.

Gianluca seemed to come alive at the sight of it. "*Mio dio . . .* ," he whispered to himself. "Someone loves you very much. John is his name, your note said?"

"Yes, John Hayden Jacobs."

"Ah, a very strong American name."

"Have you been to America?" I asked.

"Many times," he said. "Mostly to New York."

"Where Carmela lived . . ." Gianluca looked away, out the sheer curtains of the open window.

My dream for this trip had come true, but now I felt stuck.

I didn't know how to connect with this man. Suddenly my mind went to Mom: I saw her with a patient who looked very much like Gianluca, sitting at the nursing home where she worked for the last decade of her life.

Suzanne Anderson, RN, graduated at the top of her nursing school class. She was twenty years older and ten thousand times busier than her classmates, yet she made the dean's list every semester. I later learned this was the beginning of her journey to set up a life apart from Dad. She'd started taking night classes when we still lived near Santa Barbara, probably because she saw the writing on the wall with Dad's job stability—and general stability. She worked for almost a decade to finally get that degree, then in a cruel twist the universe gave her less than four years to use it.

I'd watched Mom walk patients through difficult moments many, many times over the years I volunteered as a candy striper. She approached them all the same way, with clear and deeply present patience. That sturdiness was one of the things Mom and Nonna shared. And that's what I needed right now.

"There's no need to rush anything. We can get to know each other a little first, maybe? You can ask me anything you'd like."

Gianluca nodded to himself, then smiled at me. "Thank you," he said. "So, when did you get this ring?"

"Just this July. John bought it at a jewelry store in Hudson, New York. It looks like Carmela sold it there just a few weeks before she—" I stopped short, terrified I'd started to reveal what would be devastating news.

"I know that she passed," Gianluca said.

It took a second for my mind to fit this piece into the rest of the picture. "If you know, then . . . did you follow her life all these years?" I asked.

"No," he said. "I was in her life all these years."

I literally gasped.

"Let's sit now," Gianluca said, then he motioned to the tattered sofa hidden in the corner.

"I WANT YOU to know that I'm doing this for Gianna," Gianluca started. "In your note, you mentioned that this kept her from fully knowing her mother, and that breaks my heart."

Something finally clicked in my mind. "Gianna," I said. "She's named for you, isn't she?"

"Sì. And that's why I can't bear the thought of her believing there's some horrible secret about her mother's life. Carmela is innocent of everything but protecting me."

A chill ran through me. *Protecting him from what?*

"You know that Carmela and I ended our engagement after two years of living together here in Rome. During that time, I traveled to Manhattan for a teaching position. We went together and Carmela fell in love with the city and with America. We dreamed of making a life there once my career took off. After things ended between us, I told her to sell the ring so that she could start that new life in the States. But she found a way to make it there *and* keep this piece of us."

"So you found her once she settled in New York?"

"No, she found me. Because, as she said in a letter just as beautiful as yours, we were soulmates."

I was trying hard to be patient, but the devil on my shoulder finally got the best of me. "So then why in the world did you break up?" I asked.

The words passed through my brain and out my mouth too fast to sound anything but rude. Gianluca closed his eyes and took a deep breath. *I ruined it*, I thought. But moments later, the man said something he must have uttered aloud rarely in his life, given the look on his face.

"Because I realized not long before Carmela and I planned to marry that I could never love her in the way she deserved. It was in trying to give her all of me that I realized my truth: I am a gay man."

My hand flew to my heart, thumping loud against my chest. "Oh!" I said. "Wow . . ." It was a bungled response, but an honest one.

"I know that's not something you need to hide in this day and age, especially in America, but Italy is a deeply Catholic nation, and I come from a very religious family. If anyone found out back then, it would have ended my relationship with them. Plus I made my living as a portrait artist to wealthy families; they never would have brought a gay man into their homes in the seventies. So the people who knew the truth were sworn to secrecy, and that included Carmela."

"How did she feel when she found out?" I asked.

Gianluca's face fell at the memory. "Hurt, confused. Angry at first," he said. "Years later, she told me she'd wondered once or twice, but you have to remember there were so few out gay men then. I didn't even realize it myself, until I met someone, a fellow artist."

"Did you two stay together?"

"No," Gianluca said. "Too risky, I decided. I was alone for most of my life because that was easier than losing my family. Of course, now that I am old, it seems foolish. They didn't accept me anyway because I was a 'loveless bachelor' in their minds. I needed to be married to be a man."

His words cut through me. Before meeting John I'd been asked countless times if I was getting nervous about "finding *the one*" so I could "settle down." Marriage was the accepted, standard way to be an adult, steady and responsible, even now.

"I'm so sorry," I said. "None of that could have been easy. And I'm guessing that's why Carmela kept you a secret?"

"Yes. She would sneak down to Manhattan to visit me whenever I was in the States. For the rest of the time, we communicated via long, handwritten letters. I still have them all, and I'd love to finally get them to Gia."

"Of course," I said.

But my mind was still with Carmela keeping this secret, lying to her family to honor this man. To have acted with such compassion while dealing with her own deep heartbreak showed how much she truly adored him. With that thought, I felt all the weight I'd been carrying since the moment John opened the black ring box begin to lift off my shoulders.

"The ring is safe," I whispered, holding back tears.

"What's that?" Gianluca asked.

"Sorry," I said, "I'm just relieved. Your story is such a beautiful example of love and loyalty, true connection, even if it didn't end in marriage. I can wear this ring knowing it holds all that happy, pure energy. This is everything I needed, Gianluca, *grazie*."

"Right," he said, face suddenly concerned. "You mentioned that in your letter. But, Shea, I can't give you that guarantee."

"What do you mean? You just did." My spine straightened against the back of the old couch.

"Only about my story. I don't know what happened with the woman who wore the ring before I gave it to Carmela."

All the weight came crashing back down. There was another owner. *Another relationship.* Another mystery to solve, from square one. My stomach churned.

"I'm sorry, but I can help. I know the name of the woman who sold me the ring," Gianluca said. "So you can go find her next."

TWENTY-SIX

WE WERE CUTTING IT DANGEROUSLY CLOSE to missing the train from Rome to Florence, which was timed for Annie and me to make our flight from Italy back to LA. And I couldn't decide if I wanted two more hours for Gianluca to tell me everything he knew about this second—or technically first—ring owner, or if I wanted to turn back the clock to a time before I knew about this twist.

"I'll put all I can remember into an email for you," he offered, reading the dread in my eyes. "This way you can think it through when you have more time."

"*Grazie* again," I said. "This has been so much more than I hoped for. How can I thank you?"

Gianluca smiled as if he'd been ready for this question, maybe as if it was the whole reason he'd invited me. "It would mean the world if you could put me in touch with Gia," he said.

"Of course," I promised. "I think she'll love that."

. . .

I FELT LIKE a kid fighting a dangerous sugar high as I raced down the stone steps of the apartment building to find Annie and Graham. My brain did not know where to focus first, next, or at all. Then the universe decided to push me one tick further: John was calling.

"I could kill this old Italian man," he said once I'd speed-recapped the past hour. "You were *happy*. The mystery of the ring was *solved*. Why couldn't he leave it at that?"

I said a silent thank-you for the fact that John had called me without video this time. But he was right; karma-wise, the failed engagement was a technicality. The love at its core had lasted until the day Carmela died.

"Look, I hate this just as much as you do," I said, "but neither of us is in control here."

I was hiding in the portico of Gianluca's building, wondering how much time I had before someone came to drag me toward the train. Trying not to also wonder what they'd each say when they heard what I'd learned.

"Okay, new angle," John said. "Based on your superstition, wouldn't the most recent owner erase the energy of the person who wore it prior? So Gianluca and Carmela's story washes out anything that this first woman might have experienced. Ergo, you can choose to be done."

He was making a valid attempt at logic, but I had my own.

"Imagine finding out a horrific murder was committed in a house you're considering buying," I said. "Like Golden State Killer bad. It didn't happen to the most recent owner but to the one immediately prior. Would you still want to live there?"

John went silent on the other end. I envisioned him on our living room couch, grabbing the decorative pillows so tight they'd never be the same.

"So this isn't over . . ." The rare anxious tone to his voice hit my ear like a wrong note.

"I guess it could be," I started. "Because I don't want you to be upset about this and—" I stopped myself, suddenly hearing the voice of my mother in my own. Ignoring her needs in favor of Dad's. Putting aside her feelings so he was comfortable. Being what she thought was a good wife. "Let me try that again," I started firmly. "I know we didn't expect this twist, but it's still the same plan we discussed. I'm figuring out the history of the ring."

John didn't answer right away, but when he did, I wished he'd waited longer. "Maybe the better plan would be to just get you a new ring."

As if on psychic cue, Annie appeared. She looked relieved to find me alive, then instantly aware something was wrong. I held up a finger to tell her I needed a minute. She tapped one to her wrist to tell me I didn't have one.

"Um . . . wow . . . okay," I said, stalling. I could feel my body rejecting the idea. Nudging *no* up to my brain. *Why? This would solve everything.* "Let me think about that," I finished. "We're actually super late for our train back, so—"

"I'm serious, Shea," John said. "Why not just end this now?"

"I'll think about it," I repeated, then I told him I loved him and ended the call.

TWENTY-SEVEN

W E MADE IT ONTO THE TRAIN WITH THREE MIN-
utes to spare. I'd filled Annie and Graham in
on the entire Gianluca story, including its in-
sane ending, on the cab ride over. I'd left out the call with John,
even to Annie.

"I'll get on this name Bette Silva as soon as I can connect
to the Internet," Graham said.

"And I'll try to talk you out of actually looking for her as
soon as I can find a panini," said Annie.

I slumped into my seat, grateful we weren't in the quiet
car. I needed the distraction of conversations outside my own
head. Luckily a French mother and daughter were mid-fight
just a few rows in front of us. The woman was trying but
failing to keep her voice down as she begged her child to do
something. *Listen? Understand?* I craned my neck around the
side of the seat in front of me, nosily hoping to put faces to the
sounds. It turned out I'd been wrong. It was the daughter—with
her dozen ear piercings and pink-streaked hair—imploring

her mother, a Parisian vision in head-to-toe cream. Even with zero knowledge of their language, I could tell that the young girl was making an impassioned plea for something that her parent could not, or maybe would not, understand. Their dynamic—the way the mother calmly made her case and the daughter flailed her arms—sent me instantly back in time.

I had to be around seventeen; Annie was just about to graduate from college. It was about a year after we'd lost Nonna, and Mom and Dad had finally divorced about six months prior. That should have lifted my spirits after all the years of finger crossing, but I was angry. Maybe I was still grieving the loss of my grandmother? Mad at my parents for stealing the spotlight from what I thought really mattered, once again? The fight that finally made Dad leave was just a few months after Nonna died. By that point, Pop was already starting to get sick, too. We needed to be coming together as a family, I'd thought, supporting each other through it all. Or maybe deep down I didn't want them to split up; I wanted them to be better, together.

Mom was headed out on her first date with a new man that night. A nice guy named Tim that she'd met through her nursing job. I think he'd just lost his mother, too. I remember standing in the frame of her bathroom door as she fumbled with her makeup. Mom was a natural beauty who never wore much more than mascara. It drove her own mother crazy. Nonna never left the house without completing her four-step beauty checklist: ruby-red lips, blush-pink cheeks, flawless porcelain skin, and thick black lashes. But on this night, her daughter was trying out a red lipstick almost that same color, to match a scarlet sweater dress. She was gorgeous. Excited. She didn't know I was watching until I opened my big mouth to call out the one detail that looked out of place.

"Mom," I said, "you're still wearing your engagement ring."

She jumped at my voice, then looked down at her finger. "I'm going to keep it on," she said. "Tim knows I'm divorced, anyway."

"What?" I yelled. "Why?"

"I like this ring," she said.

"You *like* it? Mom, that's nuts! That ring is from a man who made your life a living hell! You're finally free! Take it off!"

"Sweetie, I don't want to fight with you about this right now. I'm going to be late. We'll talk about it later."

"That's BS, explain it to me now!"

"Shea," Mom said, "I don't even fully understand it myself yet. Just please, let it go. I don't want to argue before I have to leave."

I complied with a stubborn slam of her bathroom door and a commitment meant to spite her: *You win. I'll never bring the ring up again.* I kept my promise. Including on that day in her bedroom near the end.

A ping on my phone broke through my memory. It was Gianluca's note containing all he knew about my ring's prior owner. I forwarded it to Graham, then stood up to make my way over to him so we could discuss. Before I could, I saw Annie walking back with two panini and a look that confirmed she was now very ready to talk.

.   .   .

"EXPLAIN TO ME why you can't just take the new ring and move on? John offered you what you wanted! No heirloom," Annie argued.

"That was before I started learning about *this* heirloom," I said. "I feel attached."

"More attached to the ring than your fiancé? Shea, it's time to consider how this fun detective work could be impacting *your marriage* long-term."

I hated the way she said *your marriage*, like it was some third-party entity, separate from John and me, a fragile but fickle thing to avoid upsetting at all costs.

"I'm not married yet!" I yelled back. *Are we now the French mother and daughter's entertainment?* "And what about how John's decisions might affect *our marriage*? He wasn't listening to me when he bought this ring. How is that setting us up for this lifetime of partnership and compromise?"

"Is that what this is about? John *winning* in some way? You losing control?" Annie asked, her voice suddenly much more worried than angry.

"I don't know!" I said. "You tell me. I've never done literally any of this before!"

"Maybe it would help to finally put yourself in John's shoes," she offered, emphasis on the *finally*.

"Maybe you could try to put yourself in mine!" I yelled back. At that, Graham poked his head up from his seat with a look that said *less volume* but also quite possibly, *I just wrote all that down.*

"I'm sorry," Annie said. "Let's take a breath, then get home.

I think things will be clearer away from the stress of this. Maybe you should even let Graham finish the research on his own." She lobbed a discerning look in his direction.

"What's wrong with Graham?" I whispered.

"I've seen him staring at you a little too much lately . . . *trust me.*"

"Oh, you'll use anything to get me off this!" I said. "Why can't you just be on my team?"

"Damn it, Shea," Annie said. She looked so much like our mom when she was angry. It was somehow both a comfort and a trigger. "I didn't want to say this, but here's the bottom line: I know you and your superstitions, and I'm scared that if this ring is tainted, even in some small way, you'll think that's a sign that you shouldn't marry John at all." She went in for the kill. "It's all reminding me too much of how you were about Mom's engagement ring. You dug in so hard and wouldn't let go."

I wondered if Annie could see every hair on my body rise. *Don't tell her*, a voice inside me said. But another said: *Mom is gone. And she didn't exactly make smart choices about her ring when she was alive. What if she was wrong about keeping this from Annie? What if Annie could help you if she knew Mom tried to give it to me?*

"I need to tell you something," I heard myself say, mouth suddenly dry.

"Oh God," Annie said. "I do not like the look in your eyes."

The only way to say it was quickly.

"Mom tried to give me her engagement ring before she died, and she asked me not to tell you." A sweet relief spread through me; the secret was finally outside my body. But in that same moment I saw the other side of the coin: it was now inside my sister's.

"When did this happen?" was all she could muster. She'd turned to stare out the train window. The postcard-perfect hills of the Italian countryside zoomed by, making it feel even more like time in here was standing still.

"Two weeks before she died," I said. "You remember how shitty everything was those last few days? I honestly forgot about it. And then once I remembered—I don't know—I got all caught up in honoring Mom's wishes because I felt like it was the only thing I could do for her anymore. I'm sorry, Annie."

"But wait, you didn't take the ring. Mom was wearing it at her funeral." Annie was arriving at what would potentially be most devastating of all. It was time for me to come fully clean.

"I didn't take the ring. And I never let her explain why she wanted to give it to me in the first place."

Annie turned away from me. She looked truly beside herself. "Shea, *why* are you telling me this now?"

"Because I keep thinking about it—having all these weird connected memories. It even came up in a nightmare I had weeks ago, and I really need your help figuring it out what it all means."

At that, Annie exploded. "*God* you're so selfish! *Always* have been! *Always* will be, apparently. Mom wanted to share something with you—for reasons that we'll now never know—and you refused because you didn't like it? Because you were *sure* you knew what she was going to say? Oh wait, it's because you've always been the expert on her and Dad's marriage and didn't think for a *second* about what that information might mean to me! That ring was as much mine as yours, but now neither of us have it!"

The sting of all Annie's words hit me, but what she said about me being the expert on Mom and Dad flipped me from guilty to defensive. For years, I'd begged Annie to understand how bad it was between them and why we should try to talk Mom into leaving. She'd told me to butt out. She'd told me to stop being selfish. Then she went back to her own life, away from it all. First in high school, where she was the president of half a dozen clubs. Then in college in Sacramento, far enough north that she only came home for the holidays.

"I think we're done here," I said. "You're obviously not the person to help me through all this." I knew that would be the dagger to her mother-hen heart.

"Let's continue this at the airport," Annie said, tucking her hair behind her ear. A conductor's voice popped over the intercom, announcing our arrival in Florence. "We'll both get off this train and let off some steam."

"I don't know that I want to talk about it anymore right now," I said, feeling stronger in her presence than I had in years. "And I don't know that I'm going to the airport."

TWENTY-EIGHT

I WATCHED AS GRAHAM HELPED ANNIE INTO A CAB, OUR fight looping in my head like my least favorite song in the world stuck on repeat. Annie looked back at me before he closed the door. Her eyes said the thing I feared most: *You're wrong.* On her neck was the Prada scarf I'd bought her on our first day, a special treat to mark the magic of getting to be back here together. Now our second trip to Italy would always end with the memory of this moment and the question of whether it was all my fault.

"You okay?" Graham asked as he made his way to the table where I was "hiding" just across the piazza.

"Not really," I said.

"We can talk about it, if that would help. Off the record."

A waiter dropped off the cappuccino I'd completely forgotten I ordered, giving me a second to think. "Maybe later," I finally said. "I have a lot of other things to figure out right now." It was genuine, not a brush-off. I'd come to really appreciate the way Graham's mind worked, even if I didn't always agree with it. "Can we go over Gianluca's email, actually?" I asked. "That would probably be the most helpful next step."

"Of course," said Graham as he opened the laptop he'd already set on the table, as if anticipating my request.

Most people don't believe this story, Gianluca started. But I swear to you it's true. He and Carmela were in Portugal by invitation of an art gallery showing his newest collection of portraits. On the night they arrived in Lisbon, the Teatro Nacional de São Carlos was showing *Madama Butterfly*, in Puccini's original Italian. Carmela took the Italian as a sign, Gianluca wrote. They splurged on tickets but saved on dinner, just grabbing a glass of wine and some ceviche at a bar around the corner. A mysterious beauty in an emerald-green dress was seated on the bar stool directly to their left, Bette Silva. Carmela and Bette quickly bonded over the fact they'd both received a Portuguese scoff for ordering an Italian red wine, then they all got to talking about their shared love for the opera. One glass of wine became several for the fast friends, which had unfortunately affected Gianluca's memory of additional Bette details.

I can picture her beautiful red, curly hair, he wrote. And I remember her Italian was so perfect it was as if she was native, but I don't think we learned much about her that night. Only that she'd spent her career mostly touring with the famous Puccini classic we were seeing that night, maybe playing one of the key roles? It's hard to remember because Bette did all the asking, and Carmela did all the talking over our drinks, telling her about our plans to move to New York, where I would pursue my art and Carmela would open her café. One of the only questions that Carmela asked Bette was about the engagement ring the woman wore on a chain around her neck.

My hand went straight to the ring at my own chest after Graham read that line. His look told me he'd also clocked the coincidence. A good detail to scribble in his notepad.

Carmela told Bette the ring was perfect, the note went on. Gianluca was grateful for the clue since buying an engagement ring was already on his mind. Shortly after that exchange Carmela excused herself to the restroom. Bette immediately took the ring off her necklace, grabbed Gianluca's hand, and placed it inside.

And she just said, "Pay me whatever you can. It doesn't matter because this ring is already yours," the email went on.

Of course Gianluca tried to protest. He and Carmela were strangers to Bette, and this ring was an incredible piece of jewelry, something that should be passed down in Bette's own family. But all she would say was that she knew the ring belonged to them.

Maybe it was the certainty in her eyes, or the fact that I was raised by a family just as superstitious as yours, Shea, Gianluca included. But I believed her.

Several months later, he and Carmela had tried to find Bette to let her know that they were officially engaged, but she was never at the phone number she'd given them that evening. And that was the end of that. A chance encounter. An incredible story. Or, as Gianluca wrote at the end of his note: fate?

"It reads like an opera," Graham said once we were through all the details.

"Don't say that. They almost all have tragic endings," I said.

Graham nodded, trying to avoid the elephant at the café table. I appreciated the out-of-character gesture.

"Out with it," I said. "What should I do next?"

"You should go to Portugal. I already have people looking into Bette and that opera house where she was performing. You're only a three-hour flight away."

I was expecting this pitch, minus one part. "Why the *you*?" I asked. "You're not coming?"

Graham shifted in his seat. "I went to Portugal a long time ago," he said. "On an assignment, I guess you could say. It didn't go so well, so I'm not eager to go back."

I tried but failed to hide my grin. "So . . . you're saying the place holds a kind of *karma* that you don't want infused into your life?"

Graham's brows popped in a way I hadn't seen yet. A *Touché*.

"Listen," I said. "I don't want to make you do something uncomfortable, even though that is essentially what you did to me by coming on this trip in the first place."

"I'll take that," Graham said.

"But I really need your help right now. And it would be my honor to help you rewrite your Portugal karma with my ring karma."

"Thank you," said Graham. "That is maybe the kindest of-fer I've ever received, even though I don't believe a single word of it."

. . .

AN HOUR LATER, I was tucked into the crowded waiting area of Amerigo Vespucci Airport leaving what probably should have been a much longer voicemail on John's phone. It was the middle of the night in Los Angeles. I'd considered sending an email, then a text, but this felt like information that needed to come with the context of the feelings in my voice: I was resolved but I wasn't thrilled.

"I need to go to Portugal to hopefully finish this whole mission," I said. Then after a quick breath, I added the trickier part: "Annie is headed back to LA, but Graham is staying on to help."

TWENTY-NINE

W E ASSUMED OUR BETTE SILVA SEARCH WOULD be easier. We were armed with her full name from go, plus all the additional intel from Gianluca. But Graham was quickly starting to worry that some—or all—of it was a lie. Thanks to airplane Wi-Fi, he'd already discovered that the woman was not a known entity in the opera world. He couldn't find her name in any press for any show that was recent enough to be mentioned online, or in several news archives.

"I'm thinking Bette used some other stage name Gianluca didn't know," he said as he chugged his third ginger ale of the flight. "Maybe that's why it's not coming up in any opera-related search."

"Well, how do we find that name?" I asked.

"I have literally no idea," he said, shocking even himself, it appeared.

"Is that why you're chain-drinking ginger ale?"

Graham responded by pushing the flight attendant call button to order another. Evidently this was not going to be as easy as buying an engagement ring off a stranger in a Portuguese wine bar.

"Is going to Portugal a waste of time?" I asked, considering my own ginger ale order.

"No," Graham said. "It's even more important we go there in person. I'm sure Bette came into contact with tons of people when she performed. We'll start first thing tomorrow at the opera house, poke around, see if someone in the building knows anything about her, then ask about their archives from old performances. That'll at least confirm that she's real and maybe give us some more bio data."

Graham was more scrappy than certain—willing to dive into something as a trial, then pivot just as quickly as needed. It was his own brand of confidence.

"You're really good at what you do," I said. The rounds of Graham's high cheeks blushed pink, shockingly. "Hasn't anybody ever told you that?"

"No," he said, straight-faced. "Nobody ever has. Thank you."

"What happened with you and Portugal?" I asked. It felt like a door had creaked open between us. Graham wasn't surprised by the question, though maybe a little impressed that I'd chosen to lean in at this moment.

"I told you my mom had an affair," he started. "That's why my parents split up. But I was the one who caught her."

"Oof, I'm so sorry," I said. "And we don't have to talk about it anymore if you don't want to."

"No, this is good," he said, nodding as if to convince himself. "I never talk about it, which isn't healthy, at least according to both my exes."

"You cannot drop that kind of bomb and expect me not to ask a thousand follow-ups . . ."

Graham laughed, then changed his order from another ginger ale to two coffees.

I spent the next hour finally learning about what made my unexpected travel companion tick. His mom was a successful documentarian who traveled the world for her work. She was powerful and persuasive, not someone anyone would think to question. But Graham was not everyone.

"I would sit on her bed while she packed for an upcoming trip. It started when I was a little kid, but it stayed our thing— our time to talk," he explained. "I was probably around twelve, maybe thirteen, when I noticed that she was packing different things than her usual work clothes. Nicer dresses, a lot of lace. The filmmaker raised a kid who paid attention to detail."

I'd been there, too. An unfamiliar, flowery scent on Dad's shirt; a fancy gift box never received by my mom; and multiple matchbooks from hotels, which seemed odd, even to a kid. I wanted to tell Graham all of these things, but instead I let him hold the floor.

"When I was sixteen she started traveling a lot more, and for longer trips. That's when I started to write things down, keeping tabs on her itineraries and then comparing what she'd tell me when she came home. She started dropping the name Emilio, apparently one of her new producing partners . . . based in Portugal."

I suddenly noticed my left hand moving toward Graham's

right forearm. I was just going to offer a supportive touch, the way my nonna always did when she was listening to me tell her something hard to say, but I stopped and slipped my hand back before he noticed.

"I asked my parents for money to go backpacking for my high school graduation," Graham continued. "And I used that money to go looking for Emilio. I knew enough by then to track him to the university outside Lisbon where he worked. But I neglected to consider one very big piece of the puzzle: that my mom would be with him."

"Oh my God," I said. "You saw them together."

"And the worst part is that my poor dad technically paid for that to happen," said Graham.

"Maybe you were helping him?"

"Yeah, well, he definitely didn't think so." Graham pinched the bridge of his nose, as if trying to clear a thought. It made me realize how raw this still was for him, even after what had to be almost fifteen years.

"I am so sorry that I made you come here," I said. "I feel so selfish." Annie's accusation was coming back to haunt me.

"No," Graham said. "It was my decision. Maybe I'll cancel out my history with our story."

Now I let my hand do what it wanted, giving Graham a squeeze that said, *I get it*.

IT WASN'T MUCH longer until we were on the tarmac in Lisbon and I was listening to the reply voicemail from John—my eyes shut to really focus on the sound of his voice.

Do what you need to do, Shea, he said, then I heard him sigh, almost as if he was breathing away what he'd wanted to say next. *Call me as soon as you can* and *I love you* were what he chose instead. John's voice was flat. I couldn't tell if it was angry or hurt, sincere or scared. I didn't know if he was stomping around our bedroom now, opening and closing dresser drawers like he did after the Dodgers lost, or curled up in his favorite corner of our sectional with my weighted blanket. And worse, I had even less sense of how *I* felt. *Anxious? Determined? . . . Obsessed?*

All I knew was that I didn't call John back as soon as I could have, like he asked. I didn't want to call him back until I knew what I had to say.

THIRTY

I WAS UP BEFORE THE SUN ROSE IN SEARCH OF STRONG coffee and a moment as a tourist before the detective work began. Lisbon had always been a dream destination, but no travel site I'd scanned captured its magic. The streets were San Francisco hilly in a way that made the sun play peekaboo with the buildings. The city's crescent shape along the river meant you could catch sparkling water from every view. And hand-painted tiles—a Portuguese signature—covered every surface in sight. Their yellow, red, and blue jewel tones gave way to delicate patterns of rosettes and diamonds. En route to a café, I stopped a dozen times to take photos, then genuinely considered buying enough tile to cover our entire bathroom back in LA. But all this beauty paled in comparison to the famous *pastel de nata*. A pillow-soft custard pastry that tasted like the inside of a Boston cream donut meets heaven. I ate two and bought six more to share with Graham.

By nine a.m. we were outside the Teatro Nacional de São Carlos for a docent-led tour. It was a stately building—more

London than Rome—with a rich buttercup façade and ornate stonework reliefs. And it had attracted just as dignified a crowd. Our group included a stuffy, sixty-something American couple from Northern California who had seen a combined fifty famous opera houses, a fact for which no one asked; an impossibly chic French couple who greatly disliked the Americans and were communicating that fact exclusively with their eyes; sisters from Sweden who were over eighty but still giggled like teens; and a dead-serious, possibly-Russian man who didn't utter a single word. Graham and I were the *two of these things are not like the others.* So much so that our guide—Beatriz—made us double-check our tickets. She looked ninety, moved like she was forty, and talked like she was a college show-off, spewing facts so fast she didn't bother with complete sentences. *Seventeen ninety-three: the year the building was opened. Neoclassical: the style of architecture. Queen Maria was the benefactor; Milan's La Scala served as inspiration for the design.* My patience bottomed out once she started describing, in detail, the life of every single Portuguese businessman who had invested in the property.

"How long is this tour supposed to be?" I whispered to Graham.

"Two hours," he said, avoiding contact with my *What the hell?!* look in response.

"Okay, everyone!" Beatriz squawked. "Now into the building for the architecture, the restorations, and the dozens and dozens of meaningful touches. Please hold your questions until the end—you can write them down in your guide as we go."

"One question before no questions," I heard Graham say.

"Is there an archive in the building? Maybe a registry where historic documents are stored?"

"Not one that you will see on this tour," she said. "Now please follow me through the main doors—not the original, but replaced in 1822, for better security after a string of crimes I'll explain inside."

Graham pulled me aside, mischief in his eyes. "What's your tolerance for breaking and entering?" he asked.

"Depends. Is Portugal more *Brokedown Palace* or—actually, I don't know a movie where people commit an international crime and just get away with it."

"All I'm proposing is snooping around to try to find the basement."

"Oh, *snooping* is fine, cute even." I didn't say that I would have followed him even if he'd suggested more. Graham seemed like the kind of guy that could bend the rules to the point just before they break, and get away with it every time.

We waited until Beatriz turned to reference out one of the hundreds of identical plaques in the foyer, then quickly slipped back through the entryway, searching for any other doors that might be accessible. We counted sixteen exterior doors in total; not a single one was unlocked.

"We can't look around inside while she's still guiding the tour," Graham said, "so I guess we'll have to wait and—" He was interrupted by what sounded like a tank engine but turned out to be a garbage truck heading toward the building. "Follow that truck!" Graham yelled, then he took off around the left corner of the property.

"*What? Why?*" I called out, trying to trail his cross-country strides.

"Because it might stop at some kind of loading dock with access to the building!"

And that is precisely what happened. The truck pulled up to a driveway at the very back of the theater. Waiting beside an open garage door was an older man in a blue jumpsuit, completely unfazed by the two tourists running after garbage.

"Nice!" cried Graham, then he threw his hand up for a high five. It shocked me so much I looked behind me to see if he was waving at someone.

"Sorry, I didn't take you for a high-five guy."

"I wasn't one until right now," he said as he tapped his hand against mine, completing the move. "Never had a partner like this before."

"Wow, so you're saying I'm the first girl you followed to Europe on a mission to steal her life story for an article," I said. "*What an honor.*"

"I'm just saying we make a really good team," said Graham.

I was so caught off guard by his sincerity that I was still waiting for the snide follow-up as Graham rushed over to meet the man beside the garage door.

Tomas, we learned, was the head of building maintenance for the Teatro Nacional and kindly promised to answer all of our questions once the day's trash collection was complete. First, the good news: the building *did* have a room of boxes stored in its basement, a fact we determined after a lot of tricky Google translating and several attempts at miming words like *box* and *basement*. Then came the bad: any documents prior to 1980 had been gifted to the Biblioteca Palacio Galveias for their municipal archives.

"I do not know what is kept and not," Tomas told us in his low, round voice.

He reminded me of my pop, wide in the center but with the slender legs and muscled arms of a man who worked with them every day. *Popeye*, Nonna liked to call him, then Annie and I would sing the song.

"This has been incredibly helpful," Graham said, shaking the man's hand.

"*Sim*," he said, "my pleasure. You are beautiful couple. Like memory of me and my wife."

I don't know why I was so shocked to hear it. Graham and I were an American twosome of a similar age, running around together in a foreign country. Objectively, we matched—Graham in his uniform of loose khakis and blue button-down, and me in whatever flowy skirt and linen top I'd thrown together that day. Without even knowing that our travel involved an engagement ring, one would assume we were together. But Tomas was the first to take note.

"*Obrigado*," I heard Graham say, deciding not to correct Tomas's assumption about our status.

Our new friend smiled and wished us "*Boa sorte*," which I assumed meant "good luck."

I was silent as we walked toward the library, but Graham read my mind.

"It seemed easier than trying to explain to him what we were doing here," he said. "And that we're not together."

He was right, of course. And maybe his journalistic instincts—that skill of saying what was needed to move the conversation where he wanted—were quicker than his other reflexes. But as half of this assumed couple, I easily could have jumped in to correct Tomas. Why hadn't I?

FIFTEEN MINUTES AND two more *pastéis de nata* later, we arrived at the library. Our hope was to find an archive of opera house performance programs for *Madama Butterfly* from the fifties through roughly the late eighties, since that's the show Gianluca thought Bette had performed in most. After that we were looking for the name of a performer with some connection to *Bette* or *Silva*, hoping she'd picked a stage name more like Michael Douglas using Michael Keaton, and not Reginald Dwight becoming Elton John. *If* we could make that connection, and if opera programs were anything like Broadway Playbills, we might learn *something* about this mystery woman's hidden life that would point us in the next direction. It was a wing-and-a-prayer plan, which took at least fifteen more minutes to explain to a group of very patient librarians. Luckily they delivered us our first win of the many-step process: we were told the library *did* have copies of all the Teatro's programs, which were wheeled out to us in a set of decomposing cardboard boxes on what had to be the oldest library cart in existence.

"Please tell me these are in chronological order," I said. Graham did not reply; he already knew they were not.

We proceeded to open *every single one* and examine *every single piece* of printed theater history until we'd narrowed it down to a group of fifteen performances of *Madama Butterfly* in twenty-some years. It was technically progress, but I didn't feel that way. Somewhere around hour two, I ran out for more coffee and *pastéis*. At hour four, the dust got to Graham so much that he had to wrap the sleeves of my extra cardigan around his face. It would have been hysterical if we weren't so utterly depleted. Finally, Graham jumped up with a piece of brown-edged paper and shouted, "*YES!*" Everyone around us jumped too, then shushed him.

On April 2, 1970, a Lisbeth Park had performed the famous "Un Bel Dì, Vedremo" aria from Puccini's *Madama Butterfly*. Alongside her name in that night's program was a photo of a young woman with fair skin, curly red hair, and kind eyes, just as Gianluca had described.

"That's got to be her, right?" I said.

"It's the closest we're going to get before I die of an asthma attack," said Graham. Then he read the words under the photo as I Google translated: *Lisbeth Park é um meio-soprano que já fez turnê internacional.* Lisbeth Park is a mezzo-soprano that has toured internationally. Or in other words, hours of searching for a *duh*. Graham started a coughing fit. "What is this woman, in witness protection?" Graham said, still choking.

"Please do not suggest things that involve crime," I begged, a tickle forming in my own throat.

"Wait," he said, wheels spinning. "This isn't totally worthless. This program has the names of people who Bette or Lisbeth or whoever she is performed with that night. We can try to find one or some of them to get more information."

"Find *more people*? What if they're not alive? We still don't even know if she's alive!"

"There would be an obituary somewhere if she was dead."

"Not if she was a recluse who died alone in some villa in Tuscany, never to be found!" Graham did not dignify that idea with a response. He just raced the opera programs over to the world's oldest photocopiers, so we could both get out of this building.

The next step of this already endless mission was to work through the list of castmates, the third time in six days that we were beginning a new search. With eighteen performers total, we focused on the traditionally Portuguese names first, hoping to connect with someone while we were here. We emailed that list over to Graham's research contact from the lobby of the hotel. The plan was to have them run names through their database, asking for addresses, phone numbers, or—though hopefully not—any obituaries. Then, finally, we went back to our rooms to freshen up before a dinner of anything other than custard and pastry dough.

ALONE IN MY room, I considered calling John. I opened my laptop, wondering if Annie's old advice about writing a letter to express all my confused feelings would help again. Instead I found one new email from Jack Sachs.

I assumed the worst, that he wasn't approving my request

for a few more vacation days to address this "family issue." Instead, I opened it and read the opposite: I was officially being offered the promotion to "Director." I stared at the words on the screen. Why hadn't my face lit up? Why hadn't I slipped into even the start of a proud smile? This odd blankness was the same as it had been when Jack first told me about the job. *Do I not want this job?* Suddenly habit took over; I grabbed for my phone and called John.

"Hey," he said. "There you are." The subtext was clear.

"Yeah," I said. "Sorry. It's been a crazy day, but we're making progress. But I'm actually calling with good news. I got the promotion."

"Shea! That's incredible! Congrats!" John said. There was the emotion I'd been missing. "Wow. Our life's really coming together, huh? Marriage. Big promotion. Soon enough we'll be in a house, finally."

"Right," I said. The relief in his voice should have been contagious. Why wasn't it?

"Why does it feel like you don't mean that?" John asked, reading me from a single word. I sat down on the hotel bed, searching for an answer. Instead John offered one. "Hey. Maybe it's a sign," he said. "The work news is saying *come home*. We'll celebrate. And we'll get you a new ring. Move forward in all ways."

"Right," I said, pulled from one minefield to another. "I'm still thinking about the new ring. I promise. Right now, I need to get something to eat before I pass out."

"Okay," said John. "Text me before you go to bed. Love you."

"Will do. Love you too," I said, then we both hung up.

I got halfway down the hall to meet Graham before I realized that I'd just fully lied to John, and maybe for the first time in our entire relationship. I hadn't thought about his offer for a new ring once since we touched down in Portugal.

THIRTY-ONE

I FOUND GRAHAM SITTING BESIDE THE BLUE-TILED WALL of the hotel patio, two Negronis on his table.

"Took me three waiters to find one who knew this drink," he said. Then immediately, "What's wrong?"

I sat down and took a half-the-drink sip. "I just got promoted. Which should be good news, but I'm . . . I don't know. And—sorry—it doesn't involve ring-gate, so we really don't have to get into it."

"Hey now, have I not proven that I am an international man of solving mysteries?"

"You have . . ."

"And do you not owe me one after my family drama over-share?"

"I do . . ."

We downed our drinks, then moved around the corner for dinner at a tiny spot serving table-sized platters of *arroz con mariscos*. The restaurant was so narrow that all its seating was squeezed along the bar facing the open kitchen. The whole place had the wild energy of a New York City deli wrapped in the scent of fresh seafood and sharp spices.

"All right," Graham said once we'd placed our order. "Tell what lead to this promotion."

"The woman in the position before me left, and my boss put me up for the job," I said.

"No, no. Back it way up. I want to know how you got into marketing at a film festival in the first place."

"You want the whole history? Why?" I asked.

Graham cocked his head.

"Right," I said. "Touché."

I told him how my love of movies began with a daily dose of the Shirley Temple canon in front of my grandparents' giant black-and-white TV and continued with Friday nights in front of the Blockbuster wall, arguing with Annie, who only ever wanted Disney. My first crush had a dad in the industry whom I worshipped way more than his son. He was the person who first told me about NYU film school. I liked more structure than the artist life generally provides, so I applied and got into their business program. After a few miserable producing internships, I found the much more artist-friendly world of film festivals. The marketing department ended up scratching my creative itch and desire to get more films in front of more audiences. I was squarely inside my dream world, I told Graham, but with the kind of stability that made me most comfortable. Then I finished by providing a very comprehensive list of the benefits to taking this huge promotion.

Graham had listened without interrupting, nodding as if

he understood it all as I'd gone on and on. But he was silent now that I'd finished. I watched as he poured us each a glass of crimson wine from the carafe that had arrived during my long career recap. He took a slow sip, the apparent windup for a curveball question: "What does John think of all this?"

"Why do you care about that?" I asked.

"Because you obviously do. Did you not hear your benefits list? *John's been wanting to buy a house, and this new salary would really help. John's considering going for his PhD, so this stability will really help. John always told me I'd end up the head of this department someday.*"

"Well, he's going to be my husband. We're making a life together. That's kind of the whole point."

"Is it?" Graham asked. Our food came before I could push back on that. We each shoveled a few bites, coming back to life. Then Graham plowed ahead with another. "Answer me this: is it your dream to be your boss?"

The answer flashed through me so fast I literally had to blink. "No," I said, then, "Why did I just say no?"

"*Okay . . . ,*" said Graham. Apparently we were getting somewhere. "Why not?"

I closed my eyes, trying to envision myself a decade in the future. A vision slowly pieced together—me standing onstage for the opening night of a very different film festival. One I was running. Then I recognized the daydream from memory. I had volunteered at the tiny Cape Cod International Film Festival after college. It had been run by an eccentric woman in a uniform of black with a different pair of glasses for every single event: Misty Ellinger. She had come up the ranks as a film festival programmer and a filmmaker herself. She was who I wanted to be, not Jack Sachs.

"I might not want to stay in marketing," I finally said, opening my eyes.

"Nice," said Graham. "Now, what would John think of that?"

His pullback to the John of it all irked me. It reminded me of Annie harping on how every decision I made was now going to affect my marriage.

"Hey. I am uncovering some major life stuff here. Why do you keep bringing it back to that?"

"I'm glad to hear you ask that," was all Graham said in response.

I took a sip of my wine, mostly so that I could more dramatically roll my eyes over the rim of the glass. "You honestly think I'm going to be the kind of wife that just defers to her husband's wants?" I asked.

"I'm still trying to figure out why you want to be a wife at all!" Graham said. The approaching waitress did a full about-face.

"Call her back, because I want the check, now," I said.

"Come on," said Graham. "Make a case. It's arguably the most important decision of your life. Shouldn't you have an answer for the question? Why do you, Shea Anderson, the superstition-ruled child of a messy divorce, want to be married?"

He'd raised a very fair point, but I felt an answer quickly forming.

"Okay, here goes: I want to marry John because there

was no drama with him right from go, no game-playing, no runaround. John was honest, clear, and direct from the very start." My words started to flow faster as the memories of falling in love came flooding back. "I didn't ever have to ask myself how he felt about me when we first started dating. He just . . . loved me, right away, and always. I knew it, and I felt it. I still do. John remembers when I have a big client meeting at work and texts me an encouraging message before. He covers me with a blanket when we watch TV, the second I look cold. He was the one who thought we should have date night every other Wednesday and rotate surprising each other with the plan. And he says things like 'I love you so much right now' at the most random times, which would typically make me cringe, but it's so genuine that I say it to him, too."

"So, you're saying that you want to be John's wife because he really loves you?" Graham asked flatly.

"Yes, but also because there was just this, I don't know, *comfort* to our whole dynamic. My friend Rebecca always said I was a commitment-phobe, but John gave me every reason to trust. And also—this sounds simple—but I just love being with him. Like, he makes every room he's in a better place to be."

"So, you knew John was the one because he loved you *and* it was comfortable." These seemed like good reasons to me, but Graham's face and tone said otherwise.

"I take it you don't believe me."

"Oh, I believe you," he said, suddenly smug. "I just don't agree with you. When you say *comfort* and *ease*, I hear *boring* and *unchallenging*."

"You, a child of a bitter divorce, think that love should be challenging?"

"Absolutely. My parents' marriage was difficult, yes, but I'm not going to swing the pendulum in the complete opposite direction to *easy*. What's the point of spending your entire life with someone if they're not going to push you to the extremes of yourself?"

"Um, how about *joy, happiness*? Maybe not being pushed, especially to whatever *the extremes of yourself* means?" I was mad now, elbows on the table, hands flying.

"Sorry, that just doesn't feel like enough to me," said Graham.

"It doesn't need to! I'm the one who believes in making a lifelong connection."

"Okay," said Graham. "So let's go with that: why? What's the genuine value in *forever* with someone?"

His question popped an image of Nonna and Pop's fiftieth wedding anniversary party to the front of my mind. I saw them cutting the cake, surrounded by generations of family and lifelong friends. In the background, one of those photo montages was playing on a portable screen. I was twelve, maybe thirteen, at the time. I remember watching as the images flipped through their life, from their honeymoon at the Grand Canyon to the proud shot of them holding the *Sold* sign in front of their first house, to Mom's birth and their first big trip back to Italy and Pop opening his mechanic shop and Nonna opening Bella Vita and on and on and on it went with them at the center. Together. That's what I'd always wanted. Wasn't it?

"Fine. You win. I can't explain it," I said. "It just seems like the best version of a life."

I watched Graham nod, then he leaned in as if he was about to tell me a secret.

"Then why in the world could something as small as an engagement ring screw all that up?" he asked.

I do not play chess, but I imagine that was what it feels like when your opponent says, *Checkmate*.

THIRTY-TWO

H OW DO YOU FEEL ABOUT CONVERTIBLES?" GRA-
ham asked as we made our way by metro to a rental
car pickup the next morning.

"I'm from California," was my answer.

"Good. I sprung for one to take down the coast. Decided it
was the best way to rectify my last trip, which involved five
angry hours on a very old coach bus."

"Then I'm going to need Grace Kelly sunglasses, stat," I
said.

"Not a Hepburn fan?"

"Audrey for the films, Grace for the look."

Thirty minutes later, we were on the road: me in my brand-
new black cat-eye frames from Estilo Armazenar—literally
"Style Store"—and him in a cheap straw fedora that I was
shocked and honored he didn't throw immediately in the
trash. We took off, sun shining through the kind of streaky
clouds that look painted. This was the setting for the refocus

I needed. No more work distractions. No more probing interviews. Just a day to tackle the mission, gain clarity.

Graham's colleague in New York had identified just one Bette Silva castmate still living anywhere near Lisbon, Carla Cardoso. Her address was listed in a town south of the country's capital, in a region known as the Algarve coast. This jagged, rustic coastline could stand in for any film locale along the classic beaches of Italy or marinas of the French Riviera. Its mountainous cliffs sat above beaches so private they didn't even have names. And there was blooming lavender everywhere you looked. The sweet, floral smell mixed with the salty ocean air in a way I wanted to bottle and wear.

Our destination was Vilamoura—a fishing community just a few hours from Lisbon. An inland highway could have gotten us there in under three hours, but I insisted on taking the winding Pacific Coast Highway–style route.

"This is taking time away from finding Carla," Graham protested.

"I don't think you rented a convertible just to sit on the equivalent of the New York State Thruway," I said.

He agreed by revving the engine of our red Mini Cooper convertible—my pick—as we headed off the main road and down a half-paved path toward the water. I made us stop no fewer than ten times to take photos, then finally convinced Graham to traipse down three flights of rickety wood stairs to an actual beach: Praia de Dona Ana. Our reward was untouched ivory sand, piles of exotic shells, and a bathwater ocean. An olive-skinned man sat alone with a bottle of *vinho*, reading a newspaper and armed with an additional pile of books at his side. A young couple darted in and out of the water and wrote words on each other's backs as they lounged across an old floral bedsheet.

"Thirty minutes," I said, a statement, not a question.

"Twenty," said Graham, in the exact same way.

We melted into the warm sand. My body started to relax as I turned my face toward the sun. Graham rolled up the pants of his baggy khakis and headed for the water. I watched as he grabbed a few stones, then stood at the edge preparing to skip them across the still ocean. The first failed with a wide splash. The second looked promising but petered out.

"Third time's a charm!" I called out from my spot up the shore. Graham blew on the stone for good luck, then launched it out to sea. It skipped one, two, three times—perfect. I cheered from the sidelines with a fake stadium roar. He celebrated by running into the waves like a kid who'd just scored the winning Pop Warner touchdown, then remembered he was an adult wearing his only clean pair of pants. The shocked look on his face made me laugh so hard that I fell back onto the sand. *This is bliss*, I thought as I scooped up handfuls of granules and watched them escape through my fingers. But with that thought came another: *When was the last time I felt this way?*

My mind searched, then landed on the obvious place: the afternoon John proposed. I pictured the nervous smile on his dewy face, the way he'd gone down on one knee so quickly he almost stumbled over. I rewound to a point in that day when the ring box was still unopened, and my heart tightened with anticipation just like it had in that moment. I'd known the proposal was coming, and—my skin chilled as a new thought broke over me—I was still filled with anxiety the moment it happened.

Why? Why wasn't a proposal from the love of my life total bliss? We'd been together for years. All the rest of our friends were already married. It was time. *Then how could five minutes on a beach, worlds away, possibly feel better?*

"Everything okay?" Graham asked. He was standing in front of me now, his tall frame casting a shadow.

"Yeah, just thinking," I said, nowhere near ready for one of his too-effective interrogations.

"Me too," he said as he sat down next to me. "For years I cursed coming to this place. But maybe that trip was the start of me figuring myself out. Maybe I owe who I am to that awful trip."

"I think that's true," I said.

"Good, then maybe you'll feel the same way, someday in the future," Graham said.

It was the kind of reassurance I didn't know I needed—not advice for what to do next, like Annie would have given, or the dose of cheerful certainty that John would have offered. This was an honest *Keep going.*

Graham and I spent the next ten minutes sitting side by side, staring out at the blurred line between sky and sea, totally silent.

THIRTY-THREE

I T TOOK US AN HOUR AFTER ARRIVING IN VILAMOURA TO find Carla's stucco-covered cottage. This was becoming an unfortunate pattern of this whole trip. Street signs and accurate maps were not a strong suit of the European countryside. Then for another repeat experience, Carla wasn't home. According to a very suspicious neighbor, she spent most of her Saturdays visiting an even-more-elderly sister in the very next town. Unfortunately, our only option was to wait outside Carla's address until she got home two hours later, at which point the shockingly tall, impressively spry ninety-something-year-old ran us directly off her property. The silver lining was that the cop she called—the portly, mustached Officer Pires—agreed to stay and help translate.

Once Carla was settled and the *bicas*—coffees—were served, our chat began.

"We're here to ask about a fellow singer that you performed with years ago: Lisbeth Park was her name in this program," Graham said as he held up the photocopy.

Carla took the piece of paper and brought it within a centimeter of her eyes. "1 know her," Carla said through Officer Pires. "Bette Silva was her name."

1 was so shocked 1 almost knocked my coffee cup onto the white lace tablecloth. Graham grabbed it before it fully tipped, like some kind of ninja.

"1'll never forget the woman," Carla went on. "She had such a *mistério* about her. Like she was hiding something."

Graham opened his notepad. 1 tried to talk myself off the ledge words like *mistério* and *hiding* had introduced.

Over the course of the next hour—much of which Carla spent discussing her own illustrious opera career—we were given three critical pieces of Bette Silva information. The first was that Bette had been in her early thirties when she sang at the Lisbon opera house with Carla. By our hostess's memory, this was in the mid-1960s, which meant that Bette could have been younger than Gianluca had suggested, and more likely to still be alive. Plus if Bette had worn my ring, it was probably during the time that she and Carla sang together. Women of that generation were married by their early or midtwenties.

The second reveal was that Bette was an American. Carla had no idea from which city or state and didn't know how long she'd lived there or when, but this meant Graham could focus his *Lisbeth* Silva research on one country versus the whole world. This was a breakthrough.

But the third detail that Carla offered prompted my string of follow-ups. Bette was offered the opportunity to join the chorus in a performance of Puccini's *Madama Butterfly* at the

Vienna State Opera—the finest in the world—but she turned down the invitation.

"Because of her *husband*," Carla told us. So there was a husband . . .

"Because he wouldn't let her?" I asked.

"I have no idea," Carla said. "She refused to discuss it. She was the most private person I've ever met."

Graham shot me a *relax* look. He already knew the narrative my mind was forming: a jealous, controlling husband squashed his operatic wife's dream of performing a legendary piece at a legendary venue.

"Did you ever meet Bette's husband?" Graham asked, taking over.

"No," she said. "I barely met *her*! We spent one week together. She talked about nothing and kept to herself."

"Did you two share a dressing room?" Graham continued.

"Yes, why?" I wondered the same thing.

"Performers usually place photos of loved ones on their dressing room mirrors. Do you remember Bette having any photos up in the room?" Officer Pires and I both perked up, impressed by his line of questioning.

"What do you know about performers' dressing rooms?" Carla said, setting the power dynamic straight. "I'm telling you, it's lucky I remember this woman at all! I only do because the director went on and on about her magic voice, but I didn't think she was anything special."

Carla's jealous tone led my mind in a new direction. I reached for the ring hanging from the necklace I was still wearing.

"Do you remember whether or not Bette was wearing this ring when you knew her?" I shifted closer so that she could examine the jewel properly, but it turned out to be unnecessary. The ring had caught the sun as it came through her crocheted curtains and scattered a shower of sparkles across the wall. It looked alive.

"No," Carla said, "absolutely not. I would never forget that ring if I'd seen it on that woman's finger."

My detective work earned an impressed nod from Graham. Unfortunately, it didn't answer the more concerning questions: *If Bette was married at the time, why wasn't she wearing this ring? Did it have something to do with the husband's refusal to let her go to Vienna? Or was Bette Silva not the ring's owner at all?*

I looked out to see the sun now starting to set behind the cliffs surrounding Carla's cottage. It was getting late, and we were all out of angles.

"Thank you for your time today," Graham said, either reading or sharing my feelings. "Is there a phone number where we can reach you if we have any more questions?"

We left with Carla's number on the back of an old grocery list and a recommendation for the *restaurante excelente* just down the street.

"It wasn't official bad news," Graham said as we navigated back to the main road.

"No," I said. "It was worse: *confusing* news. What if we've been following this Bette and she's not even the one? Gianluca met her *once*. What if he got her name totally wrong and we've been tracking a person who never touched this ring? What if we're literally nowhere?"

Graham rolled the car to a stop. "I'd tell you to count from ten to one, but I don't believe in that bullshit, so just listen to me," he said. "We're not nowhere. I've got you, and we've got this. It may just take a little more time." Then he shocked me by giving my hand a squeeze. I gripped back on instinct, but also because his touch was soothing. The warmth of his skin lingered on mine, so that I didn't even realize he'd pulled away.

"Let's get to the hotel and regroup," Graham said, all business.

"Sounds good," I said, moving on from the moment, then I grabbed my phone to check directions. "We're going to the 3HB in Faro. Must be the next town over, but this place looks *gorgeous*. Super modern."

"*No*," Graham said. His response was so sharp that I genuinely wondered if he was talking to me until he said: "Sorry, we can't go to Faro."

"Why not?" I asked.

"We just can't," he said, suddenly annoyed.

"We have nonrefundable rooms booked there for tonight, so if you have an objection, I need to hear a reason."

"I'll pay for it. And another hotel," Graham said, then he slowed the car to a stop again and pulled out his cell. "Let me find one."

Now I was concerned. "Whoa, what's going on?" I asked.

The look on Graham's face shifted from cranky to guilty to something I hadn't seen yet: sad.

"We can't go to Faro because my mom lives there," he said.

THIRTY-FOUR

WE FOUND THE FIRST RESTAURANT THAT WASN'T already closed along this sleepy part of the coast, an old bougainvillea-covered building with a Tiffany-blue door. It reminded me of the little cafés along Ocean Avenue in Santa Monica. Especially Blue Plate Oysterette, where Jack always took our team for a celebratory lobster feast on the last day of the film festival.

Graham's plan was to find a new hotel over our meal. Mine was to use all the skills I'd picked up from him to gracefully talk him out of that plan.

"All right, there are tons of places around here," he said. "Reasonable rates, too. And again, I'll cover the Faro rooms and these."

"Thank you," I started, "and that's fine, but we can also talk about all this first. You didn't mention Faro during our conversations about your mom and coming to Portugal . . ."

Graham did not make eye contact. "I knew you'd want me to go see her," he said.

"So then . . . you know where she lives?"

"Yes," he confessed, gaze still down. "Good catch."

"Do you think she'd want to see you?" I pressed.

"Oh, yeah. Though I hear phones work between Portugal and New York now, so if she wanted to have a relationship with me, there are easier ways." When he looked up for that dig, decades of frustration were painted across his face.

"So, things between you two are rocky. Is that really how you want to leave it?"

"Asks the person who hasn't talked to her father in years . . ." Graham said. I would have balked at his defensiveness, but I understood it.

"You're right," I said. "I don't have a relationship with my dad, and that's what works for me. If that's what you want, too, I get it."

"I don't think it's about what I want," Graham said. "She lives in her own world. I'm offered a viewing every other Thanksgiving. We meet at some hotel in midtown, where she goes on and on about how much she misses *American* Thanksgiving, as if she isn't still American."

"As if she doesn't also miss *you*," I said. Graham shot me a look—surprised, not angry. It was as if I'd said something he'd never even allowed himself to think. "Listen. If seeing your mom will hurt more than it could help, then we're done. Let's book the new hotel and pretend she lives in—oh, I don't know—Florida."

"Oh, Nina Shani would *never* live in Florida. She planned a trip to Disney World when I was eight. When we got off the plane, she took one look at the crowd headed for our shuttle bus and rebooked us on a flight to Santa Fe."

"That is a pretty epic move," I said, half hiding a smile.

"She is a pretty epic woman," said Graham, then he let the tiniest crack of a smile escape his own mouth. But it was gone in a second. "Or she was. I feel like I don't even know her anymore." I knew angry, knew *done*. Graham was neither. And after everything he'd done for me, I owed it to him to help him see that.

"I have a proposal," I offered. "Hold off switching the hotels until after we eat. We'll take a minute away from the heat of it all. If you still don't want to be anywhere near her after dinner, you have my full support."

"What exactly do you think is going to happen between now and the end of this fish stew?" Graham asked.

"Well, I'm going to ask questions about your mom until you tell me to stop. I'm hoping that you'll start to wonder if seeing her could maybe heal the way you feel about her, even the littlest bit. Because it doesn't sound like *not* seeing her is making you feel very good."

Graham shook his head, looking bewildered. "John is a lucky guy," he said after a long pause.

"Wow, where did that come from?" I asked.

"From this—from you. If you're this caring to someone you barely know, I can't imagine what it's like to be the person you're choosing to spend the rest of your life with."

I flashed to the fact that John and I hadn't exchanged much more than a few texts the past forty-eight hours. I hadn't made time to actually sit down and talk to him. I hadn't asked in days how his week was going. I usually prided myself on being the kind of person who lets you know how much they care, and I couldn't help but love that Graham had seen that in me. Why wasn't I being that version of myself with John?

"Yeah, well . . . ," I said. "I don't know how true that is . . ." *What kind of future wife travels Europe with another man?* I could only imagine the way Kay Jacobs would explain my whole trip to her book club friends: *Well, you know, Shea had to take care of Shea first, then my son.* Would she be right to judge?

"Thank you," I finally replied, dragging my mind back, "that really means a lot. But you're not someone I 'barely know' anymore. You're someone I care about, which is why I'm here to help you through things with your mom."

"You already have," said Graham. "I'll stop by her place to-morrow morning. Can I talk you into coming?"

"You can," I said. "But you don't have to. I'm in."

THIRTY-FIVE

N INA SHANI WAS THE KIND OF WOMAN THAT OTHER women remember meeting for the rest of their lives. She had Michelle Pfeiffer eyes that pierced through you; a silver bob like the best of the Meryl Streep characters; and a voice straight out of a Billy Wilder flick: husky, low, and spoken directly into your ear as if everything she said were a secret. She reminded me of her son, with their olive skin, long, lean frames, and lack of filter.

"You're from LA," were her very first words to me. "I see it immediately." With Graham, her candor took a turn: "And you're not getting enough sleep. What's got you worried? Money? You know I'll send you whatever you need."

Graham took a deep breath as he walked into his mother's house for the very first time in his life. It was a sun-drenched, Portuguese-tiled masterpiece that made me jealous, then deeply sad. This house represented the life Nina chose instead of the one that involved her son. And it included a man we found sleeping shirtless on the back porch, a French edition of Michael Crichton's *Jurassic Park* open across his chest. *Emilio.* Graham took one look in his direction, then avoided that section of the house entirely.

"We're studying French," Nina explained, "for a trip this summer. Two months! It's going to be just *parfait*." She finished with a finger pinch, Italian chef style. I resented her for co-opting the move from my people but found myself drawn to her all the same. Clearly, this was a woman who did whatever she damn well pleased.

"We don't have much time," Graham said, standing cross-armed as Nina placed snacks of dried fruit and fizzy wine on the aqua-tiled kitchen table.

"Right," she said, "because of this *mission* you two are on. Sounds incredibly romantic." She pulled out a chair for Graham to sit. He acted like he didn't notice.

"I told you, it's Shea's ring. I'm just helping because I'm trying to convince her to let me write a piece about it." It was the opposite of what Graham had said during our Tomas interaction, but Nina didn't care what words her son used.

"Mmhmm, so you said," she murmured. "So tell me, how long do I get you?"

"Oh, we have to be back in Lisbon tonight," I said, standing only because Graham still was. I almost folded my arms across my chest too; his energy was that contagious. "We have tickets to an opera, for research. Eight p.m." It was the wrong choice of lie.

"Opera . . . even more romance," Nina said. "And good, Lisbon is only two and a half hours from here, and it's only ten right now. We have time for a boat ride around the caves. It can't be missed, I promise you, and I have seen my fair share of the world."

"We can't, Mom," Graham said, stepping in.

"Why not?" she pushed back.

"I don't need to have a reason," was his tense response. It softened Nina, made her shift from her chair into the one directly next to her son. Then she grabbed both his hands tenderly.

"My love," she said, "I am really, genuinely happy to see you. And I would really, genuinely like to spend as much time with you today as possible. Whether I've earned that or not."

Graham's eyes lifted, really, genuinely surprised.

WE SPENT THE afternoon with Captain Nina aboard the *Eve*, a compact, four-person speedboat that Emilio had given her when she turned sixty.

"I named her for the first woman," Nina said.

"Of course you did," said Graham. But his mother smiled back, happy to have any response from him at all.

If the southern coastline of Portugal was enchanting from the land, then seeing its rugged cliff line from the water was otherworldly. The azure sea glistened as if dotted with diamonds. Nina navigated through the region's signature caves as we sipped on glasses of effervescent wine. The tour took us through a series of ballroom-sized rock cutouts that turned the liquid sapphire. One had a naturally formed skylight in the shape of a heart; another was so massive that a beach had formed inside. And in my favorite, the rocks had created a diving platform two stories high.

"I'll anchor here so we can swim out to it," said Nina. "Declining is not an option. We're all going."

"But we don't have bathing suits," I said.

"What's the difference between underwear and a bathing suit?" she asked. I got the sense the question was rhetorical. Nina killed the engine. Graham threw the anchor over.

I felt my pulse quicken, nerves over stripping down in front of him.

"You don't really have to, Shea," he said, already peeling his shirt off. I turned away like a prudish teenager who had just snuck a peek. Graham was far more muscular than his baggy button-downs let on, thick through the arms and with a broad, square chest. And not lacking in confidence. It was contagious. Giddy from the wine and the once-in-a-lifetime feel of it all, I scurried out of my own top and bottom, then stepped toward the boat ladder. *Is Graham watching me now?* I wondered. *Do I want him to?*

We splashed in the air-warm waters. We dodged in and out of the rock paths. We popped back to the boat for more delicious *vinho verde*. And then we finally swam out to the mini cliff to take our turns launching off. Graham and Nina went up together first, son helping mom navigate the rock steps. I watched from the water below as they counted down together—*three, two, one*—then leapt off, hands clasped, childlike glee on both their faces. My voice caught in my throat as I cheered. When Graham popped back up to the surface, he was smiling so wide he looked like a different person.

"That looked incredible!" I said as he made his way toward me through the chop. "How did it feel?"

Suddenly a boat's wake passed, tossing a wave over that made it trickier for me to tread water. Graham offered his arm to steady me.

"Thanks," I said, grabbing tight.

"No. Thank you. That was . . . This whole day has been . . ." He couldn't finish—out of breath, or out of words. I reached my free arm out for his to say *I know, I'm so happy for you.* But Graham did the same, so we were suddenly holding each other in the water, hugging. We stayed like that for one, maybe two heartbeats until another wave crested through, separating us.

"Sorry," I said. "I think wine plus water is a little—" *Why am I apologizing? It was just a hug.*

"No, no. It's fine," said Graham. "Go take your turn to jump." Then he nudged me toward the rocks before I could try to read his face.

————————

NINA TOOK US back to the house for a lunch of prawns purchased from a literal side-of-the-boat fish shop. Graham had finally heard from his contact in New York with Lisbeth Silva intel, so I offered to help in the kitchen.

"Your life is really incredible," I said, chopping the parsley Nina'd grabbed from her thriving balcony herb garden. It was the first time we'd been alone all day.

"Yes. This one is a fit for me," she said with a glance toward

Emilio, who was working behind the French doors of his office.

"Your other one wasn't?" I asked. I'd gotten the sense that Nina was an open book, and maybe a wise person to take a life lesson from, given how joyful she seemed.

"I didn't know who I *really* was in my twenties and thirties, so I didn't know how misguided my choices were. I think many women suffer that way because there's such a focus on settling down 'before it's too late.'"

My mind went to the marriage math that I'd heard girlfriends start to compute around the time we all turned twenty-five. *If we meet now, then date for three years, then are engaged for one, then wait two more 'til kids, then . . .*

"So you feel like you weren't the real *you* when you married Graham's dad?" I asked.

"Yes, a bit," Nina said, scooping up my poorly chopped herbs to finish the job herself. "I saw a path that looked familiar—like the choice every woman in my life had made— and I took it. Graham's father was wonderful, but once I started looking inward I came to realize that I wanted a different life, a different partnership. And he did not feel the same."

"He wasn't willing to consider your way?" I wondered if she could sense how leading my questions were becoming.

"I don't know," Nina said. "I fell in love with someone who was a better fit before I could really find out. And I *do* regret that, because I hurt people, but I couldn't live my life for them. Emilio is who I'm supposed to be with. The timing of it was unfortunate, but that doesn't make it wrong. The universe doesn't adapt to our schedule, Shea." Nina gave my hand a tender squeeze, then looked straight through me. "But you know that."

I pulled my hand back, unsettled.

"Oh, I've said the wrong thing," said Nina. "I'm sorry."

"No, you didn't. I just have a lot to think about," I said.

The truth was that Graham's mother had unearthed a question I'd never considered: How do you know when you're the right version of yourself? And how would I know if I wasn't?

THIRTY-SIX

NINA INSISTED ON QUICK *SESTAS* FOR ALL OF US AFTER lunch. The combination of wine, sun, and sea air made it impossible to say no. I closed the door on her cozy guest suite and curled onto the bed, still feeling the sway of the boat as I drifted off to sleep.

I opened my eyes to an unfamiliar place. Cream carpet. Crisp white walls. Shiny black tables in a giant U shape. Crystal chandeliers lit the space, light reflecting from glass cabinets. My eyes adjusted to take in the whole room. I was in a jewelry store. A half dozen salespeople in chic black stood behind each glass-topped case, like cater waiters lined up at a wedding. Overhead was what sounded like the smooth guitar music I'd heard all over Portugal.

"What is this?" I said—I'd thought to myself, but a man's voice answered from above.

"Pick anything you want," it said. "They're all brand-new."

My first feeling was relief. Glee even. It was like being inside a movie moment I hadn't known to wish for. A hand rested against my lower back. "Ready?" that same voice said. I flipped around, but I already knew who I'd find: Graham.

I stared at him with a wide, excited smile, then took his hand. We glided across the floor, almost floating from case to case like we were Fred and Ginger, the music swelling as we went. Ring after ring caught my eye as Graham spun me around the room. Each one was almost spotlit as I turned its way. Graham beamed at my side, proud he'd pulled off the perfect surprise.

"Anything you like?" he said.

The music suddenly softened. I homed in on the table at the far back of the room. It was glowing brighter than the rest, as if the jewels inside were the most sacred. My body pulled me toward it, my eyes fixed on the brightening light. It wasn't until I was inches from the table that I finally looked up to see the salesperson standing behind the counter. *John.*

I SHOT UP from the bed. My skin was wet with sweat. A beam of sun tried to force my eyes closed again, but I turned away from the window.

I splashed my face with cold water at the sink in the guest bathroom, then stared at myself in the mirror. All I saw was searching. I sipped in air, then let it slide through circle-shaped lips. The breath broke up the tension in my chest so I could think, but my first thought sent that squeeze right to my stomach: *Being with Graham in that dream felt so natural. So right.*

I'd had dreams like this since John and I got together. In

one I was back in seventh grade, about to be forced to play Seven Minutes in Heaven with my middle school crush, Chip Clem. But that dream-me had known about John and felt almost sick at the thought of making a mistake in that basement. In the dream I'd just left, John was the shock that felt off. *Why did my subconscious flip the script? What was it trying to tell me?*

A knock on the door let me avoid answering.

"It's me," I heard Graham say. My body knotted up at the sound of his voice. "I just heard from Tomas. He has something for us at the opera house."

"Be right out," I said, then I doused my face with handful after handful of cold water. Enough to shock my system as far out of the dream world as possible.

THIRTY-SEVEN

GRAHAM WAS FULLY FOCUSED ON BETTE BUSI-
ness for our drive back—a relief. Whatever happened back in Faro had been the product of a
sun-drenched day away from the real world.

Apparently our search had piqued Tomas's interest enough
for him to head down to the dustiest corners of the opera
house basement. There he found boxes that never made it to
the library, among them one filled with papers and photos
from sometime around 1970. Tomas didn't know what Bette
Silva looked like but said we were welcome to come see it all
for ourselves. The catch was that he would only be available to
meet us after the opera let out that night. This meant waiting
around until at least eleven p.m., unless we wanted to attend
the show ourselves, he said. My original excuse for leaving
Nina's house early had come true, with one extra detail that
seemed too meaningful to ignore: the performance was *Madama Butterfly*.

"It's eerily perfect," I said to Graham. "I think we have to go."

"We have to go home tomorrow," he reminded me. "If there's anything else we can do in Portugal, we've got about twelve hours to figure it out."

I nodded. He was right, but that also meant this was my last night in Europe after a grueling eight-plus days between six cities. I wasn't here to revel in a night at the opera, even though that would have been the dreamiest end to this whirl-wind trip. "Go," I heard Graham say. He'd been reading my mind again. "The truth is there's not much more we can do until I dig into the name Lisbeth Park, and I'm a better help as your researcher than your date."

"No," I said, ignoring his use of "date." "I'll help. We're a team."

"Right. And you deserve a night out after putting up with my mother," said Graham. "I've got this."

I finally understood; research was Graham's way of saying thank-you.

THE STREETS OF Lisbon were buzzing with New York City en-ergy as I headed out to grab myself one ticket to the opera. Scooters whizzed by carrying suit-clad men. Teenagers skipped home from school at full volume. And the tourists were in their happy-hour positions, even though there was no such thing in this country where people drink wine from brunch until midnight.

The box office turned out to be closed until closer to showtime, so I popped by a bakery for more *pastéis de nata*, plus a *sanduíche* stuffed with meats and cheese. Next door to my food find was a tiny boutique with gold-trimmed windows revealing three vintage mannequins. Each wore a gorgeous version of a theater-curtain-red dress. The one in the center called to me through the shop's door. An Audrey-meets-Grace stunner. It had a fifties waist, seventies pleated skirt, and the most delicate boatneck that draped around the shoulders and opened to a low, scooped back. It was the kind of dress one was supposed to wear for an evening out at a palatial music mansion in the center of a European capital. I raced in to try it on before I could talk myself out of it; the dress fit like an opera glove. *My kind of sign.*

I took a stroll across the yellow stone pavers of the plaza in my new look, more confident than I'd felt in as long as I could remember. An old man in a sharp blue fedora played the accordion for a group of spinning little girls. I joined them for a twirl as I passed by, imagining myself as Bette Silva working out her preshow jitters. Had she stood in this very spot? Would she have been wearing our ring? Walking beside the man who gave it to her? I grabbed my phone and snapped a quick selfie with a view of the river below. The magic-hour sun hit my curls in a way that made them look like I always wished they would. *I took this to text John*, I realized as I stared at the image. He always said I looked gorgeous in red. He even liked when I wore the scarlet lip stain that left his own skin pink when we kissed. I'd try to limit myself to a peck so the color wouldn't totally transfer, but John would pull me in for a full lip-lock. I started typing something into our string of messages, then looked up at our last exchange. A simple You doing okay? from him and Yeah, good, making progress from me. That was from almost forty-eight hours ago.

I tried to picture John with me on this plaza. To feel the tingle I always did when he came home after a trip. But before I could settle into the moment, my phone buzzed. On the screen was a new message: Got enough work done. Can I still be your opera date tonight?

THIRTY-EIGHT

I ALMOST WALKED RIGHT PAST HIM. SEATED AT THE HO-
tel bar was not the scruffy Brooklyn journalist I'd been
traveling with all week. Graham was transformed. He
wore a slim-fit navy suit over a crisp white button-down.
Shoes he had to have bought in Italy. And his hair was slicked
back behind his ears like he was a leading man at Cannes. I
felt a flutter so strong that I decided to wait before approaching him. It was only half out of my system before he managed
to spot me.

"Wow," he said. "New dress?"

"Yes, thank you," I said. "And you look great yourself. Did
you go out and buy that suit instead of all that emailing?"

"I had it with me. You never know where you could end up
in this line of work."

I laughed out loud, but I could tell Graham was completely
serious. In this moment, I found that fact—and, frankly, all of
him—impossibly charming.

We'd barely made it inside the Teatro Nacional on our

abbreviated tour, so I was stunned by its absolute grandeur when we entered for the show. Ornate reliefs of gods and goddesses peeked out from every corner. Rings of seats climbed four stories high, like the inside of a gilded colosseum. And the soft amber glow of antique bulbs made everyone's skin luminescent.

The last-minute tickets we'd purchased were in one of those coveted boxes floating above the audience. I felt like royalty in my red dress as we walked through gold velvet curtains to find our seats. This was the old-world magic of Europe in full force.

Most of what I knew about Puccini's greatest opera was the haunting storyline—young, Japanese Cio-Cio-San falls in love with American naval officer Pinkerton, leading both to devastating ends. But it was the power of the music that awed me most as the show unfolded. I listened to most of "Un bel dì, vedremo" without taking a single breath, and at the end of the duet "Vogliatemi bene," I stood straight up out of my seat, clapping as if the performers were family. Graham took in the show completely still, mesmerized. When the lights came up after the final curtain call, I saw what may have been dried tears on the very tops of his cheeks.

"I'm really glad I came," he said as we made our way out of the theater to meet Tomas. He gave my hand a grateful squeeze, lingering longer than he had any prior time and making my heart beat in a way I could not control. *What is happening?* I thought as we walked toward Tomas, who was waiting in the lobby. He had one tattered brown cardboard box in his hands.

"The show was good?" he asked.

"The show was perfect," Graham said. "We loved it." His *we* reminded me that this man thought we were a couple searching for the history of a ring Graham had given me. Tomas did not even know that John existed. And tonight my engagement ring was on fuller display, lying above the lower neckline of my new dress.

"Look through tonight," he said, handing the box to Graham. "You can bring back tomorrow." We thanked him, then started the long walk back to our hotel. The idea of a cab hadn't crossed either of our minds.

"Should we go through this in my room when we get back?" Graham said, lifting the box for emphasis, as we passed through the theater's plaza and into the moonlit city streets. His question made my step stutter. Was it an invitation?

"Maybe," I said, gaze straight ahead, too afraid to look Graham in the eyes despite how desperately I wanted to.

"Or I can do it by myself," he quickly added, "if that's better . . ." He trailed off, letting the words linger.

Maybe it was the drama of the opera or the overwhelming days we'd just had, or just the fast-paced mission with its countless emotional layers, but I finally just . . . *burst*.

"I don't know!" I said, stopping right in the center of the narrow sidewalk. "I feel . . . confused. And our time with your mom was so . . . And then—then—Graham, I had this dream about you, where . . ."

I was so focused on trying to find the words that I didn't feel the bottom of my heel get stuck inside an edge of the cobblestone. Instead, all I saw was the panic on Graham's face as I started to fall backward, right into oncoming traffic.

In a single motion, he dropped the box and lunged to grab my arm, pulling me toward him with such force that we both stumbled back into the building behind. A car whizzed by with an angry blare, but I barely heard it, just trying to breathe. I was safe, but still, neither of us moved. I felt Graham's breath on my cheeks and the grasp of my hand around his wrist. And I heard my heart beating so loudly that there was no way he couldn't hear it, too.

Graham's lips pressed against mine first, then he moved his hand to the back of my neck, drawing me in even more. Another second passed, and I began to float, somehow seeing myself from above—kissing a man who was not John. I jolted backward, out of Graham's hold.

"What?" he said. The surprise in his voice threw me.

"Why did that just happen?" I asked, taking another step back. "Why did you . . ."

Graham's face fell—a slow sinking from eyelids to chin. He seemed like he was putting the pieces of something together, but he stopped short and looked up, livid.

"Because I thought it was *very* clear that's what you wanted, Shea." I felt cornered. Accused. Maybe even gaslit? I wasn't sure, but something in the tone of Graham's voice enraged me.

"Don't talk to me like that," I said.

"I can't believe you're surprised!" said Graham, turning from me to pick up the box of documents. "This—whatever this is—has been building for days!"

My whole body shifted into a higher gear—blood pumping, fingers tingling. Was he right? "You don't get to decide what I want," I heard myself say. It was as if my mind were reading a different script than my body, maybe too afraid to follow the suggestion that Graham's assumption was right.

"Maybe take a look at your actions over the past twenty-four hours," Graham barked back. "I think you're making a lot more moves than you realize."

Part of me wanted to lean in. To agree. To let myself feel what I had pushed away these past few days. But the other could not stand being told what I was feeling before I'd fully figured it out for myself. *Then why does this heat in me feel energizing?* I wondered. *Why do I want to keep fighting?* Maybe Graham and I were pushing and pulling each other toward the truth?

"Even so, you had no right to do that," I said. Facts were safety.

"Fine," said Graham. "Forget it happened." He started to walk again, cutting it all off.

"What if I can't do that?" I said, refusing to follow. "Then what?"

"Then I guess our journey ends here. Or mine does." He didn't even look back to deliver that blow.

"I didn't peg you as the type to just walk away!" I called out, still charged. "I guess divorce-kid habits die hard." I knew it was hurtful, but I wanted him to come back.

Graham turned toward me, now at least ten paces ahead. "Well then, I guess we were both wrong about each other," he said.

Headlights from an approaching car suddenly lit up the street, exposing us. It was a taxicab. Graham quickly stepped to the curb and raised his hand. It screeched to a stop right in front of him. Graham opened the door, motioned for me to get in the cab, then walked off into the dark Lisbon night.

THIRTY-NINE

I SAT FOLDED INTO THE LAVENDER FLORAL CHAIR AT THE
window of my hotel room. It reminded me of Wendell and
Winnie's, my very first stop on this wild goose chase. Part
of me wanted to start all over again—to make different choices
all along the way. But another wondered if I would have ended
up in this exact same place no matter what.

Outside, the bulbs of the black iron streetlights flickered.
Across the alley, a young couple strolled by, entwined in each
other and their shared middle-of-the-night whispers. I could
just make out the Tagus River lapping against the stone wall
that hugged the crescent-shaped city. It helped me finally
find the rhythm of my own stilted breath, the space I needed
to think.

Those seconds with Graham lingered on my skin, making
the corner of my mouth twitch. *Why didn't I stop him more
quickly?* My mind answered as quickly as it asked: *Because it
felt right.* The chemistry between us was undeniable. I'd started

off annoyed at his gruffness and skeptical of his charm, but I'd come to adore the way his mind worked. His determination. His intensity. Graham pushed me, yes, but he had been propelling me forward, forcing me to face things I'd buried or hadn't even realized. Our differences didn't feel like friction; they were like a spark, an Elizabeth-and-Darcy tête-à-tête. I'd never loved *Pride and Prejudice*, annoying every other woman I knew. But maybe that was because I'd never experienced that feeling. My body tightened, anxiety landing. Was this just cold feet? Or was it totally normal to have feelings for other people before you got married? Maybe Graham was just a mirage, an opposite-of-John built to test my feelings?

I WAS STILL wide awake when the envelope slipped under the door of my hotel room.

I slogged over to pick it up, expecting to see checkout papers. Instead there was a small photo, worn around the edges, and a note.

"Oh my God, that's her," I said aloud. Bette Silva, posing proudly in front of an old brick house, a large bouquet of flowers in her hands and a streetlamp in the background. I opened the folded piece of hotel stationery, already knowing I'd find Graham's scratchy handwriting inside.

This was in the box from Tomas, by some miracle. It must have been a collection of stuff that people left in their dressing room, which means . . .

"This photo was important enough to Bette that she kept it in her dressing room," I said, guessing almost the exact words Graham had written next.

Take a really close look at the picture, his message continued. *You'll see where you should go next. Turns out your obsession with signs was smart.* I stopped and looked at the image again, seeing nothing that made sense. *What did he mean?* There were only a few more lines in his note: *I think it's best for me to leave it here. Good luck, Shea. And thank you.*

It was the right move. But I didn't feel like we'd left things with any kind of closure. And this cryptic note wasn't helping. I looked at the photo again, scanning my eyes more slowly across every single detail. *There.* In the far-right corner, no bigger than two centimeters, was a tiny, square real estate sign. *Downtown Boston Realty*, I could make out if I squinted. *A sign.* My mouth turned up at the trick of Graham's message. I knew this was him trying to leave things between us on a less difficult note.

Boston, I said to myself as I looked into the eyes of the much younger Bette in this photo, desperate for her to tell me what to do next. The right thing to do would be to keep my flight from Portugal to Los Angeles. To go home to my fiancé. To call my sister, work through the fight we'd had, and ask her to help me clean up the rest of the mess I'd created. Instead I grabbed my laptop and started searching flights to Massachusetts.

It was the end of the school day in Los Angeles by the time I was done booking. John would be wrapping things up in the classroom so he could head out for afternoon bus duty. I could try to catch him with a call, but he'd have two minutes to talk. Email felt like a ridiculously formal option, even if it did give me time to think through how to justify my next move. Plus, there was much more I needed to explain. I would tell John what had happened with Graham; I would not be my father's daughter. But that confession needed to happen in person. And the sooner I solved Bette's piece of my ring's puzzle, the faster I could get home.

I grabbed my phone and started typing a text. Making progress but need to make one quick stop in Boston before home. Will call when I land. Love you.

I would gain nothing by cutting off my mission at this point. Messy and confusing and painful as things were, I felt as certain as I had when I'd first suggested coming here to Gia back in Hudson. The *why* wasn't as powerful as the clear and remaining nudge from within. *I have to get to the end*, I thought. Then I put my phone down and started to pack.

FORTY

REBECCA PICKED ME UP AT LOGAN AIRPORT WITH A giant Dunkin French vanilla, an old-fashioned glazed donut, and one of her old L.L.Bean puffer vests in tow. I'd texted her just enough information to turn her into her anxious mother.

"You'll need that by sundown. And careful. Coffee's hot. And, Shea, I don't want to push you to tell me everything right now, but, you know, I obviously do because I'm pretty worried about you," she said as she swerved through the streets of downtown Boston, gulping down iced tea.

"Can we actually stop for breakfast?" I asked. "I'll tell you everything, then we can come up with a plan."

"Right," said Rebecca. "To find a probably dead woman in a city of six hundred and seventy-five thousand based on a decades-old real estate sign. Yes, I looked up that number. 2020 Census data, but still."

"Honestly," I said, "I've done more with less."

We went back to Rebecca's neighborhood for her favorite

brain fuel: chicken soup with rice at Zaftigs Delicatessen. I walked her through the biggest pieces of what had happened between Italy and Portugal: the Maria meeting and Gianluca hunt, the reveal of Carmela and Gianluca's modern fairy tale, and the shock of learning about Bette Silva before them. I even told her about Annie leaving and the tension with John. But I did not mention what had happened the night before. I wasn't sure how to explain that piece yet. Rebecca's reaction to everything was so simple but so exactly what I needed to hear. "I'm just glad this whole thing brought you to me," she said.

I was feeling revived enough to jump in again. I ordered one final coffee refill, then paid for our check while Bec popped to the bathroom. That's when John finally texted back. I heard my phone ping and knew it was him. My mind started to spin—why had he waited almost twelve hours to respond?— then I read his words on the screen: I want to trust you, Shea, but it's getting really hard. Even I have limits. Call me, ok? Love you. Ice ran through my hands. I almost dropped the phone. This was not my John. But was he right?

I was rereading the text for the sixth time when Rebecca came back to the table.

"Everything okay?" she asked.

"Yes," I lied, shaking it off as I shoved my phone into a jacket pocket and got up from the table. The sooner I finished this, the sooner I could figure out everything else.

"ALL RIGHT. GO time," said Rebecca as we hopped back in her car. "We have a house and a realty company sign to work with.

I see two paths." This kind of team-leader thinking was why she'd always been my desert island person. Give Rebecca five minutes and two sticks, and she'd have built a giant fire. "Old brick row houses like this aren't in every neighborhood of the city. We could start with the most obvious spots—Back Bay, South End, Beacon Hill, Charlestown—and drive around until we hopefully see it."

"What's the second path?" I asked.

"We call the realty company and see if they have a Bette Silva in their system . . . from fifty years or so ago, based on her dress in this photo . . ."

We decided more was more. Bec served as driver and lookout while I tried to explain the situation to a very confused operator at Downtown Boston Realty. It turned out to be a completely different company owned by completely different people as of twenty years ago. Unfortunately, Plan A was turning out to be just as much of a bust. The house was not in the Back Bay or the South End or the North End or Charlestown or the two other neighborhoods we added to the list as we went along. It turned out *brick row house* was the dominant look of this entire metropolis.

We stopped for a pick-us-up at The Little Crêpe Café in the next neighborhood on our list: Cambridge. The almost-fall sun was already low in the northeast sky, so dipped that the street lanterns were starting to pop on one by one down historic Garfield Street, even though it was only four p.m.

"Let's not panic," Rebecca said. "The city is only eighty-nine point six three square miles—*yes, I did just look that up*. We can get this done in a few days. Teres can help." I could have kissed her for the total dedication to my cause, but I was too busy formulating a new plan. I grabbed the Bette photo from my bag and stared at the details again. On the curb in front of the house was a streetlamp. It had stood out to me the first time I looked at the image, but I hadn't thought much about it until I saw the street lanterns turning on just now. Most lamps were a single pole with a single light. The one near Bette's house had three lanterns at the top forming a round crown.

"These lights can't be everywhere in Boston, right?" I asked, holding the image up.

"Doubtful," she said, then she scrunched her face to think. "We need some kind of old book on Boston city planning or something. Something with archive photos we can match it to." As if on cue, we both looked out the window of the café to find two bookstores on this one block. Becca turned to me with a smug smile. "Don't you ever complain about my town being too nerdy again."

The answers—according to several photos in *Planning the City upon a Hill*—were the North End, which we'd already covered, and Brighton, a neighborhood half a mile from Rebecca's own apartment. We drove there immediately, then slowed down and put the flashers on to start scanning each property. I held the image up between us for a side-by-side comparison. Rebecca put on the classical music station to try to keep us calm. Within ten minutes of circling, at a spot five minutes from where we'd had chicken soup hours prior, Bec slammed on the brakes and screamed.

"THERE!" she pointed.

"YES! We found it! Omigod, we found it!!" I screamed.

"I know! This is *insane*!!" Becca yelled back.

"I KNOW! Why don't they ever scream like this in detective movies?"

"Good point!!" Bec replied. "Now, what do we do next?"

My elation collapsed back to reality. "I guess I go knock on the door? See if the people living there have any idea who Bette Silva is?"

"Unless she's there . . ." Rebecca was willing to say what I was too scared to think.

We walked up to the front door together, for safety's sake. I clenched my teeth to stop them from clattering from nerves. The house was an absolute classic with the type of red brick façade they feature in glamour shots of old New England. This one had emerald-green shutters and a Kelly-green door that made it feel like a set piece out of *Oz*. I ran over my opening line in my head one more time and rang the doorbell. Then we stood there, for *several* moments.

"Um . . . how long should we wait?" Rebecca mumbled.

"Um . . . three to five more minutes?" I guessed.

But the front door creaked open. And on the other side was an old, thin woman with auburn wisps laced through silver hair: Bette Silva.

I was so stunned that my brilliant opener ended up being, "Oh!"

"Oh *what*, dear?" she asked.

"Oh, hello," I recovered. "My name is Shea Anderson. I found you thanks to a photo from an opera theater in Portugal, and I would love the chance to ask you a few questions about something we share. It turns out I am the most recent recipient of your engagement ring."

Rebecca gave me a little side shove to say *Well done*. But Bette's eyes quickly filled with tears.

"Looks like it found me again," she said with a very knowing smile.

FORTY-ONE

I WAS ENCHANTED BY BETTE SILVA FROM THE MOMENT she walked me through the long hallway connecting her foyer to a back room filled with floor-to-ceiling windows and ceiling-to-floor plants. *The solarium*, she explained. I adored the way she held her left arm behind her back as she moved, as if performing each step on a stage. I coveted the loose bun that sat atop her head. And I worshipped the fact that she called me *dear one*, as if she were my long-lost great-grandmother. All my worries suddenly felt lighter in this perfect room, tucked within the safety and warmth of her ancient green velvet couch.

"I know that you're a very private person," I said after a brief explanation of how I'd come to be here and who Rebecca—now waiting out in the car—was, "so please don't answer any questions that make you uncomfortable. I'm sure this is all strange enough."

"Surprising, yes," Bette said. "But not strange. This ring

guided me for years. Of course it would lead someone back to me."

I didn't know what Bette meant, but I couldn't hide what her words made me feel: hot tears sprung to my eyes and began running down my face.

"I'm sorry," I half sobbed. "It's just that no one else has . . . and it's been so . . . and I'm just . . ."

Bette moved her chair closer to mine. She took my right hand and placed it over my heart, taking a long, slow breath in as she did. It looked so soothing that I followed suit. With that, the tears stopped.

"There, dear one," she said. "Little trick from my days on-stage to recover from the heavy scenes. Now, let me tell you about our ring."

Bette Silva's life was an unlikely triumph. She was raised in a tiny Northeastern Pennsylvania town by an Irish mother and Portuguese father. They noticed her gift early on and scrounged all they could for vocal lessons. Her poise and range made Bette the perfect fit for opera. By the end of high school, she was performing with the celebrated Pittsburgh Opera. That's how she met her first love—a young stagehand named Nathaniel Park.

"That's why you went by Lisbeth Park onstage!" I said, connecting the dots.

"Exactly. Lisbeth was my grandmother's name. Park was for Nathaniel." I thought to press on why she hadn't just called Park her *married* named but let Bette continue instead.

Nathaniel was immediately smitten, too, she explained, but he didn't think this star-in-the-making would ever give him the time of day, so he started leaving letters in Bette's dressing room for her to find after every show. He'd sign each with a different name so Bette would think she had dozens of fans.

"He did it to woo me, but it ended up changing my life. Those letters gave me the confidence I needed to study here in Boston at the conservatory, so I could pursue opera full-time," she said.

Nathaniel proposed after two years of dating, and the ring was—of course—breathtaking.

"He swore up and down that the man who sold it to him in Pittsburgh promised it was a Harry Winston straight from New York, but Nathaniel could have never afforded that. I think we both knew it was a tall tale. We called it my Larry Winston, as a joke."

Graham will roll his eyes at that detail, I thought as I looked down at my phone to make sure it was still recording. Then I shifted back to Bette, trying to ignore why I was preparing notes for someone I should probably never see again.

"We planned a wedding, and I bought a little white dress, just like I imagined Grace Kelly would wear," she said. I smiled to myself at our shared style icon. "Then we booked a honeymoon to Portugal, where my father's family had emigrated from in the twenties. But five days before we were due to walk down the aisle of the theater where we first met, Nathaniel was stung by a hornet and died."

My hand hit my chest, shocked. "*My Girl*," I whispered. "I'm so sorry."

"It shocked us all," Bette said, not catching the reference. "You can imagine. You have a fiancé yourself."

An image of John flew to the front of my mind. He'd had surgery for an old shoulder injury about a year ago and taken longer than was typical to come out of the anesthesia. Every nurse assured me there was nothing to worry about, but those two extra hours beside his hospital bed before he woke up were absolute torture. My heart swelled at the idea of losing John so early in our life together. We had made so many plans for the future: from turning last year's camping trip in Cambria into an annual event, to someday owning an apartment back in my old New York neighborhood. We even had a list of names for dogs and kids, some interchangeable depending on what life brought, John's idea. Had I put myself at risk of losing all that?

"I took our ring off and put it in a box the day after Nathaniel's funeral." Bette's voice pulled my focus back to her story. "Didn't even look at it until what would have been our one-year wedding anniversary, when it felt right to wear it again in my love's honor." Later that same afternoon, a courier dropped off the tickets for their honeymoon to Portugal. Bette hadn't remembered to cancel, and the travel agent had apparently gotten the date wrong by an entire year.

"I took it as a sign," Bette said. "And off the ring and I went."

In Lisbon, Bette met a charming bartender, a statue of a man with long hair and wire glasses, Vincenzo. Over her week-long trip, she learned that he was a fan of the opera and had always dreamed of marrying a beautiful American girl. Three years later, that very thing happened, twice.

"A ceremony in America at my home church, and another in Lisbon right inside the bar where we met," Bette said.

"I was just there," I said. "Hoping to learn more about you. I wonder if I even walked by that very bar."

"I'm sure you did," Bette said. "That's the power of the ring. That's why I wore it into my marriage with Vin."

I bristled at this detail, thinking immediately of Mom. But this was also the third or fourth time Bette had alluded to the ring's mysterious power. What exactly did she mean?

"Were you and Vin married very long?" I asked, assuming *Were you happily married?* was too direct a question.

"Not long enough," Bette said. "Vin died ten years later of complications from a routine back surgery. The doctors told me there was a one-in-ten-thousand chance of something like it happening, almost the same number given after Nathaniel died. That's when I started to wonder about our ring."

Bette had skipped to the ring connection, but I had to stop my hand from flying to my mouth a second time. This poor, sweet woman had lost not one but two great loves. And within what couldn't have been more than a decade of each other. How could a person survive that, let alone sit here and recount the devastation to me with such calm? I now understood the kind of inner strength that made her such a great performer. But envisioning Bette onstage led my mind down a new path: her story was a full operatic tragedy. One definitely filled with my greatest fear: *very bad karma.*

"How did you survive all that?" I asked, refocusing on her story and not my growing fears.

"I went back to the stage. I thought I could mend my broken heart through the characters I played," Bette said.

That's when she met Carla in Lisbon, but after just a few

shows she realized a quiet life was the only thing that suited her. Hence no Vienna. Bette returned here to Boston, and our ring remained in the top drawer of her dresser until there was finally another occasion to wear it, and, as she explained, "test my premise about its powers."

It was years later, on a trip back to Pittsburgh to celebrate the retirement of a beloved vocal teacher. Bette put the ring back on for her performance at the memorial service.

"I wanted Nathaniel and Vin with me onstage," she explained.

That night she was introduced to the incoming music teacher, Charlie Grant. Sparks flew immediately.

"And that's when I truly knew," she said. "I'd been connected to a new love because I was wearing the ring."

It took a second for me to catch up to her point.

"You're saying you believe the ring had the power to bring men into your life?" I asked, hoping I'd used my least judgmental voice.

"Absolutely," Bette said. "On the night I finally wore the ring again, I felt the same thing I had when I first met both Nathaniel and Vin."

I was captivated but confused. Bette believed in a portion of my premise—that this ring held energy, even spirits—but to her, the power didn't come from the karma, it came from the actual ring. She believed it was in full control, and she wasn't afraid; she yielded to its magic.

"At that point I decided enough was enough," Bette went on. "I took the ring off and said goodbye to Charlie that very night. I wasn't personally afraid of loss—in case that was the pattern again—but it has such a ripple effect on the other loved ones in your life. I decided it was time to end those kinds of journeys for me." It wasn't until her final trip back to Europe—to Lisbon, of course—that she even brought the ring out of safekeeping in her dresser drawer.

"I couldn't imagine visiting my sacred city without it," Bette said. Naturally, as far as she was concerned, the ring guided her toward its intended new owners during her trip—a handsome man named Gianluca and his beautiful girlfriend, Carmela.

"And I just knew. I was absolutely certain the ring was for them," Bette said.

My forehead tightened as I put the pieces together. "But why give it to them?" I asked. "It had brought you so much heartache."

"Well, that wasn't for me to decide. The ring knew what it wanted. It compelled me."

"Didn't you feel guilty passing along bad luck?" I asked. I worried I was pushing things, but Bette didn't react negatively in the slightest.

"No, you're only seeing half of the story. The ring brought me as much joy as it did heartbreak," she said. "If not more."

I don't know if it was the magical setting of her green-filled room, Bette's soft whisper of a voice, or the fact that I was just so desperate to believe in someone else's clarity, but I felt myself wanting to lean in. Her faith was just a small step beyond my existing superstition. The ring held energy, and the energy compelled its wearer. Was it really so impossible?

Especially considering Gianluca and Carmela had a beautiful, lifelong relationship?

"I can see that you feel what I'm saying," Bette said to me. "Maybe the ring has already compelled you?"

"I . . . I don't know," I said, suddenly spinning. "That's what I'm trying to figure out. Because there's John, my fiancé, but then I met someone else, because of this ring, and then he kissed me and, oh God, I hadn't said it out loud yet and—"

Bette reached over and placed *her* hand on my heart. "Breathe, dear one," she said. "Breathe and listen, and things will fall into place."

Then she tapped her palm to my chest, right at the spot of my heartbeat. It calmed me instantly, *magically*. So much so that it was a moment before I realized the Nonna connection: *Listen. Ascolta.*

"Thank you," I replied. "I wonder if I could ask you just one more question."

"Of course," said Bette. "Anything."

"Do you wish you'd never been proposed to with this ring in the first place?"

Bette's mouth shifted into an unexpected smile. "No," she said. "I had two beautiful relationships and my own rich, full life in between. So little is within our true control, dear one. All you can do is allow life to live through you and make yourself strong enough to be ready for whatever it brings. I'm lucky that this ring taught me that."

FORTY-TWO

RE YOU IN A STIFF-DRINK MOOD OR AN HERBAL-tea mood?" Teres asked once Bec and I finally made it back to their place.

"I literally have no idea," I said, and so she made me a hot toddy.

I finished the entire mug, then stole away to the guest room to finally try for a phone call with John. Finding Bette had given me the confidence to tell him I was flying home tomorrow, even if that was all I was ready to report. The phone rang what felt like a million times, then went to voicemail. This time I opted against the awkward message.

Out in the living room, Rebecca and Teres had set up a life-restoring buffet of Chinese food on the coffee table, just the feast to get me through the very long story I had to tell them.

I walked through every detail of Bette's biography in between bites of lo mein. My rapt audience was enthralled by the twists and turns of the story—their doodle mutt, Louie, especially—but the humans were ultimately suspicious of its narrator.

"Bette sounds really sweet but . . . not fully with it," said Rebecca.

"I hear you," I said. "It's a bit of a stretch. But she was so certain. I guess I could cross-check her story, but I can't imagine a world in which she was lying."

"What about delusional?"

"I'm less interested in Bette and more interested in Shea," said Teres. "You're a patient presenting with too many symptoms. What is the most pressing issue here? Because that's where we need to focus our efforts."

Teres was an infectious disease specialist with a Harvard education and an obsession with crime podcasts. *I should have taken her to Italy instead of Annie*, I thought as she looked around the kitchen counter for what I could only assume was a pen and paper.

"Okay," I said, picking up a fortune cookie, then quickly deciding against it, "the most pressing question . . . I think, is, am I completely insane for agreeing with Bette that this ring has power over my life?"

"Yes," Rebecca said, then just as fast, "Sorry, I meant no. I mean, that's not the right pressing question. It's why, after all this, aren't you just getting a new ring from John? He offered! And you haven't technically put that ring on your finger, if that's the concern." I now remembered why Rebecca and I had become such fast friends: she reminded me of my sister. That also made me terrified to answer her honestly right now, given my last attempt to be brutally honest with Annie.

"I don't know if a new ring will matter," I confessed. "I'm worried that magic powers or not, this one has already led me away from John."

"Now we're getting somewhere . . . ," said Teres.

"Graham and I . . . had a kiss . . . in Lisbon," I said.

The shocked silence lasted for a moment too long. I wanted to run away.

"Define *had a kiss*," said Teres, but Rebecca's frozen look told me she knew that wasn't the part that mattered.

"Oh, Shea," she finally said, a devastating mix of anger and sadness in her voice. It sounded like I felt.

"I know. But it's even worse than that, if that's possible. I can't stop thinking about him! I recorded my entire conversation with Bette and sent it to him for his take, even though we had a huge fight in Lisbon!"

Rebecca sat straight up on the couch. I got the scary sense she was flipping into courtroom mode. "Are you saying you think this . . . thing with Graham is real?" she asked. "You just met him!"

Rebecca was John's biggest fan. When he came along, she turned into a total yenta. *When is he proposing? What is he waiting for? Do you need me to talk to him? I will absolutely talk to him.* Her affection was part of my trust in our relationship from the beginning. But right now, her certainty only spun me out more.

"I don't know!" I said. "And I don't know how I'm supposed to figure that out! But isn't the fact that I did what I did evidence that I'm not ready to marry John? Isn't that what matters more?"

"I think it's too early to know that yet," Teres said quickly, a confusing tone to her voice.

"What do you mean? Isn't the decision to let someone else kiss you all you need to know?"

Teres turned her eyes toward Rebecca, then almost looked like she was asking for permission. Whatever the question, Bec nodded.

"I cheated on Rebecca before we were married," Teres confessed.

I hoped my face didn't match my brain in that moment. "You *did*? Bec, why didn't you tell me!"

"It was complicated," Rebecca said. "And I was afraid of being judged for being the feminist who took back a cheater." I guessed my shocked reaction, even years later, proved her right.

"What happened?" I asked.

Teres reached for her cocktail, then reconsidered.

"I was a mess," she started. "My mom had died a few months before, and Bec and I had just moved in together, which was sooner than I was ready for, apparently. I was just . . . lost. That's not an excuse, but it all led me down a bad path. I was drinking way too much, numbing out. Going out a lot to stay distracted. It happened once, on a night that I barely remember, with someone in my residency."

"Omigod, I did not know *any* of this," I said. "Does anyone?"

"No," said Rebecca. "We were too afraid of the unsolicited advice. Everyone shames cheating. It's painful. It's a huge breach of trust. It is one hundred percent worthy of making you stop and question whether you're in the right relationship. And when I did that, I ultimately realized that I was, and I wanted to marry Teres more than I wanted to let this mistake ruin our future."

"Wow," I said. "Sorry, but *how*?" The teenage version of me was speaking. The one that stopped looking my dad in the eyes after I found out how many times he'd cheated.

"I got into therapy," Teres said. "I learned that what happened told me something huge about how my body reacts to stress and my lack of coping mechanisms, not about how much I loved Bec."

"And I read seventy-five thousand books on forgiveness because lawyers study instead of going to therapy. Even lesbian lawyers," Rebecca said. We all laughed at that, *finally*. "But at the end of the day, our dream of marriage was bigger than our problems. It was this huge political statement for us. Our way to have safety. And kids. And that right was just a few years old at the time. Remember reading that section of *Obergefell v. Hodges* at our ceremony?"

I thought back to their Cape Cod beach wedding day, now five years ago. I remembered how struck I was as I looked up following my reading of a section of that Supreme Court decision. Everyone was crying, me included.

"Look, our situation was specific," Bec said, "but all I'm saying is that one mistake doesn't have to spell the end." Then she leaned over and squeezed me into her. "And also, I love you, and I'm sorry you're going through this."

"Thanks," I said, hugging back hard. "I'm sorry you did, too."

"*Okay!* I think that's enough of our drama for the hour," said Teres. "Shall we break for the biggest ice cream sundaes of our lives?"

I didn't know if I was ready to move past everything that had just been unearthed. "Do you mind if I get some air before we have dessert?" I asked.

"Of course," Rebecca said. "Want to take Louie for a spin around the block? He'll love you even more." As if on cue, their little brown bear dog appeared at my heels, tongue wagging.

LOUIE GUIDED ME left out of the apartment building, then down the street toward a little park at the corner. I was grateful for the guidance. The night air was chilly like Bec had warned, but I still found myself hot with stress. It felt good to put one foot in front of the other. We made it down to the square, then around the paved path. All the while, I kept trying to dig into my feelings about Graham, but my mind kept going back to Rebecca and Teres.

They weren't perfect but their relationship was still what I'd always dreamed of, like a modern Nonna and Pop. Connected. Compatible. Deeply loving. And *fun* together. They'd done it. Made the commitment. Walked down the aisle. But I could not imagine surviving what they had along the way. Forget a superstition; Teres had given Rebecca a real reason not to trust. How could she get over the fear that it would happen again? Wasn't that the most important part of marriage? Feeling safe in your love, forever? *Did John and I have that before all this?* I stopped, realizing I should have been asking myself a very different question: *What did I do to the trust John and I used to have?*

Louie pulled at the leash, itching to chase a taunting squirrel in a nearby tree. I scooped him up into my arms and nuzzled my face in his silky fur.

"Tell me what to do, Lou . . . ," I said as I turned us around to head back.

We were still five or six buildings away when I saw a cab pull up to Rebecca's. I stopped. Instinct kicked in, quickening my pulse. Then my mind jumped to an answer: *Graham.* Of course he couldn't let the story go. He'd found Rebecca's address. He'd come here to hash things out.

I rushed Louie toward home as a male figure stepped out of the cab. I moved faster, letting my hope build without question. He closed the cab door behind him, then turned to face me. Time stopped as my eyes met his.

"Hi, Shea," said John.

FORTY-THREE

H I," I SAID BACK. IT TOOK A SECOND FOR ME TO DO what should have been immediate, run to hug him. Once I did, I felt a stiffness between us. "What are you doing here?"

John's face tightened. "Sounds like you wish I wasn't," he said.

I heard the building door open, saving me from having to reply. Then I saw Rebecca coming out. She must have been watching from the window.

"Hi, John," she said as she took Louie's leash from my hand, then, "Come in when you're ready."

"Did she know you were coming?" I asked, now wondering if this was some kind of setup.

"No," he said. "Let's sit. You look . . . let's just sit."

It was a devastating déjà vu of the moment right after John proposed. Part of me was thrilled to see him, like walking into your own home after a long time away. But the rest was terrified of what was about to happen to us. Because of me. That must have been the look John read on my face.

I motioned for us to sit down on the front stoop of the building. John followed, adjusting his black-framed glasses as he did. He always looked even more handsome in those than in his contacts, I thought, then, *He's only wearing them right now because he just flew clear across the country to see you.* I could tell he was deciding what to say next. John always thought before he spoke.

"I came because you had me that freaked out, Shea. You fly from Italy to Portugal and then suddenly you're headed to Boston. What is going on here?"

"I know . . . it's a lot. But I'm so close to finally finishing this. And I just really needed to—"

"Yeah," John said, cutting me off. His voice was sharp. "You said that in your text. Did you read what my last text said? Because I've gotta be honest, I was pretty shocked to get radio silence from you after that. Honestly, that's why I got on a plane." Now his voice was almost unrecognizable.

"I'm sorry," I said. I thought to reach for his hands, but that felt wrong. "I've been so focused. And . . . a lot has happened." I couldn't believe how vague and awkward I was being— treating John like some old college friend I was trying to evade.

John looked away, considering his words for a longer moment than usual.

"Did something happen with Graham?" he finally asked. "Is he here, too?"

I've often wondered what it feels like to be faced with the

exact moment you have to choose between hiding the truth and hurting someone you love. I've tried to imagine how my dad did it all those years, what it felt like for him to stand in front of my mom, look her square in the face, and choose the lie. On days when I've found compassion for him, I imagine he was doing it to protect her feelings. He really did love her; he'd just made another mistake. And he truly believed it was better for them both if she didn't find out about the latest affair or failed business venture. But as I stared into John's searching eyes, I knew that was all wrong. The lie isn't to spare whoever is looking back at you; it's to protect yourself.

"He's not here," I heard my cracking voice say. "But yes. He kissed me. It was quick, and I stopped it, and that's all that happened—I promise you. I left Lisbon right after. Alone."

My heart left my body entirely. I watched through tear-clouded eyes as John squeezed his own closed, then shook his head back and forth in a way that I didn't expect. The gesture wasn't *What?* or even *How?*

"I knew it," he said.

The hurt in his words pierced through me. I felt nauseous. *Fix it!* my brain screamed. I shifted my legs, then my body. I considered standing up just to move the pain until I could figure out what to say.

"This wasn't something building all along," I said. "And I didn't go on this trip because I was looking for anything other than the history of the ring. It just—I got confused. John, I am confused."

"That's not what I meant," he said, his voice so much quieter now. "I knew I never should have gone with the heirloom ring in the first place. It seemed so right at the time, and it had that sign—that connection to our history I knew you'd love—but it was the wrong move. I just—" He suddenly stopped himself short, then pressed his hand against his forehead. "I just wanted you to pick me over some fucking piece of metal."

That was the blow that sent tears spilling from my eyes. I knew just how heartbreaking it was to have someone not choose you over whatever they'd deemed more important. I knew you didn't recover from that.

John suddenly stood, propelled by his very rare anger.

"Bottom line, Shea, it was me—no, *us*—and everything we've built over *years* together versus a superstition! And you didn't choose me! You couldn't! So maybe that tiny voice inside my head was right when I picked the ring."

"What did it say?" I asked. I wanted all the torture out on the table now.

"*If you pick this ring, you'll know if she's really ready to marry you.*"

Suddenly my body stiffened. My tears stopped. What John said should have been devastating, but it landed in my brain, not on my heart.

"You set me up," I said.

He raised his brow at my shifted tone. "No, it wasn't a conscious decision, it was just . . . I guess part of all the things I was feeling before I proposed."

"Why didn't you share any of those feelings with me?" I asked. Now I was standing too, even with John's darting eyes.

"I . . . I don't know," he said. "I didn't want to scare you, I guess."

"With what? Your uncertainty about getting married? That sounds like you were lying to me, not protecting me!" I hated the feeling of this heat rising in me, against John. This was not us.

"No, Shea," he said, his voice calmer. "I was sure about you. I was afraid you didn't feel the same about me."

"Right," I said, putting the pieces together. "Sounds like neither of us was ready."

Now tears welled in the bottom of John's eyes, an even rarer sight than his anger. I reached out and looped my arm through his, pulling him into me. John brought my head into his neck so that my nose touched the spot that I always nuzzled to wake him up in the morning. Both of our anger had been quelled, by heartbreak.

"Maybe you were right about the ring," I whispered. "Maybe it was the right choice because we needed it to get here."

We stood in each other's arms for another minute, choosing to stay frozen over whatever unknown would come after we let go. John pulled back first, then he kissed me just as tenderly as he always had before he turned and walked away.

FORTY-FOUR

W HAT CAN I DO?" REBECCA ASKED AS I WALKED back through her front door.

"Tomorrow," was all I could say as I made my way to the pullout bed in her office. I didn't even take off my clothes before climbing in and curling myself into a ball so tight it was hard to breathe. I thought maybe that pain would make all the rest hurt less. But I was wrong.

I must have drifted off to sleep because the next thing my mind registered was standing on the concrete steps outside Rebecca's apartment. My feet were—very oddly—in white satin sneakers. I looked up and out into what should have been the town houses across her street, but instead I found a crowd. Fifty or maybe even a hundred people in suits and dresses.

I tried to move my feet to get closer to this audience, to ask them what was happening, but my legs started to twitch, throwing me off balance. "Pink Moon" by Nick Drake started to play. I turned toward the sound and saw an orchestra on a floating stage. *Is this my wedding?*

Suddenly, Annie was standing beside me.

"You look perfect," she said, a Mom smile on her face. "Are you ready?"

My legs shook violently. Quick gasps of air were all I could take. *John just walked away!* I thought. *This isn't happening.*

"Is this real?" I asked Annie.

She laughed as if I'd said something sweet but expected. "It's a big feeling, right?" she said.

I looked down to see what I was wearing on my body—hoping something would trigger the end of this chaos—but I caught the sight of something completely foreign on my left ring finger instead: a simple gold band holding a single, round-cut diamond.

"This is my ring?" I asked Annie.

She looked at me as if I were insane. "Yeah. Come on, it's almost our cue."

I could hear the music crescendo.

"I'm marrying John?" I heard myself ask. "There was no heirloom?"

"Yes, correct. You are marrying John," Annie said, worry rising in her voice. "What heirloom?"

"And no Italy and no Portugal and no Graham."

"What are you talking about, Shea? This is freaking me out! Let's go!"

She held tighter to my arm now, trying to move me forward. I felt my legs strengthen. The shaking had stopped. I looked out onto the crowd, now filled with familiar faces. I took one step forward, testing myself. I could do it. I was fine. Everything was back to normal. Then I turned in the opposite direction and ran.

I didn't stop, despite Annie's cries. Suddenly the concrete became sand below my feet. *Am I back in Portugal?* No . . . I saw dunes. And cars in a parking lot. This was California. This was Emma Wood State Beach. Mom's favorite. The place she would take Annie and me when she needed to get away.

I ran up over the hill where we used to sit with a picnic of fried seafood, through the tall grasses where Annie and I would hide, then down the beach until my feet hit the freezing-cold water. Only then did I finally breathe. And wake up from the dream.

All the covers were thrown off the bed, and my heart was racing as if I'd actually just run all that distance. Morning light beamed through the window. I'd slept through the night.

I reached over to the nightstand and grabbed my phone, hoping to see a text from John at least letting me know he was safe at some hotel. Instead, there was one from Graham: Call me as soon as you can. I found the real first owner of the ring.

FORTY-FIVE

ETTE'S LINE ABOUT HARRY WINSTON CAUGHT MY ear, and I couldn't let it go," Graham said. This was his attempt at calming me after the string of obscenities I'd just yelled. I was still in bed. Still out of breath from my nightmare. Still reeling from the night before. Now my search for the heirloom's complete history had been cracked wide open *again*. And Graham was back. Or was he?

"Turns out someone at Harry Winston is familiar with the story," he continued.

"Wait, the ring is actually a Harry Winston?" I asked, the charm of that detail briefly trumping my confusion around how and why Graham had dug that fact up.

"I'm not sure. Something seems weird about the whole story, but I've got a guy at the brand willing to help. He's in New York. If you want to go. Or come, I guess I should say."

"Alone?" I asked.

"Only if you want to be," was his answer. A cop-out.

"Why did you look into this, Graham?" I asked. "What are you doing?"

I heard him take an out-of-character shaky inhale. "Maybe I'm trying for some closure," he said.

"For the ring or for us?" I was in no mood for ambiguity.

"Maybe both?" Something about the way Graham asked and did not tell oddly made me realize just how serious he was.

I walked circles around the room after we hung up. Seeing him was a risk. Wrong even? But terrified as I was to throw more gasoline on this fire, I wanted every single piece of the mystery solved, including whether what had happened with Graham was worth what happened with John. If Bette was right, then it was already too late to stop this train from taking me whichever way I was bound anyway. If I ignored this— God willing, final—open door, a new one would just pop up somewhere else. Besides, a whisper inside me said, *Haven't you gone too far to stop before the end?* Or, in this case, the beginning.

I slinked out to grab something to fill my queasy stomach. Rebecca was at the table in her robe holding a cup of coffee.

"You have to go to New York," she said. "Sorry, but I heard everything. *Yes*, because I was listening at your door, but still."

"You think?" I asked, collapsing onto the chair beside her. "Even with Graham involved?"

"Especially with," Becca said. "Shea, I am very sorry to tell you that the saying is one hundred percent correct; unfortunately, the only way out is through."

I took her words in, grateful for the affirmation but no less terrified. Just then the text I'd been waiting for from John finally appeared on the phone in my hand.

Headed back to LA, he'd texted. Let's talk when you're back.

Okay, I replied. Safe flight. Love you.

It didn't hit me until hours later, as I sat staring out another train window as another set of buildings and trees blurred by. I had been replaying my last moments with John—over and over and over—but until now I hadn't fast-forwarded to remember our text exchange this morning. *John didn't say "I love you" back.* And maybe for the very first time since we'd started saying it to each other. The realization left me reeling. I'd been in the driver's seat since the moment we got engaged—consumed with what I thought would help protect our relationship. But after everything I'd done, was our future actually in John's hands now?

FORTY-SIX

L ATE THAT SAME AFTERNOON, I MET GRAHAM OUT-
side the very intimidating doors of Harry Winston.

"Hi, how was your train?" he asked. His voice was missing its signature boom of confidence.

"Okay," I said, then awkwardly left it at that. We were both struggling to navigate this reunion.

"Let's see what we find here," Graham said, "then we'll get dinner . . . and talk everything over." I nodded, grateful for the baby steps as we made our way into one of the world's most famous temples of jewels.

Bette's mention of the Harry Winston connection had piqued Graham's interest because, at the time Nathaniel Park would have purchased it for her, the brand wasn't nearly as well-known outside certain circles. He'd cross-checked with antique jewelers in the Pittsburgh area, and only one had a single option from the brand, even now. It made Graham wonder if there was some truth to the story, so he sent an image of the ring to the public relations team that worked with

Harry Winston corporate. They didn't have anything in their archive of designs that matched my ring exactly, but some vintage pieces were close enough to inspire one curious young employee to consult an unofficial historian in the building: a Mr. Nolan Jones III. He'd taken a look at the images Graham sent over and, according to the PR contact, made one incredibly intriguing statement: "I'd need to see the ring in person." We were now headed to meet the man himself.

I was not prepared for the opulence that is the Harry Winston flagship Manhattan location. Shockingly, my time living there as a film festival assistant hadn't lent itself to much diamond shopping. Ornate black iron doors at the entrance. Black-and-white marble tile made the floors look like they were wearing tuxedos. The main sales room was decorated like a parlor in Versailles. The perfection of it all made me wonder if this final stop might somehow redeem every other choice.

"We're supposed to head downstairs to meet Nolan Jones in his basement office," Graham said.

"The basement?" I asked.

"Apparently Nolan Jones is the head of security," Graham said.

"Then what does he know about a single ring from decades ago?"

Graham shrugged; my shoulders fell.

We had been treated to conversations with many one-of-a-kind people over the course of our investigation, but no one could compare to the great Nolan T. Jones III. He was sitting straight up at his carved mahogany desk in a three-piece suit when we arrived at what turned out to be his mini basement apartment. This man clearly spent a lot of time in this building, and clearly loved it very much.

"Welcome to Harry Winston South. Coffee?" Nolan asked. His voice boomed à la James Earl Jones as Mufasa. His white hair and beard glistened against his dark skin. He had to be at least six and a half feet tall. I wondered if he'd ever been approached to act.

"Yes, please," Graham answered for us both, as I noticed a small espresso machine on a vintage bar cart. Beside it was a framed photo of Nolan III with people who had to be Nolans II and I, all outside the front gates of this very store. I had a similar photo of Nonna, Mom, Annie, and me standing outside Bella Vita. How rare it was for three generations to share one special place.

We got the brief history of Nolan's tenure at the brand, but it was clear the real center of the story was his grandfather, Nolan I. He'd started as a Harry Winston security guard in 1946, at just eighteen.

"Gramps was one of the first Black men to be hired here," Nolan said. "And by Mr. Harry Winston himself. He loved to brag about his brilliant boss, the 'King of Diamonds.'"

This ended up being the first and only job of his entire working life, and he took it very seriously. Nolan I worked in security but made himself a student of the brand, and he shared that love of its history with his son and grandson.

"So that's how you're familiar with this ring?" Graham asked, moving the conversation along.

"Yes. May I see the ring?" he asked.

I reached for it under the lip of my shirt like I had count-less times over the past weeks, took the chain off my neck, and passed it over. Nolan reacted with an excited raise of his pure-white eyebrows.

"See the baguettes on the sides, around the center stone?" he launched right in. "The tongs of the setting are thicker than anything we ever released. I thought that might have been the case when I first saw the pictures you sent over. And that difference was supposedly how someone first discovered the forgeries."

"What forgeries?" Graham and I both said, him with curi-osity, me with panic.

It turned out Bette's Nathaniel was given partially correct info. The ring was not a Harry Winston original, but it *was* designed to pass as one by a man rumored to have created knockoffs. The alleged con artist gained access to the designs he copied thanks to a security guard named Chet Hastings.

"It was all just whispering back then. No one here wanted it to get out that fake Harry Winston rings were flying around the city, if not the world," Nolan explained. "I remember my gramps telling me that the papers were paid off so they wouldn't publish stories about the ordeal."

Graham's face fell at that. "So, you're saying there's no way for us to prove this?" he asked.

"Not necessarily," Nolan said, a tiny sparkle in his eye. I got the sense he was secretly thrilled to be asked to come to the defense of his beloved employer. "That security guard Chet was from my family's old neighborhood on Staten Island—that's how my grandfather found out about the open job here in the first place. The whole thing was big news for our little part of the city, and we had a little paper that was probably too small-potatoes to have gotten a bribe. I've got to believe there was something written about it in the *Staten Island Advance*, especially after Chet skipped town on his wife and kids. Maybe you can find something in the paper's archives that connects the dots between this story and your ring?"

I may have audibly groaned.

"*If* we find this article, it *might* provide a link to my ring, so we can *maybe* figure out who first owned it?" I asked. I felt Graham's hand on my forearm. It was a sweet gesture—reassurance—but his skin on mine made me even more uneasy.

"Sounds like you've been at this for a while," Nolan said. "I'm sorry I can't help you more."

"Thank you," I said. "And you have helped so much."

"We'll figure it out," Graham added.

"Well, I'm wishing you two luck. Tough way to start out your engagement, I imagine."

There it was again.

"No," Graham said, surprising me. "It's Shea's ring. I'm just a journalist covering this story."

It was the truth and what he should have said to Tomas back in Lisbon. And yet it left me with an awkward pang now. *Why? Do I want him to still want me?*

"Well, then," Mr. Jones said as he looked from Graham to me, then me to Graham, "seems like this ring has continued to collect interesting stories."

FORTY-SEVEN

RAHAM AND I FOUND OURSELVES WAITING IN line at the reference desk of the New York Public Library, our second library in our second country on our second continent in a week. And once again, I was running on criminally strong coffee.

"The good news is that all five boroughs had their newspapers digitized sometime in the eighties, so we don't have to go to actual Staten Island," Graham said.

"I think the real good news is that you know that, because I'd be waiting in line for the ferry right now."

Graham smiled, then did a little *at your service* bow. We'd slipped right back into our rhythm.

It took ten minutes to be assigned a computer within the wood-paneled walls of the building's famous Rose Main Reading Room. Then, with only three minutes of searching, the universe—as if finally giving us the break we desperately needed—delivered the very thing Nolan thought might exist: an article from the *Staten Island Advance* about Mr. Chet Hastings.

Local Chet Hastings Fired in Harry Winston Scandal
November 14, 1946—Staten Island, NY

Mr. Chet Hastings of the Spring Lake neighborhood is in hot water with one Mr. Harry Winston. The former security guard was fired from his position at the famed Manhattan-based jeweler because of his alleged connection to a Mr. Frederick Jonathan Quinn of Newark, New Jersey—a man accused of stealing ring designs so they could be copied by a Diamond District con man.

Mr. Quinn's crime was first reported by his family's house-keeper, a Mrs. Jane Caldwell, who found details of her employer's black-market business dealings in his home of-fice. According to a second source inside the home, Mrs. Caldwell was hoping to use the information as blackmail for a pay raise. Authorities quickly confirmed her accusa-tions and arrested Mr. Quinn for forgery, a crime punish-able as a felony in New York. He is currently awaiting trial on Rikers Island.

As for the counterfeit rings, the quantity produced, and their locations, are unknown. Mr. Quinn only confirmed that he sold the one remaining in his possession—his own wife's, Mrs. Celia Quinn's—to a pawnshop near the home where he was raised in Pittsburgh, Pennsylvania.

"Wow. There it is," said Graham.

We'd read the same confirming details. A forged ring had been sold in Pittsburgh—exactly where Nathaniel purchased it for Bette, where he was told it was a Harry Winston in the first place. Case closed. That ring was my ring. And with that, I now knew that this heirloom had been worn by exactly three women prior to John's proposal—first this Mrs. Celia Quinn, then Bette Silva, and finally, Carmela Costanza. Three lives. Three relationships. Three sets of karma. I breathed in deeply, letting the musty smell of shelved history fill my lungs.

"What do you think?" he asked.

"I don't know yet," I said. "I guess I'm relieved that the story connects?"

"Yeah, true," said Graham. "We did it. Which is pretty incredible, huh?"

He was celebrating our efforts. My mind had shifted to what it all meant. I looked down at the ring—*my* ring now. I'd gotten used to catching its stunning sparkle as the diamonds bounced against the light, a happy sight despite my anxieties about the unknown. Why did it feel somehow dimmer now?

"I have my answer," I said, mostly to myself. This ring was and had always been filled with bad energy. It started as a con from a crook and was given to his wife as a lie. Even if I bought into Annie's old suggestion that each owner somehow erased the previous history, the tragic deaths of Bette's two loves and Carmela and Gianluca's dear but unrequited love didn't feel like they could stand up to that task. Graham must have seen the distress in my eyes.

"Hey," he said. "What if you could look at the ring as the

thing that finally brought this guy Quinn down? It's, I don't know, like a truth omen? It was for Gianluca, too. Maybe that's its power?"

"Then what does that mean about Bette?"

"Um, okay . . . that Bette found her true loves?"

"And then the ring killed them?"

"Right, that's one way of looking at it, but—"

"I'm sorry," I said. "I appreciate what you're trying to do. Let's just finish reading the article and get out of here."

Graham nodded, then clicked through to the final paragraph of the piece.

Neither Mr. Frederick Quinn nor Mr. Chet Hastings was available for comment by the time of this paper's publication, but Mrs. Celia Quinn was reached at her Bronxville, New York, home. When asked for her reaction to the scandal, Mrs. Quinn shared these words: "Mr. Quinn is my husband. We exchanged a sacred vow. And we will address what's happened between us privately. As for my engagement ring, I regret greatly that it's left our family. I would have liked to someday give it to my son for his future wife."

Graham responded with a chuckle. "Sounds like Celia Quinn was a spitfire."

He was trying to be positive, to lighten the mood, but that's because he hadn't seen what I saw in Celia's quote. I felt like fate had just slapped me across the face. I stood up from my chair, desperate to escape the haze of the library's yellow-bulbed chandeliers.

FORTY-EIGHT

W E FOUND A PRIVATE SPOT IN NEARBY BRY-
ant Park. The grass was filled with couples
cozied up on blankets, squeezing in the last
alfresco picnic dinners before true fall set in. We sat on a bench
off the grass, a street pretzel between us.

I gave Graham the short version of what had happened
with John in Boston. He listened without commenting, without even asking a follow-up question.

"I'm sorry, Shea," was all he said once I finished.

"It's not your fault," I said. That was a truth I'd started
wrestling with on the train ride from Boston to New York,
when I considered how it would feel to see Graham. "I chose
this. All of it."

"What do you mean?" asked Graham.

I spoke as I thought, letting my words be messy. Wondering if Graham would help me make sense of it. "John wasn't
wrong from the beginning. If I'd been really secure in our relationship, then I wouldn't have been so insistent on finding

"What? What happened?" Graham asked.

"She stayed married to him," I said, gathering my things. "And if that isn't bad enough, she wanted to pass the symbol of all his lies along to her son and some unsuspecting woman."

"Right . . . but—" Graham tried.

"There is no *but* here. He was a bad guy, but she stayed because of their *sacred vow* and somehow still thought the ring was worthy of offering to her future daughter-in-law!" Then I really snapped. "I can't believe it! Of all the origin stories! Of all the possible beginnings this damn ring could have! *Why, why, why* did it start with a woman who made the exact same idiotic decision as my mother? I'm all for signs, but this is *way* too much!" By that point every set of eyes in the room was shooting daggers in my direction.

"I'm sure there's more to the story," Graham whispered. "We should do some research on Mrs. Quinn. Try to get some first-person accounts of her situation."

"No!" I said, walking out now. Graham quickly followed. "I've been delivered a glaring red blinking strobe light of a sign that I should run in the opposite direction of this ring, if it isn't already too late! Except it obviously is too late because I practically cheated on my fiancé, and he knows!" Thankfully I'd made it to the hallway before that bomb drop.

"John knows?" Graham asked.

"Yeah . . . ," I said, kicking myself for broaching this topic in this way. "He came to Boston. I told him there."

"Well, now I think we should definitely go somewhere to have that talk," said Graham.

the ring's karma. You said it, too. I would have just let the superstition take a back seat to what I knew was more important. So . . . I don't know . . . I love John but something in me can't trust that, I guess? That's got to mean something, right? I mean, the fact that I let you—" I stopped, not sure if it was worth revisiting that piece. Graham looked down at his hands, then back at me. It seemed as if something had finally come together in his mind.

"Shea, I believe in almost nothing, literally. And I certainly don't believe that rings carry magical energy. I'm a facts guy. I do the research, I add it all up. And in this weird way, I've been doing that with you since the minute we met way back in Hudson. I had this curiosity about you from go, and I have ever since. It got stronger once we figured out how much we had in common. And then—I don't know—we just click in a way that makes me want to go on a thousand more adventures with you. I'm sorry I blamed you for leading me on in Lisbon. That was wrong. Immature. I was just . . . trying to avoid whatever this panic-attack feeling is, I guess. I think I've been trying to avoid this my whole life. But I think we're going through something similar right now. Because I keep thinking that the fact that I don't want to let you go must mean something, too."

I was too thrown to do anything but sit there and stare back at him. This was a different Graham. To think that he'd changed because of me was so flattering. It satisfied a part of me that had always hoped people would evolve for love.

"Are you saying you want to be with me?" I asked, snapped back to reality.

Graham reached out and grabbed both my hands with his. I went to tuck my thumb in, like I would have with John, but our palms were squeezed together too hard. The warmth of his skin seeped through my own. I felt his heart racing through his palms and was sure he could feel mine matching the pace.

"I'm saying so far, all I know for sure is that I'm a guy that's never believed in *the one*, but you make me want to be wrong."

I glanced down to see all four of our hands trembling, then back up to meet the terrified honesty in Graham's eyes. I'd never fully bought that moment in the mist of the London countryside when Matthew Macfadyen as Mr. Darcy tells Keira Knightley's Elizabeth that she's "bewitched him, body and soul." How could she just believe him after all that came before? Turns out, it is intoxicating beyond reason to have a man tell you that you are the reason he believes in love.

Part of me wanted to be pulled in the direction of everything Graham was saying, to acknowledge that I felt so much of the same. He'd genuinely opened me to wondering if our shared backgrounds would actually make for a stronger couple. Plus I felt so alive around him—this inexplicable, edge-of-my-seat energy.

"Shea? Say something . . . please . . . ," Graham asked in a soft, worried voice.

I'd heard that line before. And the fact that it reminded me of John was as sure a sign as any of my uncertainty. Right now, I couldn't even look Graham in the eyes. I didn't even feel like I was there with him in that park. Then where was I? And why did his tone feel so oddly familiar?

It hit me as I looked down at our hands, still clasped together. I'd held John's just like this when I first felt the kind of
certainty Graham was expressing. It was the moment I said *I
love you* in front of the very Hudson shop where John eventually bought the heirloom. He'd made me so certain I could say
those words, for the first time to anyone but Annie as an adult.
With John I felt secure. Protected. *Cherished.* Like I had the
chance to love and be loved in a way I'd only dreamed about.
Graham was like a lit sparkler drawing me in, but in my heart
of hearts, I'd always been the kind of person who wanted to
curl up beside a warm fire.

"Thank you," I said, giving his hands a squeeze before re-
leasing my own. "And you're right, there was something going
on between us. And I've loved what we've shared—"

"But . . . ," Graham said, two steps ahead as usual.

"But you met a specific version of me," I said. "One really
thrown by some things and caught up in others. I need to re-
solve all that—and probably more—but I don't think we'll be
the perfect match once I do."

"So, it's still John?" he asked, clearly stung.

"I don't know. And I don't think I will until I get to the bottom of some things I've been confused about for a very long
time."

Graham nodded, not surprised, then offered a thought
that reminded me what had made him such an important
part of this whole journey.

"Makes sense. You're technically the fourth owner of the
ring. It's only fair for you to examine yourself the same way
we did the others."

. . .

I STARED UP at the pink-streaked clouds for a few minutes after Graham left. Their glide across the sky made me itch to move. I chose to walk west, following the sun as it slipped closer and closer toward the Hudson River. Green lights served as my only route for ten or so zigzagging blocks until I finally knew exactly where I needed to go.

The High Line had started construction in my first week living in Manhattan and finally opened in my last. I followed every single piece of the development, from fundraising to ribbon cutting. It always felt like we were keeping pace with each other, growing up together in a weird way.

I told John all of that on one of our first dates in LA, then I brought him here the first time we were in New York together. We walked the full length of the elevated park—from Thirty-Fourth Street to Gansevoort, stopping to take ridiculous selfies with the art installations and sneak kisses behind plants.

John proposed on the High Line because I loved it, but also because it was the place where he said he really fell for me. *But what does that even mean?* I wondered as I finally made it to the entrance at Thirty-Fourth. To *fall in love*. It's based on pheromones and lust. You become infatuated. Or maybe enchanted? You start to envision your future with that person. I knew I was falling when I started to wonder if John was the missing piece in my life. Would he be the calm to my anxiety? The rational to my emotional? Would his guidance and counsel be the reason I pushed to become the best version of myself? Would I do all that for him? And how could either of us be sure that'd be true forever?

I strolled south, passing the Plinth, where the newest sculpture commissions lived; then the four brick arches now covered in wildflowers and ivy; and finally the giant picture window that looked out onto Sixteenth Street. In front of it were the stadium-style benches where people sat to chat or read or think. I'd sat here the very first time I visited and thought about whether or not I was truly ready to leave this city—the biggest life decision I'd made, to that point. Now I was sitting here thinking about something much, much bigger.

I'd set out to see if my heirloom was cursed. The answer was yes, as far as my superstition went, but that resolution led me to another, more important question: Was the love between John and me wrong from the start? Not cursed. Not doomed. Just . . . not right? It felt impossible to walk away from everything we had built over the past three years, but what was three years in the grand scheme of life?

"Do you know that one of the synonyms for *superstition* is *delusion*?" Annie once asked me. We'd gotten into it about the fact that I'd held fast to so many of Nonna's rules during a walk on the Manhattan Beach pier.

"I did not," I said. "But I take it you're telling me for a reason."

"Because a delusion is a lens we use to process things. Sometimes it's not our choice—a psychotic delusion, for example. But in your case, I think it is. I think you holding so tight to these superstitions is you finding rules to live by."

"Yes," I said. "I like rules. What's the problem with that?"

"Rules are just an attempt at control, Shea. And I hate to be the bearer of bad news, but control is a total illusion. We never really have any. Over anything."

I understood what she was trying to say, but I didn't agree back then or now. Weren't my rules protecting me right now? Wasn't I taking control of my future?

FORTY-NINE

WHEN I LANDED BACK IN LA, I FELT DEPLETED in a way I hadn't since Mom died. My sister had the same drained look on her face when I arrived at her front door.

"I'm glad you're home," Annie said. Her voice was stiff, but that was fair. A lot had been said in Italy, and nothing since. Still, she scooped me into a quick hug.

"I'll set up the guest room, then I have to get back to school. We'll talk about everything tonight." It wasn't a question. Annie was not the type to let things linger. Nervous as that left me, it did at least mean one mess in my life would start to get resolved soon.

I spent the day sleeping off my jet lag. When my eyes finally opened, it was dark outside; I'd successfully made the entire afternoon disappear. The smell of hot pizza pulled me up and almost right out of the room, until I heard Annie and Mark's voices.

"I'm obviously going to talk to her about how long she's staying," Annie said.

"Good," he said. "I know she's your sister, but I really don't want to get in the middle of this."

Mark's bluntness wasn't a shock. He was the oldest of four brothers, each one more loyal than the next. Over the years, they'd made John an honorary fifth.

"Go to racquetball," said Annie. "I'll talk to her."

I waited until the front door closed before making my way into the kitchen.

"Hey," Annie said, plating slices of mushroom pizza, our favorite.

"Thanks for letting me come right here," I said. "I wanted to give John some space, for reasons I can explain . . ." Queasiness rolled over me; my body obviously did not cosign the explaining.

"Mark saw John," said Annie. Something in her voice made me feel even sicker.

"Before or after he came to Boston?" I asked, but her pivot away from me answered.

"Can I tell you the whole story?" I asked, following her into the living room and taking my usual spot on her couch.

Annie took the world's smallest bite of pizza. I didn't know whether to be grateful or devastated that this was affecting her insides as much as mine.

"Okay," she finally said.

I KEPT THE recap short, considering, taking her through the details of the ring search she'd missed since Florence. Then I went back to explain what happened between Graham and me, then John and me.

"That's a lot, Shea," Annie said once I was done. It was her counselor's training in action, a compassionate response. But the older sister in her was holding back.

"It's fine," I said. "You can say it. None of this would have happened if I'd just listened to you."

Annie shrugged. She looked more defeated than righteous. I'd pushed off really thinking through my fight with her until now. I still didn't know who was right or wrong, who was supposed to apologize first or for what. But I decided to ignore all that, for once. Annie deserved for me to play the big sister.

"Annie, I'm really sorry," I said. "I should have told you about Mom's ring, or at least *not* told you during a fight in the middle of an Italian piazza fifteen minutes before a flight. It was cruel. And you were right: I was being selfish."

Annie turned to face me on the couch. She was softening, but the wall wasn't all the way down yet.

"Thanks for saying that," she started. "And you know you only frustrate me so much because I feel like it's my job to protect you, a job that you do not make easy."

I smiled, finally. "Consider it free motherhood prep?"

Annie sighed, overwhelmed at the thought, before turning serious again. "But I get it," she said. "About Mom's ring. And, Shea, there's something I need to tell you, too."

"Okay . . . ," I said, crossing my legs under me to settle in.

"It's also about Mom," she continued. "I wanted to tell you in Italy but I thought it would hurt more than help at that point. Honestly, now I wish I'd told you years ago, but Mom asked me to keep this to myself, too."

My heart rate did not like her tone. "I guess we were both just trying to be loyal to Mom," I said carefully.

"Yeah. And in this case, Mom was just trying to be loyal to Nonna." Annie inhaled deeply, then let everything spill out: "Mom tried to leave Dad years before it actually happened. She had divorce papers drawn up when we were maybe eight and thirteen, right after we had to sell the house up north, which was when she first found out Dad was cheating. She was fully prepared to leave, but . . ." Annie's voice trailed off.

"But *what? Why didn't she?*" I asked, teenage rage rising up.

"Nonna convinced her not to." She said that part slowly, knowing how hard her words would hit me. "I don't know all the specifics—Mom told me after starting on the morphine drip at the very end. Something about the shame it would bring to the family, the sin of breaking her marriage vows. You know Mom wasn't super religious, but I guess deep down she just believed her mother, or was at least convinced to stay married until Nonna passed away."

"That's . . . I can't even . . ." I was standing up now, shifting my body as if I could punch something. "How could Nonna do that? How could she let Mom stay in all that pain?" I covered my eyes as if my palms held an answer, then a thought struck me back down to sitting: *Was the hero of my favorite love story the villain of my mother's?*

"Why didn't Mom want me to know?" I finally asked.

"She didn't want you to resent Nonna. That's actually the thing she said most clearly. She knew how much you loved her and Pop, and how much the fairy tale of their marriage meant to you. I think Mom decided it was more important for you to hold on to that."

I was listening to Annie but rewinding through the tapes in my mind, trying to see any tensions between my mom and hers. *How could they have stayed so close despite Nonna ignoring what Mom needed?* "Did Mom blame Nonna? Or secretly resent her all those years?" I asked.

"I don't know. All Mom told me was that she wished she'd been stronger in a lot of ways. The married person in me wonders if Nonna's 'rule' was easier for Mom to follow than divorcing Dad would have been, in her mind at least."

Annie's comment pushed my freight train of thoughts in a new direction.

"Wait," I said. "If Mom had wanted to leave Dad for so long, the fact that she wore her engagement ring *for the rest of her life* makes even *less* sense than before! Why wouldn't she want to get rid of the constant reminder?"

"I don't know. But I think we have to live without an answer," said Annie. I nodded, hoping she saw how grateful I was that she hadn't included *because of you*, but she'd gotten up and was heading to the kitchen, maybe rightfully still struggling with that piece.

"Why would Nonna do that to Mom . . . ," I thought aloud.

"Nonna was from a very different time, with very different beliefs," Annie answered, glasses of water now in hand. "She probably thought she was helping Mom. And as you know, Nonna could be very convincing when sharing her beliefs, especially if she thought she was keeping her loves safe."

It took a second for the irony of Annie's comment to finally land on me, but once it did, I face-planted directly into a pillow.

"Are you okay?" Annie asked.

"I'm not really . . . ," I mumbled, still face down. "But that feels right, considering."

"It is," she said. "Both clinically and sisterly speaking. Now, can we make a promise right this very moment?"

"Can I do it from inside this pillow?" I asked.

"No," Annie said as she pulled me back up. She kept my hand in hers, preparing to shake. "No more secrets."

"No more secrets," I echoed. "Especially from this new generation in our family line."

Annie looked to her belly, then gave it a sweet rub. "This new generation of women," she said.

"It's a girl!?" I screamed.

"It's a girl," my sister said. "God help me . . ."

With that I hugged her—and my future niece—so hard we almost all tumbled off the couch.

———

I DECIDED TO finally call John before bed that night. At the very least, I figured, we could work out some apartment logistics. At the most, one of us would know how to begin what would come next.

"Let's just take a few weeks to think," I said after our stilted hellos. "I can stay at Annie and Mark's."

"Yeah. Time would be good," said John. "And thanks for

that. I'll be at school late tomorrow for final Science Olympiad prep, if it would be easier for you to grab stuff at the apartment while I'm not home." I had to tighten my grip on my phone. *Has it really come to that? Avoiding each other?*

"Would that be better for you?" I asked, desperate to not have to decide.

I wished John had needed much longer to think before he said yes. But then I remembered indecisiveness had never been his problem.

FIFTY

T HE NEXT DAY WAS MONDAY, THANK GOD. GETTING
back to work after two full weeks away was the distraction I needed. Though Jack Sachs did unfortunately
pop by during one of my many sessions staring at the computer screen. Luckily it was on the same side of the cubicle as
my giant monthly calendar with all my color-coded meetings
and events. I cocked my head to the side as if I were considering adding something, then grabbed a green pencil from my
desk for effect.

"Welcome back, Anderson," he said. "You doing okay?"

"Um, I will be," was the best I could do.

"I can give you a day to settle in, or I can dump a ton of
new RFPs for potential activations on your desk. What's more
helpful?" he asked.

"Staying as busy as possible, please."

"Gotcha. See Julie. She'll talk you through. And we'll talk
about the other stuff top of next week."

It wasn't until he was halfway down the hall that I realized he was talking about the promotion. The huge new title that I now wasn't sure I wanted. I'd replied with a simple Thank you to his email offer while I was away, a nearly rude bare minimum. *This is not who I am*, I thought as I got up to go find Julie.

The hours slogged by until it was time for the next gut punch: grabbing some things from my apartment. I found it just as tidy as always. John preferred all spaces a full ten degrees colder than me, but aside from that stereotypical divide, we were very compatible roommates. His bathroom cleanliness alone put every roommate I'd ever had, Rebecca included, to shame.

I looked around the living room, remembering how we'd barely even redecorated after he moved in. The space had me written all over it, from the mustard velvet couch to the bold green-and-gold wallpaper behind it. *Is this what John wanted or was he just appeasing me?*

On the entryway wall was the photo gallery we'd painstakingly hung together. The memory of John sweating over his newspaper print map of all the frame sizes and positions made me laugh, but the photos occupying those frames were what drew me in now. Us on a tuk-tuk in Bangkok. Us with Annie and Mark at Christmas, the four of us in ugly sweaters. Us in the exact Florence piazza I'd walked through a week ago, alone. We were a happy couple. We had always been a genuinely happy couple. What were we now?

Unable to answer, I turned away toward the bedroom. I shoved clothes and toiletries into my luggage without a clue how much I would need. I thought about taking a shirt of

John's. *To have as some sort of security blanket? To see how much I missed him?* He had been right, I thought, this was better to do alone.

Finally, I went to grab our spare key to Annie and Mark's place from the key hook by the front door. It wasn't there. An awkward laugh flew out of me: *Of course. John has it.* Apparently, the universe did not want me to get away without seeing him in person. I decided I was in no position to question its authority.

JOHN WAS IN the school's auditorium when I arrived, prepping his team for their big state tournament. I'd texted him that I was stopping by for the key, but he hadn't replied. Part of me wondered if popping by anyway was a mistake, but another part had to see him in person. I slipped into the back of the room silently.

The kids were seated at a long table, fake buzzers in hands. He was at a podium, playing tournament host. He'd even put on a blazer and tie to make the character official. I smiled. He always looked so handsome in a blazer and tie.

"Ladies and gentlemen, welcome to the annual Southern California State Science Olympiad Tournament," he said, then he covered his hands and breathed into them creating that *crowd going wild* effect. All fifteen kids went wild with laughter.

"All right, our first topic today is biology. Franklin Middle, are you ready?"

"Yes!" the team screamed in unison.

"I like that spirit!" John said. "All right, please turn to the screen for your first question." They obeyed like little soldiers, nerves visible in the shifts and twitches of their preteen shoulders. *How does John do this?* I thought, my own blood pumping.

John pressed the clicker in his hand. But it wasn't the text of a quiz question that popped up on the screen, it was a picture of Jayden—one of the eighth-grade team members. He was in a Hulk pose on the stage of last year's tournament. The kids lost it, pointing and laughing at the screen, then at Jayden, who was now mimicking his own move.

"What?!" said John. "How did that get . . . Just one second here." He held the clicker up and pressed again. This time it was a shot of Kira and Jess jumping out of their seats after nailing a super-tough question during that same event. I knew because I'd been in the audience that afternoon, nervous and excited like one of the parents sitting next to me.

Ha!!! Whaat? Mr. Jacobs!! the kids yelled.

"I have *no* idea what's going on," John fibbed as he clicked yet again. Next was Teddy being squeezed by his parents post-tournament, then Alex holding the team's second-place trophy just as tightly, then shot after shot after shot of these kids bursting with excitement and joy and pride. I watched the looks on their faces as they cheered like they were right back in those moments and the look on John's face as he took in their total delight.

John ended on an image of the entire team posing with a classic range of middle school silly faces. He was dead center, cheeks puffed out like a faux blowfish. I covered my mouth to avoid laughing out loud—or maybe crying? I honestly wasn't sure. John left that one on the screen as he came around the podium and up to the table.

"No quiz questions today," he said. "These photos are all you need to prep for the tournament. You've worked hard for months. You know your stuff inside and out. *Except* for the periodic table, but those noble gases are a killer," he teased. "So if we win, amazing. But this fun we get to have together is what it's all about. And I'm honored to be a part of it."

The kids beamed, then started in on a slow clap. John beamed back, then joined in. And I stood silent at the back of the room, most shocked at the fact that none of what I'd just seen had been a surprise to me. *This is John, through and through.* I had so much respect and admiration for him in that moment that it was hard to imagine it not crashing straight out of me and over him. And maybe that's just what happened, because the moment the rowdy cheer finished, John finally turned and caught my eye.

"Oh, hey," he said, startled. He had not seen the text. And from the look on his face, he did not want to see me.

"Hi. Sorry," I stumbled. "I texted you. I think you have Annie and Mark's apartment keys?"

John shook his head, frustrated to have forgotten that detail in our exchange of things. "Right. Sorry. They're in my glove compartment. Car's in the parking lot, but it's locked."

"It's okay, I have—" I started, but John cut me off.

"Right," he said, shaking his head again. Of course we each had a set of the other's car keys. We had shared a whole life up until now.

"Who's that?" a kid I'd never met asked.

"Um . . . that's my . . . uh . . . ," John started.

His search for the word made me want to disappear. My eyes closed, maybe trying for just that, but then I heard the start of a very specific sound, one I hadn't heard since I was probably the exact same age as all the kids making it: all fifteen members of the Science Olympiad team finishing John's stumble with a classic middle school, *oooohhh*. It made both John and me blush.

"Good luck tomorrow," I called out, unable to hide my smile.

"Thanks," he said with the tiniest hint of one, too.

————————

JOHN'S SLIDESHOW HAD me thinking about old photos as I lay wide awake for hours in the middle of yet another night. Mom had kept incredibly organized albums from the second Annie and I were born. She and Nonna even went through a phase of making fabric covers for them, themed by the time of year or event. Little pink flowers for our baby albums. Holly-printed material for Christmas and our ski trips to Big Bear. I started to wonder if they might contain some clues to answer questions still lingering from my chat with Annie. The ceiling fan spun above me, its center chain clicking at each turn as my mind continued down this path. *Didn't Annie take all those albums after Mom died?* I thought. I could picture them in a set of old boxes labeled with thick black Sharpie. *Could they be in the closet right in this room?* There was no sense not checking, considering I still felt hours from tired, even though the clock had long since ticked past midnight.

I got up and slid open the mirror-faced closet door. Inside was Annie's *incredibly* well-organized storage space. Even her old stuffed animals had their own cubbies. I found her very ragged monkey staring back at me, like I was sure he always had. Then, on the very top shelf, I found the exact boxes I remembered.

I managed to pull the biggest one down without dropping it. Its side said *1980–1987.* I stopped at first—*I wasn't even born yet*—but something in me wondered if that range might actually be most helpful.

I grabbed the first album, then leaned up against the nearest wall to leaf through. The first thing I saw was the exterior of Mom and Dad's first apartment—the studio in Marina del Rey that Mom said they should have never left. This must have been the album from their very first year married. On the next page were pictures of the newlyweds themselves. Mom was tiny and tan and rocking a perfect Farrah Fawcett cut. There was a shot of her cooking in the one-wall kitchen, then showing off a piece of art they'd just hung, and finally, with Dad on the couch. She was sitting on his lap, smiling like a girl who had just gotten pinned by the football captain. But it was his face that drew me in closer. I hadn't seen it in almost ten years. Of course, this wasn't the man I'd known. This guy had slick eighties hair, strong arm muscles, and a mustache I'd never even known about. He was squeezing Mom tight, like he'd just won the best prize at the fair. *I never saw him hug her like that*, I thought. Something about seeing them so happy felt wrong—like they had to have been faking it. Were these the parents Annie knew? Is that why she'd wanted them to stay together?

When I'd exhausted that album, I grabbed another, this one white with a thin gold border—their wedding album. I flipped through picture after picture of my parents on the happiest day of their lives to that point. Mom was a blissed-out hippie bride, down to the wildflowers in her hair, and Dad looked the most put-together I'd ever seen him, in a white tux and clean-shaven. I couldn't stop from smiling back at their bright, young faces. When had it gone so wrong?

I finally stopped at a larger-sized picture midway through: the two of them up at the church altar during their wedding mass. Dad held both of Mom's hands in his, looking at her with total adoration. But my eyes went to the obvious image in the photo, for me: the engagement ring on her finger.

An unexpected thought dropped into my brain. With it came an idea that snowballed into a plan. Charged with a sudden urgency, I found myself up off the floor, changing out of my pajamas and into clothes. Minutes later I was on the road, driving east just as the sun rose. An hour after that, I was knocking on the door of a run-down condo. Finally, an old man in his pajamas opened it.

"Shea?" he asked, baffled.

"Yeah. Hi, Dad," I said as he opened the door wider to let me in.

FIFTY-ONE

E SAT FACING EACH OTHER AT HIS MESSY kitchen table, as if I were a vacuum salesman imposing on some guy who just wanted to eat his damn breakfast. Amid small-talk questions that began but abruptly stopped and uncomfortable, forced smiles, we also had too much tense silence. Dad made instant coffee, but he didn't have any milk, so we drank it black. Or he did. I was too stiff to even sip.

He'd heard from Annie about my moving back to the West Coast years ago, making a point of mentioning that she always checked in with him during the holidays. I already knew that and wasn't here to be guilt tripped; I was quick to clarify.

"I'm really glad you are here—for whatever reason, Sheaby," he said. He used to sing that nickname to the tune of his favorite Frank Sinatra cover: *Yes, sir, you're my Sheaby. No, sir. I don't mean maybe. Yes, sir. You're my little Sheaby, girl!* I'd do a little spin at his cue.

I felt myself start to smile at that memory but quickly

turned my mouth back into a line. I didn't want to give in to his charm, but even I had to admit that Dad seemed softer than the last time we'd spoken. He actually looked me in the eyes as we talked and kept asking if my coffee was still warm. I was starting to wonder if I'd been wrong to cut him off so fully, then he brought up the wrong memory. Or maybe the right one.

"God, Shea," he said. "I don't think I've seen you in person since Mom's funeral."

Dad had been drunk that entire day, which was typical for that time in his life. He'd leaned all the way in to his vices after the divorce, a revolving door of much younger women and a series of failed side businesses. Annie and I had both tried to keep in touch at first. She even convinced him to try rehab for a stint, but then Mom got really sick. I was just about to graduate from high school; Annie was only a year out of college and had just moved in with Mark. Neither of us had time to try to save both parents, and there was a clear choice. Dad didn't visit her. He didn't call. Mom didn't want him anymore, he once told Annie, so why would he come around? He'd been just as selfish at her funeral.

"Now that you've only got one parent, you think you could find some time in your busy schedule to call?" he'd said during the luncheon Annie and I had arranged and paid for. The only redeeming aspect of Dad's presence was that he agreed to handle the final logistics at the funeral home. We couldn't bring ourselves to do that part. It required making choices that would never be good enough in our minds, and worse, being present when the casket was officially closed forever.

Mom specifically told us not to feel guilty if we couldn't do that part, still haunted by her own experience with Nonna.

"All right, you be good. And remember, Mom's better off not suffering," Dad had said as he practically ran out of the room that day. I looked out the door to where he was headed so quickly. A gorgeous vintage Mercedes was parked out front; a woman much younger than Dad was at the wheel.

"She would have been better off not suffering for her entire fucking life!" I screamed after shutting the door behind me. I'd told myself he heard me, but the truth was he was already in the car.

I was surprised by how hard it was to connect with all that anger right now. Annie always told me time heals most wounds, but I didn't believe that applied to this man. But Dad had visibly aged. He had almost no hair left, and his sagging, ruddy skin revealed a man who drank too much and ate too little. There was a deep hunch to his back, and his wide brow furrowed in cavernous lines. He was my enemy, but in the body of an old man—and the only family besides Annie and Mark I had left in the world.

"So, you still with that guy Annie told me about in her Christmas card? What's his name?" Dad asked, filling the silence.

"John," I said. "And . . . it's a long story."

"I see," said Dad. It was quite possibly the first time in either of our lives that I'd said something he truly understood.

"Dad, I came here to ask you some things about Mom, about her engagement ring."

"Okay," he said, nervous. "Whatcha got?"

I took a deep breath, knowing that I couldn't undo what I said next, no matter what he might have to tell me.

"I know she tried to leave you years before you got divorced." I watched his eyes glaze over at the reminder. It pained him. That, shockingly, pained me. But I couldn't let the little girl who thought her dad would take her for a train ride if she behaved run this moment. "I need to know if you have any idea why she refused to take off her engagement ring after you split up."

Dad's eyes widened, surprised but in a strange way. "Why do you want to know that?" he asked.

"Because I need to know," I said. "And she can't tell me."

He looked like he was seeing something he couldn't believe. "Good," he said, mostly to himself, then, "I probably should have done this a long time ago. Gimme a second, okay?"

He stood up slowly, then disappeared down the hallway off the kitchen. I sat, bewildered, tapping my foot so fast my ankle started to cramp. Minutes later, Dad was back with a crumpled-up ball of tissue paper in his hand, and a surprisingly tender smile on his face.

"Here," he said. "Seems like it's finally time for you to take this."

I unwrapped the paper, confused. Then I recognized the shape within: Mom's engagement ring. I couldn't bring myself to finish taking it out of the paper, especially not with Dad there. I didn't want him to see me seeing it after all these years; I needed privacy. But that thought prompted another.

"Wait. Why the hell do you have this?!" I yelled.

"Calm down, Shea."

"No, this didn't belong to you, or with you!" I quickly constructed a narrative. "Oh my God, you *stole* this! It was on Mom's finger when she died, and you took it! Did you take it off her when you were at the funeral home? What kind of sick, twisted person does that?"

He nodded. "I deserve that. But I took the ring because that's what the funeral home director said to do. They don't like to bury people in good jewelry. Grave robbers or something, I guess. But I also took it because I thought it was probably the right thing to do, in case one of you girls would want it someday."

"Someday? What, you were holding it for just the right special moment?" I asked, blood still boiling.

"No. I was holding the ring because I had too big a chip on my shoulder about it after your mom sent me this."

Dad reached into his back pocket, pulled out a folded piece of stationery, and handed it over.

"What is this?" I asked.

"The answer to your question about why your mother kept that ring on all those years," he said.

My hands shook as I started to peel the pages open. Then I stopped. I'd heard the last words my mom would ever speak on the day she died, over a decade ago. Now I suddenly had more of her, *words directly from her.* This was the wrong place to read them.

"It's yours to keep," Dad said, as if reading my mind. "And you can call me after you read, if you have any more questions. Or come by again?"

The hope in his voice suddenly consumed me. Tears pooled in my eyes.

"Shea, I'm sorry," Dad said. He went to reach out a hand, to maybe hold mine, but he pulled it back. "You didn't deserve everything I did. And didn't do. I promise you I wish I could go back in time to give you and your sister a better father. I would if I could, Sheaby."

That apology was all I'd ever dreamed of hearing from this man, but after all I'd come to realize these past weeks, it was the wrong one.

"I'm not the person you should be apologizing to," I said, then the rest of the words spewed from me as if they'd been waiting, alive in my throat, fully formed. "I can have a better life. You know who can't? *Mom*." I was standing now, gripping the table for support. "You stole the best years of her life. You stole her chance to know what real love was. And when you finally left, we only got a few years with her before she died!"

Dad stared back at me, not a whisper of shock on his face. "You're right," was all he said, holding back tears. "I hope you won't ever let somebody do that to you."

I felt his words sear into me, no doubt leaving a permanent mark. Then I grabbed Mom's note and her ring and I walked out the front door.

FIFTY-TWO

I WAITED IN THE PARKING LOT FOR ANNIE TO ARRIVE, trying to remember an occasion in which I'd been to Emma Wood State Beach without her. The only time we came without Mom was for our *just us* memorial. That afternoon we played Linda Ronstadt too loud, ate tomato and mozzarella sandwiches from our favorite Italian deli, and read old cards she'd written us on our birthdays. Then we nailed a little sign Annie had hand-painted into the fence behind the patch of dunes where we'd always sit together. *Suzanne Anderson State Beach*, it said. Mom loved this little enclave of coastline most because it was the only stretch in all of California named for a woman.

After a few more minutes Annie finally screeched into the lot, slipped her car in next to mine, then leapt out of the driver's seat.

"I have a thousand questions about everything with Dad, but I can't even think straight until we read this note!" she said. "Also, I called out sick from work, which I have never done before."

I grabbed her hand. "Annie, I just fled your house at day-break without even leaving a note, then made you drive an hour north to read a letter with me. It's an unprecedented time."

WE FOUND MOM'S hidden placard, then settled in on the beach towels we kept in our cars, like good California girls. I ran my hands through the long grasses, letting them tickle my skin like I used to when we were kids. Annie took her sneakers off and dug her toes into the soft hills of sand, her favorite feeling in the world.

"Okay. I'm ready. But . . . you don't have to read aloud if you don't want to," she said. "We could take turns?"

"No way," I said. "We hear it together. But if I start losing it, you have to take over."

Annie looked out at the ocean, so I did, too. The water rolled in long, slow waves, falling apart right where the line of shells met the sand—the world's most soothing sound. Annie sucked in air for strength. I followed suit, then I unfolded the thin piece of stationery. Mom's initials were at the top in black, pressed cursive. I glanced down the page at her per-fectly loopy penmanship—the mark of a strict Catholic school education—and I started to read.

Jerry, it's come to my attention that you have some opin-ions about me—specifically the fact that I still wear the ring you gave me almost three decades ago and that I might die still wearing it. I hear from these "friends" that you think it's because I'm still pining for you. I thought I'd set the record straight.

The truth is that I didn't used to know why I couldn't take the ring off. At first it was just because I felt naked without it after two dozen years of marriage. Then it was because I wanted to ward off any new men. But a lot more things have started to make sense now that I'm faced with the end of my life, and one of those is that the engagement ring you gave me is not yours, and it's certainly not ours. It's mine. I wear this ring because it holds all the strength it took me to learn to take care of myself. To leave you. So to correct the rumor mill: The ring has nothing and also everything to do with you. Yes, it was first meant to be a symbol of our promise to each other, but when you broke that promise, my enjoyment of its beauty became a symbol of my ability to keep going, despite all the obstacles you put in my way.

Jerry, your weaknesses ultimately made me strong. And that's another reason why I'm still wearing my ring. Because when I look down at my finger every day, I'm reminded that I can always find the other side, and that's a fact I've raised our daughters to know, too. So no, I do not wear this ring because I still love you. I wear it because I know how to love myself.

"Wow," Annie said, one hand clutching my arm and the other her own chest. "I can't believe you got through that without breaking down."

"I know," I said. "I felt . . . almost possessed. Sorry. Is that weird?"

"No. I knew it was you reading, but I heard it in her voice the entire time. It's incredible. I always knew Mom was that strong."

I didn't have the heart to admit to Annie—or myself—that my reaction was the exact opposite. I looked down at Mom's words, letting my eyes find the line that had gutted me most: *your weaknesses ultimately made me strong.* That was a version of my mom that I didn't feel like I knew. I wondered when exactly she wrote this and who, if anyone else, she'd shown it to. Then another thought gutted me.

"This is what she was trying to tell me that day in her bedroom," I said, my voice catching. Annie looked at me as if she'd been waiting for me to put those pieces together.

"Maybe . . . ," she said.

"Is this why she wanted me to have the ring? Was she trying to give all this energy to me?"

"I don't know, Shea," Annie said. I could tell how much she wanted to offer a more solid answer. "I think that's a part of the past you're going to have to make peace with, just like Mom did with some of the parts of her life."

I looked down at the note again. This time I landed on a sentence that I'd brushed over during the first read: *The engagement ring you gave me is not yours, and it's certainly not ours. It's mine.*

I took it in, then turned toward the water again, letting the meaning roll over and over with the waves. After a few seconds, I closed my eyes to better hear the slow whoosh, then the break. *Crash.*

"Mom could define her ring's meaning," I finally said.

"Yeah. It's pretty badass," said Annie, smiling now.

"But it also tracks with what Wendell said about metals and energy." My mind had jumped to the other heirloom. "They can hold it, but also conduct it, and then"—suddenly my gears started spinning so fast that I couldn't get the words out—"the meaning can change. Like for Carmela . . . First romantic love but then like a soulmate, without romance."

"Okay . . . ," Annie said, trying to follow.

"And for Bette, too! Whether or not it's true, she *thinks* the ring guided her life toward these big loves, so that's what it meant to her. It was *hers*, not theirs. Omigod, Annie! For Celia, it could have been the exact same reasoning as Mom's! The ring had meaning beyond her husband's lies, enough for her to want to pass it along to her son. Like Mom with me!"

"You're saying the ring carried her karma, not her husband's?"

"Right! And not the karma of the marriage, which makes sense because—of course!" The idea hit my brain so hard that I reached out and grabbed Annie's arm. "Annie, the *woman* wears the ring!" I yelled.

"Jesus! Shea! That hurt!" she yelled back.

"Sorry, but this is huge! This changes everything! Because the symbol sits on *her* finger, not theirs. It's only *her* energy inside the metal—not the energy of the relationship. So it's only *her* spirit that carries forward. It's *her* ring!"

I fell back onto my towel and kicked my legs in the air.

"I can't believe I'm going to say this, and I'm not endorsing

your magical thinking, but that sort of makes sense," Annie
said.

"I *know*! Which means my ring wouldn't be giving me the
bad luck from all its tainted relationships, it would be passing along the strength and wisdom and beauty that made up
the lives of the women who wore it first! Strong, self-assured
women!"

"Just like someone else I know," Annie said with a smile.

My hand rushed to my neck, searching for the ring. It was
nestled into its spot in the center of my chest. I held it up,
squinting at the emerald-cut diamond as it caught the light
from the cloud-streaked sun above. I moved it around in my
fingers, letting the dozens of pale blue rays shine out from its
edges. *Lifelines.*

"Earth to Shea," Annie said, waving her hand in front of
my face.

"Sorry, did you say something?" I asked, focus stuck on this
revelation and the women I now wanted to know more about,
especially Celia, whom I'd judged so quickly and so harshly.

"I asked if I could see the ring," Annie said. "Mom's."

I hadn't looked at it yet, either. I was too worried it
would transport me back to the last time I'd seen it, on Mom's
dresser top. I reached into my bag to find the tissue paper Dad
had given me, then handed it to Annie. I still couldn't look. I
only now realized just how much pain and confusion—and
more recently, regret—I'd been holding on to, all connected to
this other object that had never even belonged to me. This
heirloom.

"I didn't remember it being so elegant," Annie whispered.

I peeked over, relieved to feel like I was actually seeing the beautiful ring for the first time. I tried to picture our mom wearing it as she washed the dishes or drove us to a Friday night movie, ready for those same emotions I'd had back then to resurface. But in the place of all the anger and frustration was just gratitude. *A piece of her. With us, right now.*

"Maybe we should take turns holding on to it," I suggested. "Or give it to your daughter! We could share the note when she's old enough?"

"No," Annie said, handing me the ring. "Mom wanted you to have this, and now that I know what it meant to her, I agree."

"You do?" I asked. "Because I'm still a little lost. And also—" I barely wanted to say it. "The John of it all . . ."

"Your ring, your choices, your life," Annie said with a cryptic smile, then she popped up, tucked her hair back as the perfect punctuation mark, and sprinted down to the water.

Without a beat, I unclasped the gold chain around my neck, took Mom's band, and looped it onto the necklace, right alongside my ring from John. Then I ran down the beach after my sister.

FIFTY-THREE

I WOKE UP THE NEXT MORNING FEELING FULLY RESTED for the first time since I got engaged. One clear thought was running through my mind as I lay staring up at the ceiling in Annie's guest room: *I have to tell John what I figured out.* But the thought of how our conversation might go *after* my revelation stopped me. I'd resolved *my* superstition, solved for *my* beliefs. But that had so little to do with us. John and I had agreed to spend time figuring that piece out before getting back in touch. So far, I didn't have any answers.

I quickly brushed my teeth and showered. I grabbed a blueberry muffin from the pile of groceries I'd purchased as part of my thanks to Annie and Mark. Then I did what any lost twenty-first-century woman does as I drank my morning coffee: I bought a dozen self-help books online.

Over the next few weeks, I did as they said: Move your body, rest your body. Spend time with wise friends. Meditate. Journal. Journal more. Cry rereading your journal. Cry again while meditating about what you journaled about while you were last crying. One book suggested I buy myself lilies weekly, so I did that. Another offered to help me place myself in the room with John without actually having to be in a room with John. I did that too, then I journaled while crying *a lot. Work on and with and for things that bring you joy*, my favorite of the stack directed, which is exactly what I found myself contemplating on the day I was meant to sign the contract for my new work title: director of film festival marketing.

"We'll have you covering American Express and Verizon now. It's big-time, Anderson," Jack Sachs said with a proud smile.

"That's—*wow* ...," I said. I scanned the room, stalling. On one wall were framed photos of Jack's family. On the other, his two college degrees. How many times had I sat here and not realized there wasn't a single movie poster in Jack's office? "So, um, weird timing," I said as Jack prepped to go over the final terms. "I'd love to discuss spending some time with the programming team as part of my promotion."

"Like, *socially*?" he asked, head buried in his computer.

My career dreams had made their way into a few stream-of-consciousness writing sessions over the past weeks, starting with the one where I challenged myself to answer the prompt "What kind of spouse do you want to be?" (thank you, Esther Perel). The first descriptions that came to me were lovely but obvious—*respectful, attentive, considerate, supportive*. But the more I thought, the more I realized there were words that I'd thought, then actively avoided writing: *Independent, self-sufficient, adventurous, self-satisfied. A person who follows her own path.* They were qualities that seemed more like a single person's than a wife's. I wrote them down anyway, because they felt right. Because they felt like *me*.

That's exactly what I needed to do right now—stay with what would bring me joy personally, even if it meant I had to transition who I'd been professionally.

"No, professionally," I said. That got his attention. "I'd like to start learning those ropes, too."

"Okay . . . Want to tell me why?" I got the terrifying sense that Jack had no idea what I was going to say next. In fairness, neither did I, really.

"Because it's my ultimate goal to work in that arm of the festival," I heard myself say, as clearly as if it had been on the tip of my tongue for years.

"Well, that's not where you are right now," Jack said. "You work in marketing, where you've been promoted to a position that doesn't allow time for a ton of career exploration, Anderson." His tone was the kind of fatherly that I did not appreciate.

I nodded, stalling again. Jack took my pause as a sign that he'd won.

"All right, so let's go over compensation first—"

"I need some more time to consider," I said. I was met with a sharp stare. It served as just the right fuel. "I'm truly sorry for the timing, but I need to consider whether or not I want this promotion. I've just recently been willing to admit to myself that it's a priority for me to pivot into festival programming someday. I think I can start to learn while managing this new role, but if I can't grow in that direction, then I'd like to stay in my current position."

Jack looked at me as if I were a very silly child. "Shea. This is a good, stable job at a really important juncture in your life. Trust me, this is the kind of contract you want to be signing at the start of a marriage."

He meant well, but I still let myself say the words that came flashing at me next. "I think we have different definitions of stable," I said. "And marriage."

The next day I sent three emails: one asking each of the programming department leads for a pick-your-brain coffee session and one to Jack Sachs suggesting I take on just one big-fish client and a more modest promotion. My request was denied by HR later that week—maybe it was too tough an ask, or maybe I'd bruised my mentor's ego. Either way, moody Julie got the gig, but staying in my old job offered me ample time to let a side project start to percolate. I started writing ideas down in my journal nightly, zero crying.

A FEW WEEKS later I found myself plating the Italian feast I'd cooked my sister and Mark, so they'd be in generous moods for my pitch: to host a mini film festival at Annie's school. It was inspired by my new programming friends' DIY guide for how to break into film festivals: *program a film festival*. This little event would be more slumber party in a school library than red-carpet affair, I explained via a truly killer deck that Mark helped me display on the TV. Annie was skeptical about the attention span of thirteen-year-olds for anything but social media clips, but I hooked her with my interactive viewing games, then sealed the deal with my final slide: a picture of us smushed together on the plastic-covered couch in Nonna's living room. We were blissed-out watching *Sleeping Beauty*, our very first favorite movie.

"You dragged me to that same spot every single day after school until we wore out Nonna and Pop's VHS," Annie reminded me as she dug into my spinach and bechamel lasagna.

"My first movie was *Indiana Jones*," Mark said, head shaking. "Man, you girls really are screwed from the start."

"We *were*," Annie and I said in unison.

"My niece will be raised on a healthy diet of the badass princess movies," I explained.

"Like what?" Mark asked.

"Like *Aladdin*," we said, jinxing again.

That night the first annual Seventh Grade Cinema Sleepover was born, with my promise to Annie that my lineup would sneak lessons about healthy communication into her stubborn students.

By the end of the month, I'd forced my new roommates to watch—or listen to me watch—three to five films a week. It got so bad that Mark joined a second racquetball league.

"I think we've got to include *My Best Friend's Wedding*," I said to Annie as we settled into our Friday night routine of one large mushroom pizza and a glass of Tuscan red for me. "It's got a gay/straight friendship, real consequences for lying, an epic catfight, and a rousing musical number!"

"Sure, but I don't need to watch it," Annie said. "You've made me so many times I could recite the script." She sashayed past me holding our beverages up à la Julia in the baseball stadium scene, then nailed the exact right line: *"I've got moves you've never seen."*

"It is my favorite rom-com to rewatch!"

"It's the only one you'll rewatch. And also it's not a rom-com."

"Of course it is. There is romance. There is comedy. Also, I like other rom-coms. We were raised on them."

"You don't really," said Annie, mouth full of pizza. "And you always have a critique of the endings. You're the only human in the world that's ever argued that Harry should have taken a beat before running to Sally." The relevance of that now practically shoved me back against the couch.

I opened the "Movie Notes" doc on my laptop to avoid responding. Annie was right. I did not swoon for the classics of our nineties youth in the same way as most women I knew. Of course, the film lover in me respected their pitch-perfect structure. You always knew Julia and Meg and Sandra and Jennifer were going to have it tied up in a bow at the end, after just the right roller coaster of trouble. But I realized now—as my mind went to every single orchestra crescendo at a Tom Hanks kiss—that the magical end was my least favorite part. What did I have against a happily-ever-after?

My email pinged as if to reply. But I found the exact opposite of an answer when I clicked on the mailbox: a message from Graham. The subject line was My article. I clicked through to find a website link, then three infuriating words: Thank you, Graham.

"You've got to be kidding me!" I yelled, tossing my computer down on the couch as if it were about to detonate.

"What?" asked Annie. "And also don't shock a woman without bladder control!"

"Graham wrote the article about me! Without my permission! What a *snake*! He signed an NDA, right? I can sue him, right?"

"Wow. That's bold . . . ," said Annie, examining my screen.

"No, it's *criminal*! *Ugh!* You have to read it for me. Because I cannot imagine what he probably has to say about me after everything . . ."

I stood up to shake off steam as Annie grabbed my laptop and clicked through to the article. Her eyes settled, then squinted, then narrowed, then widened, then her eyebrows lifted into a sort of surprised arch. It was a wild ride.

"That bad?" I asked.

"No," she said, smiling with odd tenderness as she finished skimming. "It's actually really, really good. And even better, it doesn't mention you at all."

Annie flipped the laptop so it was facing me, then patted the couch for me to come take a look. I sat tentatively, then scrolled back to the top of the piece. The first line made my brows arch, too. *I was sixteen when I started writing my first piece of journalism, a self-assigned investigation into what was making my parents so miserable with each other. I was thirty-six years old when I finished it, two months ago.*

It was about him. His journey. His lessons. *His heirlooms.* I read with relief for myself, but also for Graham. These two pages of text contained a lot of healing. Then I realized Annie was wrong. He had mentioned me. Somewhere in the middle, I found a line about me being the person who encouraged him to go see his mother in Portugal. Next to it was a description: *Shea is a person who trusted all her superstitions about love over her feelings, and for good reason.*

I read it. Then reread it. Then read it a third time. The meaning bore further and further into my center with each pass, picking up connections along the way. He was right. I did not trust my feelings. *But why?* Finally, Graham's words settled down into a place inside me that I'd never been before, a place of total certainty. *Because I do not trust love.*

"I don't believe in them," I suddenly said.

"What?" Annie asked.

"The rom-coms. All love stories, really. The ones in books. The ones in real life. I think Nonna and Pop were a total fluke. I'm afraid you and Mark either won't make it or will just end up miserable." I couldn't believe what I was saying, but I couldn't stop. "And that's why I'm so terrified to marry John. I don't believe our love is strong enough. I don't believe *any* love is strong enough to last forever."

I felt like I needed to sob after all that, but I just stared into space, numb. My sister was not having the same experience. Tears streamed down her rounder cheeks.

"Am I broken?" I asked.

"No," she said. "I think you're in deep, deep grief, Shea. And I am so, so sorry that I didn't see that."

I whipped my sleeve at her. "No, no. It's not your fault," I said.

"You're right, it's not. But I'm your sister. And I have a degree in this!" I grabbed Annie a tissue off the end table, then went back for the whole box. "Thinking about Mom and Dad since we read her note . . . You lived with a very different version of them than I did. Those four years of difference between us were a lifetime."

"So this is all about their divorce? Or is it Mom's death?"

"It's both," said Annie. "And, combined, they created this block in you—like a fear that's almost covering the truth."

"Is the fear that I'm going to end up like Mom?" I asked. It was a worry I'd had worked hard to keep at bay.

"Maybe," said Annie. "Or . . ." She looked at me then like I could imagine her looking at her own little girl sometime in the future. Her face said, *This is going to be so hard to hear, but I've got you.* "Shea, you might believe that you shouldn't have a forever love because she didn't get one."

My body understood her instantly. Sobs suddenly arrived from a place that I hadn't known existed. Annie gave me a moment, then pulled me into her lap and stroked my hair as I let it all out. I don't know how long it took me to finally pull myself upright. But when I did, it was prompted by a thought that had broken through the pain: did tapping into this fear mean I might finally be able to move on from it?

"I want to be a person who believes," I said to my sister. "How can I change?"

Annie responded with a proud smile that told me I'd just taken the very first step.

FIFTY-FOUR

THERE WERE MIXED REACTIONS FROM THE SEVENTH graders when the credits rolled on *My Best Friend's Wedding*. Turns out Dionne Warwick songs don't hit quite like they used to, but I was all smiles anyway, especially after I noticed the person clapping from the back of the auditorium. I'd invited John to our closing ceremony party because I couldn't imagine celebrating such a proud moment without him in the room. The feeling was obviously mutual.

We met up at the dessert table after most of the kids had trickled out. Annie pretended to follow them into the school's front hallway, but I could see her fully-popped belly peeking back through the door.

"Looked like a huge success, Shea," John said. "Congrats." He shifted on his feet like he was going to hug me, but then he didn't. My arms went to cross in front of my chest, but I stopped them, ending up with a hand clasp that I hoped read more like what I meant to communicate: *Thank you*.

"It was amazing," I said. "And technically inspired by you. I was going to do a mini festival for industry people, but I remembered you always saying people underestimate what kids can handle and need."

"*Ha.* That sounds like me," John said with a half smile.

I couldn't get a read on him. It was killing me. This was a man whose sushi order I used to guess by the way he cocked his head at the menu. I stress-grabbed a chocolate donut off the table, then let a question fly out of my mouth.

"Should we get together? If you're ready to get together?"

John did not look surprised. Maybe accepting the invite here tonight had been his way of saying he was ready, too.

"Yes. Let's get together," he said.

WE MET THREE days later, in the M-section bleachers of the Hollywood Bowl. These were the exact seats we'd been in for Tom Petty, which I knew because I'd saved the ticket stubs. They were in a box with hundreds of other memories, from restaurant menus and bar coasters to that one rock John illegally stole from Petrified Forest because I said it looked like it was laughing. I'd been through it a dozen times over the past few months, in between journaling sessions.

"This spot looks familiar . . . ," John said, knowing in his voice. *Of course he knew.* John was the kind of guy that had space in his brain for things like which flowers I said were the prettiest at a wedding we'd been to or the name of the really good bottle of wine we had at one of our anniversary dinners.

Or maybe, I thought as I let myself swoon over his always-just-messy-enough hair, he was the kind of guy that made space in his brain.

"I couldn't resist, given its historically good karma," I said. He smiled at my awkward icebreaker, then looked down the steep incline of the amphitheater to the half-moon stage below. I turned in the same direction, noticing the California poppies that had bloomed in clusters on the hill behind the arena.

"John, I need you to know that I'm really, truly sorry for my part in what happened between us. I never, ever meant to hurt you." I'd gone back and forth, but simple seemed best right now.

He nodded his thanks. "I need to apologize, too," he said. "I'm sorry I kept things from you. I thought they would push you away, which is what happened anyway. I was just . . . afraid."

"Me too. In my own ways," I said, relieved that we'd come to the same realization. "Turns out I've been afraid of love since long before we met. In fact, it's why my entire heirloom-ring superstition exists in the first place."

John perked up. "Huh. How'd you figure all that out?"

"Um, it's a pretty long story involving three countries, ten cities, five nightmares, a surprise reunion with my father, and a secret letter from my mother. Oh, and *two* heirlooms, as it turns out. But also Annie helped me uncover some things, then found me a really good therapist."

A massive, booming laugh flew out of John, thank God. Then his eyes lowered to the ring still looped through my necklace, overlapped with my mother's. John had never seen that second ring but seemed to instinctually know what it was.

"I'd like to hear the whole story," he said. "But I think I need to talk about us first. I've got to be honest, Shea, I'm still out of my depth here. I've been trying to work through it, talking to friends; I even read a self-help book."

"Which one?" I asked.

"Something about *Us*?"

"Probably *Us, Again*. Way better than *Us, Still*, so you can skip that one."

It felt so good to slip back into our familiar cadence. I could almost envision us surrounded by thousands of people right now, just another couple laughing over wine and cheese before a show. But John pulled me back.

"I don't know how to fix this, Shea. And . . . I don't know if we're even supposed to."

I had a plan for how this talk was supposed to go, one I may or may not have written down in a notebook and tried to test out on Annie, who cruelly made me test it out on Mark instead. But my mind jumped back to a very simple question I'd once been challenged to answer. "John, how do you know that you want to be married?" I asked.

He sat up a little taller on the bench, not expecting that. "I don't know. I honestly never considered the alternative," he said, then something seemed to occur to him. "The stuff with Carrie made me struggle with trust, but I still wanted to get married. I never had a reason not to."

His answer unlocked another question. "But how did you know you wanted to be married to me?"

John's eyes widened, but with care, not curiosity. It looked like it almost hurt him that I had to ask that question.

"Shea, I barely want to be in a room without you," he said. "When we're together, I feel . . . I don't know. You just make it so simple for me to be the best version of myself. I'm not sure I even knew who that guy fully was until I met you. And since then we've just *fit*, like we were meant to do this life together. I can't explain it, but I can feel it. And I think the best part has always been that I know you can, too."

John's words landed deep within my heart, but in a space that he'd already carved out to hold them. He'd delivered the perfect answer, most of all because none of it was a surprise. But that made what I had to say next all the harder to confess. I reached my hands out toward him, a reflex. I half expected him to pretend he didn't see, but instead he locked his fingers inside mine, tucking my thumbs under like always.

"You're right. I feel it, too," I said, voice shaky. "But I've discovered that I have a deep, stuck fear our love won't last for the rest of our lives—that no love really does. That it's all too big a risk. And when we got engaged, that fear became stronger than all the other things I feel about you and about us."

John nodded yes, then his head dropped into his hands. This made sense to him, it seemed, but it also clearly devastated him. I grabbed one of his hands back to let him know I wasn't done.

"I don't want to feel this way. And I promise I'm going to work really hard to heal these parts of myself; I already am. But I'm not there yet." I closed my eyes for a second, preparing for the most painful thing I had to say. "And I understand if you need to move on because you're afraid I never will be."

John took a very long, very deep breath. He looked out to the poppies and up at the sky, then down to his feet. Finally, he looked back at me.

"I need some time to think about it," he said. "But I understand. And I'm sorry."

I knew the apology wasn't for anything he'd done; it was for everything he couldn't do to change my past. The security, the safety, of knowing what he meant washed through me as John leaned over and wrapped my body into the warmest, deepest hug.

I cannot explain what happened inside me as he did. It felt as though some tunnel or portal suddenly opened, giving me access to a crystal-clear sensation. It trickled down from my head through my entire body until it overwhelmed every other still-conflicted feeling inside. It was light and bright and only so—I knew—because of how dark things had been before.

Hope.

EPILOGUE

JOHN AND I WAVED GOODBYE TO ANNIE, MARK, AND baby Louisa from the little front stoop of our condo. I watched my sister gently ease her daughter into the car seat. Our tiny family had finally expanded. Now my stand-in mom needed caretaking from me as she raised her own little girl, and I was so ready to give it to her.

"Beach walk tomorrow?" she called from the car window.

"Eight a.m.!" I yelled back. "I'll bring coffee!" Then Mark beeped twice as they drove off to their own house just five miles away.

"I think Louisa really liked the new place," I said as we closed the front door.

"I don't know," said John. "I saw her side-eying the kitchen cabinets."

"*Ha ha*," I said, shoving him through the entryway. "I am right, though. They are *way* too eighties. Luckily I have a plan."

"Luckily you always do," he said, draping his arm over my shoulder as we stepped inside.

It was June again, almost one year since John proposed.

In December, I'd heard from Gianna. She'd taken her husband and daughter to Italy for a family trip. They spent a week with her *zia* Maria and the entire *famiglia* in Borgo San Lorenzo, then took the train down to Rome so that Gianluca could finally meet his namesake. Gia sent me a picture of the two of them standing beside the portrait of Carmela, tear stains on both their faces.

Rebecca's birthday was in February, and I flew out to Boston as a surprise. While I was there, I popped in on Bette, who was preparing for heart surgery. She asked for a photo of the ring to have with her in the hospital—visual strength. So I had Bec connect me with a photographer friend who came to her house and shot it like a museum piece. We sent copies to Gia and Gianluca, too, with a note from Bette included.

AND SOMETIME IN April, I finally heard back from one of Celia Quinn's relatives. He turned out to be the son of the son that she'd wished could have inherited the faux Harry Winston. And he completed her story: His great-grandfather spent a few years in prison. His great-grandmother, Celia, visited weekly. And when he got out, they very slowly reconciled. On their fiftieth wedding anniversary, he bought her a new diamond ring.

JOHN AND I stood together now, surveying the home we owned. It had the old, dark wood floors of my dreams, a huge

kitchen island so John could fulfill his of hosting Thanksgiving, and just the right wall for new wallpaper. For now,
though, the task at hand was unpacking our Everest of boxes.

"I want to get one thing done in the bedroom," I said.
"Let's order in so we can push through a bunch tonight."

"Chinese food?" John asked.

"*Tons*," I said, then I kissed him quick before heading into
our new bedroom.

I went immediately for the small box labeled *Shea nightstand*. There were a few things I needed to place in the room
immediately, for good karma, of course.

First, the Murano glass jewelry box that I'd bought on my
very first trip to Italy. The deep blue and pastel green colors
had reminded me of the sea glass we'd always find on Emma
Wood beach. I opened the lid to make sure its precious cargo
was still inside: Mom's engagement ring. I placed the box on
the little wood nightstand we'd already moved into the room.
It wasn't mine to wear, but I didn't want it far from sight.

Next, a small, gold frame was peeking out from under my
favorite eye mask and slippers. I grabbed it, then rubbed a
smudge off the glass. Under it was a piece of Graham's article,
the mention of me that had unlocked the most important
truth. *Shea is person who trusted all her superstitions about love
over her feelings, and for good reason*, was what Graham had
written. I'd found a print version of the article, cut out that
section, and crossed out *all her superstitions about love over*.
Now the sentence read like the woman I intended to be: *Shea
is a person who trusted her feelings, and for good reason*.

"Shea, can you come look at something?" John called from the other room.

"Yeah, one sec," I said as I placed that three-by-five-inch reminder next to the ring box, then walked toward the living room.

Up until the very moment John proposed—again—I didn't know what true certainty felt like. A warmth started from my center and radiated out, as if turning me a new color. I was squarely inside pure, calm joy as I took a thousand snapshots with my eyes. On one knee before me was the man I loved, asking a question I'd hoped was coming. We'd done so much growing over the past year—thanks to time and space and honest conversations and very helpful therapy—but it didn't all land on me until the moment we'd officially closed on the condo, committing to a space we both owned. The purchase was a risk that would forever change us—an investment in so many unknowns. But that day, my hopes for our future were crystal clearly bigger than any of my fears. And so that night, I'd put the heirloom back in its original box, then left it on John's nightstand. My silent way of saying *I'm ready now, when you are*. Turns out I was wrong to question Harry's famous New Year's Eve sprint. When you realize, you really *do* want the rest of your life to start as soon as possible.

Tears clouded my view, but not my mind.

"*Yes*," I said as I ran from the bedroom doorway directly into John's arms, almost bowling him over.

"I didn't even ask yet!" he mumbled from under my grasp.

"Right! Sorry!" I said, then I stood up to give John the

proper moment. He steadied himself, then looked up into my eyes.

"Shea Anderson, will you marry me?" John asked.

I took his hands in mine and guided him up off the floor so our eyes were in line, so I could see into him like I had the very first day we met.

"Yes," I said again, then, "but can I please say why?"

John cocked his head. "You want to explain your answer?" he asked.

"More like defend it," I said. "I think *forever* deserves that." Then I steadied myself for what I'd rehearsed to say next. "John Hayden Jacobs, I will marry you because all my clearest dreams include an image of you by my side. Because I have all the evidence I need that we're safer and stronger up against the world together than we are apart. Because marriage is the biggest way I have to say that I believe in *us*, until the end. And—most importantly—because I am a person who chooses to believe."

John wiped the tears from his eyes, then held the ring box up to my beaming face. Inside it was that gleaming diamond ring that three other women had gazed at from this same view. A deeply meaningful piece of jewelry with energy I was proud to take on. An object that would give me strength as I charted my own *ever after*.

I watched as John moved it from the box to my hand, almost in slow motion. Then, for the very first time, I let him slip our heirloom onto my finger. It fit just right this time.

acknowledgments

The idea for this book has been with me for over a decade, but the dream of *a* book has been with me since I was a very little girl writing stories that my mom would "publish" inside cereal box covers bound by ribbon. My path has been filled with the kind of support that makes a person lose sleep over how to order her acknowledgments. Here, mostly alphabetically, is my sincere gratitude:

My CAA Team: Mollie Glick & Lola Bellier redefined the word "agent" for me. Mollie, your belief in this book drove me to give it the dedication *you* deserve. Lola, your notes turned it into something we could take across the finish line. And many thanks to Sarah Harvey and Gabby Fetters for your hard work making me an International author, in record speed.

Early readers: Angie Rosen, Nat Rosen, Sara Rosen Glynn, Geanna Barlaam, Jenny Anderson, and Lindsey Martin were so gracious about my first draft that I wrote a second. Special thanks to Sara for reading that one with a baby in her arms. And to Geanna who stuck with me until the end(s).

Fairy Godpeople: Blair Singer, Carol Lokitz, Cindy Chupack, E. Jean Carroll, Julia Newton, Kim Kaye, Matt Pierson, and Paul Flanagan unexpectedly dropped into my writing journey at a most critical moment, whether they knew it or not.

My Haven Entertainment parents, Rachel Miller and Jesse Hara: Rachel, I only write books because you told me I could and should. That I *would* is because you work tirelessly to make my dreams come true. And Jesse, I never forget what matters most because you embody it: doing work you love with people you love.

Jessica Walker: The idea for this book (coincidentally?) landed right around the time you became my therapist. The fact that it is out in the world is due in very large part to the paths you've helped me find and walk ever since.

Kate Dresser: my editor +++: I was right; ours will be one of the greatest partnerships of my life. I am wowed over and over by your conviction, enthusiasm, and ability to turn both into brilliant action. Let's do this forever. Thanks also to Tarini Sipahimalani and my entire Putnam team, who have already made me feel so at home.

Kathleen Carter: As I write this you've only just become my publicist, but I'm already certain by the time the book is out I'll want the world to know how hard you worked to make it a success.

Melissa Cassera: my fellow Jersey girl and forever inspiration. Our weekly Writing Therapy sessions changed my life. It is an honor to be walking this (new!) path with you, getting misidentified as sisters the whole way.

Susan Hyatt & the BEYOND Coven: You were there in the

months right before and days right after the book sold, and I don't believe that's an accident. Thank you for seeing me so clearly.

My sisters—Danielle Rosen, Sara Rosen Glynn, and Alexandra Rosen Kanefsky—never make me question whether or not they believe in me, which is a big part of why I believe in myself. Ruby, Emma, and Lucy are the luckiest.

My writing sisters—Ally Hord, Amy Heidt, Carley Steiner, Hayley Terris, Juliet Seniff, Melissa Hunter, and Molly Prather—*get it* in every life category that matters. You are the tribe of my little girl dreams.

Dad: If you could engineer a father that would raise a daughter to be a writer, you'd end up with a clone of Nat Rosen. I never gave up because you never would, and because I secretly only do it for your pitch-perfect emails of encouragement.

Mom: Every so often, for *seven years*, you—and only you—would ask, *What's going on with that* Heirloom *idea?* I know that's because you loved the concept, but part of me believes we're connected in some magical way that let your unconscious know mine needed to write this book. That part of me is you.

And finally, *Robby*: You are the reason I believe in forever—the possibility and the power. Thank you for not proposing with an heirloom. Happy 10th Wedding Anniversary.

© JENNY ANDERSON

Jessie Rosen got her start with the award-winning blog 20-Nothings.com. She shifted from writing essays in New York to television in LA, selling original projects to ABC, CBS, Warner Bros., and Netflix. Rosen balances quiet days writing with nights performing at live storytelling shows, including her own—*Sunday Night Sex Talks*, once featured on *The Bachelorette*. She lives in Los Angeles, with her favorite Italian wines, nineties rom-coms, and *karmically safe* jewelry.

JESSIEROSEN.COM
JESSIEROSENWRITER